ALL THE
Part One

By KEISHA POWERS

To Angela
Thanks for your
support
-Keisha Powers

Acknowledgments

First off, taking time to give thanks to all of the Royal NRT and ancestors who have paved the way, who have weathered the storm so that we of the new generation could marvel at the beauty in the prism of rainbows. Ashe.

I would like to thank my parents, The King Father and Queen Mother, who have not only provided me with the flesh and blood necessary to create my very being, but have pushed me, teaching me to never turn a blind eye to what's inside. Everyone has some form of talent. Some gift.
It shows up in the form of passion, something that you can do effortlessly. Hone in on that skill, that gift...it is where you will find your purpose.
You will always be called to it. You can't escape it.
 It's branded into your cosmetic makeup. Your own unique and individual fingerprint. Tap into it. Utilize it. Find yours!!! Mine just so happens to be my vividly, extraordinary imagination, combined with my ability to write.

I would like to thank my ride or die, Ty, for having the patience and for providing a listening ear during the many days and nights that I sat him down like a Kindergartener, reading bits and pieces of this story to him, asking him to "tell me how it sounds." LOL. I so appreciate you.

Thanks to my Big Sister, Neicia and BIL, Khammy, for also taking time to read as I penned, giving feedback regarding the storyline, the selection of a book cover and just ultimately being involved.

Thanks to my niece, my Pooh, for providing the encouragement necessary from your constructive review, that I needed, to know that I was somehow headed in the right direction and on target with the storyline.

To my review committee, Mo, Esha, Gerald, Janet, Martice and Apple, you all have been supportive from the VERY start. Thanks for having the availability, the patience, the excitement...All of you have been a true help through this entire period of creation and I will forever be thankful.. Love.

To everyone else, who have taken the opportunity to purchase this book, may this story make you laugh, may this story make you think, may this story touch your heart in some way or another.
It's YOU, that's the REAL MVP!!!

ALL THE STARS PART ONE

Chapter One: Zaire (Here)

Alessia Cara- Here (Album: Know-It-All)

Zaire Jefferson took a sip of the Lemon Drop Martini in which she was holding in her hand and savored the taste of the slightly sour and not overly sweet beverage. The soft sound of the live Jazz band created a smooth vibe within the dimly lit lounge. Allowing her eyes to slowly scan the room, she noticed that a few couples had taken advantage of the newly installed dance area by swaying intimately in their own rhythmic dance. Several other patrons were scattered throughout the room engaged in what looked to be light conversations while enjoying the after work set of Happy Hour.

Boy had it been a long, uneventful day at the office. It had seemed as if time had come to a full stand still after the 10am meeting that she had attended at the request of the department's Director, who was also her own direct supervisor. The meeting had taken a mere 2 hours from the workday, when really it should have been scheduled for a much shorter time frame. Her focus: to give an updated report to the department heads regarding the recruiting efforts to fill 100 new positions that had become available on the warehouse floor. After she and the two other Human Resource Managers gave their updates (30 minutes), the rest of the time was spent gossiping about "he said, she said" rumors that had been circulating around office regarding various employees on staff. These were the types of conversations that she had made it a point to "duck away from" and had learned to conquer the goal as time had progressed throughout the 5 years that she had been with the company.

Zaire had been in her role as Recruiting Manager with Narvo Corporation for a total of 5 years. Although she truly enjoyed the work that she did, she often times experienced burnout from the long days and failed attempts to keep long-standing, skilled employees with a company whose turnover rate was whirlwind high for production staff. Tackling the task of creating requisites and posting them on the local job boards that were most frequently visited by job seekers had taken up the majority of her day and on the flip side, had caused the day to drag due to the boring nature of completing the task. Her fingers were crossed in hopes that upon returning to work the next day, she would be notified that a large response to the postings had come in overnight. That would definitely affirm that the tedious theme of the day was well worth it.

Shifting on the brown leather stool in which she sat, Zaire tugged at the rim of her skirt as she uncrossed her right leg from over her left, instead comfortably switching, crossing her left leg over her right. The 4 inch heel of the Marc Jacobs pumps that adorned her feet clicked against the metal trim of the foot rest that circled around the lower perimeter of the front bar. Thick thighs save lives, or so the saying goes. Zaire begged to differ, with the tingly sensation from not receiving proper oxygen from circulation (or the "un"circulation) of blood flow under the weight of where her right thigh once sat upon her left offered confirmation to her claim. But even with knowing the fact that she was definitely not "typical" model thin in size, she smiled at the knowledge that she was yet still " one BAD and BEAUTIFUL sista!!!" Her smooth, almost candy coated, caramel complexion, almond shaped eyes with a deep set slant in the inward corner, full, heart shaped lips (courtesy of her African heritage) and thick, voluminous, naturally, kinky-coily crowned Afro that seemed to defy gravity causing everyone to stop in mid conversation and take notice, told no lies. She was as gorgeous as she was curvy in all the right places, (another courtesy of that same African ethnicity). She was an undisputed show stopper.

From the time that she had entered the lounge, she had caught the attention of more than five guys who in turn, wanted to return the favor by almost comically trying to catch hers. But Zaire hadn't come for company. This was, like Monica once crooned on her chart topping single, "just one of those days", where she wanted to be left alone.

Grabbing her glass by the namesake signature long stemmed handle, she took another sip of her drink. She slowly felt her mood lifting as the fluid rolled down her throat. She allowed her foot to tap to the rhythm of the now catchy tune that the band was currently playing.

She mentally noted the time and dedicated herself to spending a few more minutes in the lounge before heading out to the comfort of her Downtown condo that overlooked the vast blue waters of Lake Michigan. She knew that by that time, the rush hour traffic would have died and the commute to her apartment would be much less of a hassle.

The blinking LED light, accompanied with the vibrations from her iPhone notified her that a text message had come through. The bright, blinding light nearly sparked the entire dimly lit room which caused others who were sitting at the bar to glance over in her direction. Offering a smile for apology, she tapped the screen of the phone to end the frantic flashing, and to reveal whom had sent the message.

The simple "Hey You" tugged at her heart strings.

Such a simple message, from a much less simple sender. Pharaoh. His name was as appropriate as the sun shining on a hot summer morning. From the incredible intellect of his mind to the crafting of his being as if made from the finest of Milk Chocolate, everything about him screamed King. Ruler. Most high. Her best friend and toughest critic.

She hadn't heard from him in weeks. Their last exchange wasn't the most pleasant. Zaire didn't take well to being told what she should and should not do. Unfortunately, Pharaoh had a pocket full of change and was also known as being the generous KING of giving away two cents here and there to those he felt were in need, particularly Zaire. But, yet still, she had to admit that she had missed being able to confide in her friend. Her bestie since high school, they had shared the same home room her freshman year. He, who should have been a sophomore at the time was held back the previous year which had given him the advantage of learning the layout of the classrooms from top floor to lower level. Zaire, who had never had the best sense of direction had needed his help locating her classes for the first few weeks of the school year and was appreciative to have Pharaoh who had offered his time as her personal tour guide. They had been friends ever since. From sports tryouts, to skip out parties, field trips, to broken hearts, they had been inseparable. Pharaoh had been "most sought after" by the girls at school. He had transferred to Milwaukee by way of Brooklyn, NYC at the start of high school and Brooklyn was branded in his blood. Cocky attitude, huge ego, hard cut accent and swag on ten thousand, he was a certified trend setter with good looks, a great sense of humor and an incredible eye for the latest style. He was always first to rock a new fashion and gave "life" to the definition of B-Boy with his always fresh pair of Tims, then baggy clothing and shoulder length dreads before dreads had even made a come back in mainstream fashion. Never changing, his neat, well groomed locs now fell well past his waist, not worn in keeping up with the urban trend, but always more in tune with the prideful African customs that were instilled in him from birth by receiving culturally based education from both his Dad and his GrandDad. Many had tried befriending Zaire in hopes of being able to get closer to him, but Zaire was always ten steps ahead of the game and was able to recognize the ingenious interest in wanting her friendship immediately. Alongside her own personal judgement, Pharaoh had always had her back by protecting her from the phony pursuits of his numerous groupies.

Zaire tapped the cursor field of the SMS app and replied "Wassup homie?"

It took 15 seconds tops for Pharaoh to respond. "Trying to figure out why dafuq I haven't heard from you…"(sarcastic emoji)

Reaching for the signature, platinum diamond ring that hung from the matching platinum chain in which she wore every single day around her neck, she rubbed the beautiful piece while she sucked her freshly whitened teeth and shook her head in disgust. The violins from the once sweet moment that tugged at her heartstrings now gave way to what could have been the deathly tune played in each and every movie moments before Michael Myers face appeared."The nerve of this idiot" she mumbled under her breath.

She angrily replied "I'm so sure that you already know the answer to that question." She followed the message using the exact same sarcastic emoji for emphasize.

Zaire knew that even with her response, Pharaoh, who always pointed fingers outward and never inward just somehow wouldn't get it. He had grown so accustomed to interfering in her life that she was more than sure that he wouldn't recognize that he had done anything wrong.

Just two weeks ago, Pharaoh had taken it upon himself to perform his duty that he rightfully assigned himself which was to so called "Keep her safe from the goons." This safe-keeping had resulted in a dispute at one of her favorite restaurants and had ultimately gotten them barred from returning. All the poor guy had wanted to do was to buy her a drink while they sat at the bar, waiting on a table. Pharaoh took it as being disrespectful, pointing out that the guy had known that she was sitting with him and had assumed that he was "a soft ass nigga" by approaching yet still. Pharaoh referred to some stupid ass "man code" in mentioning that the guy didn't care whether she was with him, and that he disregarded what was a possibility that she could have been his date in an attempt to test his manhood. Needless to say, an overabundance of testosterone led to an argument that caused their removal from the premises. Not understanding her anger at the time, he made sure to mention that the guy was nothing more than a "ran down reject ass nigga" and that he would have been no good for her anyways. And of course, Pharaoh always knows best.

Zaire shook her head just thinking about it. Although she appreciated his protective nature, he did have a tendency to go way too far at times. Most times. That part of him picked like the devil's pitchfork at her soul.

But even still, she had truly missed her bestie whom she had long ago grown accustomed to speaking with daily.

"Really Z? You still hot about that? Tbt I saved you from Ole' Kev Hart. Lil extra wack midget ass nigga. (laughing emoji)"

Zaire burst out laughing, catching the patrons' at the bar attention once again. She had to admit that yes, the guy was quite tiny in size. Going up against Pharaoh was like watching a Chihuahua nipping at the ankles of a Bull Mastiff and somehow, missing every time.

"Where are you?"

She waited for his response. Looking up from her phone, she unintentionally looked directly into an awaiting stare of one of the guys who had been sitting across on the opposite side of the bar. He smiled.

Damn. Not wanting to be rude, Zaire smiled back and quickly broke the eye contact. Persistence. Men never gave up. Their poles were always baited, pitched and ready to reel one in.

The vibration pulled her attention back to her phone.

"Chillin up here at the spot with Tre and Reg. Where you?"

"Headed home," Zaire responded after swallowing the last of the fluid within her glass and standing to grab her sweater from the back of the stool. Almost immediately, a guy sitting a couple of seats down jumped up, rushing over to her side.

"Let me help you with that Beautiful," he beat her to grabbing the black, cashmere duster and held it open for her to slide her arms into.

Zaire obliged although a bit irritated. "Thanks. Have a great night." She turned, walking quickly for the door, not entertaining any advances from the grinning guy.

The warm air greeted her at the open door. It was unseasonably warm for the end of May in Milwaukee. Zaire would not complain at all and welcomed the 70 degree day.

Walking to her Cream colored Lexus coupe, she checked the message that caused her phone to vibrate once more.
"From where?"

Opening the door and sliding onto the Peanut Butter colored leather seat, she strapped on her seat belt. Cracking the windows

& the moon roof just a bit. Her phone connected seamlessly with the car's BlueTooth capability. She used the U Connect system to respond to the message via the dash screen before pulling off.

"The bar." she kept her reply as simple and vague as possible, knowing that Pharaoh would have a million questions whether she was open about her location or not.

It wasn't often that she went out. Especially not alone. Pharaoh would be concerned about her reason for deciding to make the stop today. But, pulling into the Fond Du Lac Avenue traffic, Pharaoh would have to wait with his interrogation.

Driving down the city street, Zaire took note of just how many people were out. It wasn't often that warm nights occurred so early in the year, and it was obvious that the residents were taking full advantage of the mild and breezy day. The down side to enjoying increased temperatures was that along with it came increased crime levels, with homicides topping the list of offenses. What was once a beautiful, flourishing town back during the 1970's Industrial Wave, (which brought a large number of young adults to the city looking to make an honest and decent living) Milwaukee, WI was now suffering from the impact of loss, with large local manufacturing companies either shutting their doors for good or relocating overseas where labor costs left a much smaller dent in the pockets of higher level executives. This separation, in particular, affected the North side of town, where the population was primarily dominated by those who were highly melanated in complexion, leaving the now impoverished community suffering, struggling and desperate to make a way, and to make a way by any means necessary. Increased stress brought increased trauma which impacted the attitudes of the individuals who felt trapped in the overrun North side ghetto. Noone had enough to lend a hand to their neighbors and could barely support themselves. This caused neighbors to feel alone in the struggle and community to fall apart, quickly crumbling at the seams. Noone felt supported by anyone in anyway, including by the government officials. Every man for himself, became the new mantra. Tempers flared, hatred spread like wildfire. Fathers, feeling as though they were not fully capable of properly supporting their families, checked out. Single moms were left to pick up the pieces, managing both roles of mother and father within their households taking on sometimes 3 and 4 jobs just to keep a roof over their heads due to the dead end low employment wages that being uneducated beyond high school offers. After working all week, having no time for themselves, yet still having the need to feel wanted and to be wanted, young mothers opted to spend the weekend focused on being in the places where receiving what they view as "flattering" attention, accompanied with loud music, binge drinking and drug use was the norm. For these mothers, picking up guys wasn't an issue. Getting them to stay and take in an already made family when nine times out of ten he had recently abandoned his own, now that was a completely different tale of mythical nature. Women, focused on being loved by a population dominated by guys who were being raised without having a clue how to genuinely give love or even what love truly looks like, and how to be a man with Dads never at one point being present in their lives, sacrificed the well-being of their children for needs of their own. Mom's only example: to have random men in and out of her life, her home, and in front of the watchful eyes of her children. This unfortunately created a horrible, never ending cycle of abandonment that has carried through generations. This left children suffering from lack of parenting, lack of guidance and proper support needed to strive to become their greatest. Children were forced to raise and care for themselves. To fend for themselves in this unforgiving environment.

The anger brought upon escalated attitudes. Escalated attitudes brought upon instantaneous reactions. Instantaneous reactions drew guns. Drawn guns made headline news. The shootings occur regularly. Broad of day. The latest of night. Murders committed by those who were distressed and depressed and had come to the conclusion that life, as they have known it, has very little, if any value at all. Life in prison or even death had to be a better option then the hell that then had been born into.

Zaire shook her head in sadness at surveying the lively North side street. A group of teenage girls were yelling and wild, clad in far too tiny short shorts, long colorful weaves reminiscent of characters from The Jetsons cartoon, foul mouths laced with every four letter word known to curse men and nasty attitudes. The car in front of her displayed temporary license plates that had expired 2 months before. The driver was one of young twenties in age, Lil Boosie BadAss blasted from the speakers while he weaved and ducked in and out of traffic trying to recklessly and impatiently get around. Speeding ahead, running the fresh red light heading East on Fond Du Lac Avenue, crossing the busy North Avenue intersection, he nearly caused an accident in his lack of consideration for the safety of other drivers.

Zaire loved her hometown and loved her beautiful candy coated people but she hated the selfish, careless, angry, pitiful attitudes that many had development.

Stopped at the red light, Zaire searched for her favorite R&B Soul station on Satellite radio. The smooth voice of Kem told her how he just "Can't Stop Loving" her, causing her to relax in a mellow, cool groove. Continuing East, the beauty of the Downtown skyline approached in the near distance. Passing the newly constructed ramps that led to the Expressway, it took seconds before she had arrived at the 6th Street traffic stop. Directly in front of her loomed the magnificently designed Fiserv Forum Stadium, home to the Milwaukee Bucks basketball team and the upcoming Democratic

National Convention. There was so much construction being done in preparation of giving downtown a well overdue face lift. She was excited about what the creation of new businesses would bring to the struggling city. She took the avenue as far as she could, turning South onto Water Street. It took her all of 5 mins to arrive to where she could turn into the underground parking that served the tenants of the building in which she resided. She waved to Enrique in the security booth and proceeding around the winding structure to her parking spot. Removing her belongings, letting up windows and locking the doors, she stepped into the elevator closing and pressed the button that would program the car to carry her up. The elevator was awaiting her arrival as the doors opened immediately. Stepping on, she pressed in for the 7th floor.

Inside her unit, she was greeted by Nala, her Bengal cat, as she flipped on the kitchen light and locked the door behind her. Nala purred while brushing up against her leg, looking for attention and affection. Zaire bent to plant a kiss on top of her soft, furry head using her finger tips as transferring device.

She set her designer bag down on the mini bar style island that separates the kitchen from the wide open living space. Blinds pulled, since letting the morning light flow in, the view was amazing of the tall buildings that made up the downtown area. Being that her apartment was further toward the top of the building and facing East, she had the most amazingly scenic view of Lake Michigan just blocks away. When selecting her unit, she had the choice of facing West and being located directly above the Milwaukee River or taking the 7th floor apartment, facing in the opposite direction, giving her, her current view. Her decision came without hesitation.

Her phone had chimed 3 times since exiting her car and arriving inside of her pad. Picking it up, she scanned the screen of her SMS app.

"Bar? What bar? With who?

"Was going on witchu?"

"It's only been a couple weeks, you missed me that much Boo?" (Laughing emoji")

"Boy bye." She responded. Honestly, she expected a series of more probing questions from her overprotective friend. Happy to see that he wasn't in his usual drilling mode, she sat the phone on the countertop and headed to the refrigerator to retrieve a bottled water.

Looking around her always immaculate apartment, she lovingly admired the decor. Beautiful red, black and grey shades were coordinated throughout the entire unit. Most of the pieces came by way of the local Goodwill stores. Vases, pictures, various ceramics.....the color theme flowed perfectly throughout every room. Her home was so well put together that the building manager often called on her to use her unit for viewing purposes when interested tenant prospects came for tours.

Heading to the large master bath, she turned on the faucet and allowed hot, steaming water to fill the jacuzzi style tub. While the water ran, she dropped a Lavender scented bath bomb inside before undressing, hanging her 2 piece designer suit on the hook attached to the back of the door. Removing the chain from around her neck and placing it on the counter next to the sink, she tossed the rest of her garments into the wicker laundry hamper. After the tub was filled halfway and the soothing scent filled the room, Zaire shut off the water and climbing inside. Pushing the button in the top left corner, the jets kicked into full action.

The long sigh escaped her lips unintentionally but still intentionally. Just what the doctor ordered. Happy that she had decided to pull her thick, coily hair up into a top knot for the day, she rested her head back against the soft, plastic pillow that was Velcro attached to the wall right above the tub.

If only Calgon could take her away. But away to where? Zaire hadn't traveled in God knows how long. Last trip she had been on, Pharaoh had randomly popped up at her apartment early one Saturday morning, pulling her from the comfort of her bed and out into traffic for the 5 hour drive with a destination of Minneapolis to visit the Mall of America. They stayed for a few hours, shopping and hanging out before returning home later that night.

Vacations were not something listed at the top when it came to necessities. Zaire had worked hard through grade school, high school and all through college. She was extremely focused on building her career and ladder climbing. She had put in entirely too much work to get to the position that she was currently in and she still had so much more to do before retirement.

Zaire received her hard working traits from both parents. Her Mom and Dad had always gone hard in ensuring that their kids were well provided for. Zaire, being the oldest of her two brothers, she was in charge of caring for them during the evenings while her parents worked. This responsibility ran welcomed interference in Zaire's social life which wasn't as important to her as adhering to her parents plans to set their children up into situations where they themselves didn't have to work nearly as hard to survive. College and education past high school was an ongoing topic of discussion at the dinner table. And she had always had one goal, to set the example and to make her parents proud.

Having to fill the role as Big Sister, taking care of the younger ones, Pharaoh had always made it a point to be the one to look out for and care for Zaire. He had spoiled her rotten, always picking up the tab everywhere they went. Zaire never had to go in her pocket for anything so long as he was around. No matter how much she protested and declared that she could take care of expenses on her own, Pharaoh would always beat her to the punch. Even times when she specifically planned to treat him in some way or form, he would agree in the beginning, but somehow manage to weasel his way in, covering the costs before Zaire had a chance to make an attempt at paying on her own. That was her Pharaoh. So giving. So caring.

Zaire was motivated most by success. She had always had the best grades and the reputation as school nerd in high school. Thank God to Pharaoh, being her saving grace, and helping her with having more experiences during high school than what she would have mustered without him. He had always been a first invite to all of the happening parties and hot inclusions around school. Although with force most times, he would make it a point to pull her reluctantly with him to whichever gatherings he decided was worth attending. It was his popularity where hers was gained. The girls never understood why he was so pressed on her. But as Pharaoh was never shy to admitting, "Z is realer than most these niggas in this wack ass town." Pharaoh was her bestie, her ride or die til the end. Her love for him went without words. And she knew that the feeling was unquestionably mutual on his side.

The relaxing scent of the lavender engulfed in the steam rising from the water transported Zaire to another place. Reaching for her Himalayian Salt Scrub, she took a decent portion into her hand and spread the formula onto her face. The salt was one of the best exfoliating agents that she had ever come across. With regular use, it kept her skin bright with a healthy glow. After gently rubbing the scrub into her skin, she rinsed off the residue and applied a Dead Sea Warming Mud Mask. She loved how the black mask activated once the oxygen in the air touched it. The warming effect was extremely pampering and provided her skin with an extra treat from daily environmental elements that were often damaging to the skin. Zaire's skin was smooth and blemish free for a reason. Proper care, inside and out along with an overload of water intake kept her pores clog free.

She was always big on women, especially African American women, going above and beyond to take care of themselves and to keep themselves looking their absolute best. She had accepted many opportunities to attend local Sistahood groups as a special guest in the past in order to inform ladies about the various All Natural products available and how to obtain 100% raw ingredients directly from the motherland.

After her long soak, Zaire dried, dressed, tied a satin wrap around her mane to prepare for bed. Nala took her usual spot snuggled in tight next to her favorite human. With her body, weightless and comfortable on the length of the memory foam mattress, it took just minutes before Zaire drifted off into a blissful and well needed slumber.

Chapter Two- Pharaoh (Already Home)

Already Home- Jay-Z (The Blueprint 3 Album)

Pharaoh Knight looked down at the phone in his hand for the tenth time since sending the last text message to Zaire. Why in the hell was she not responding?!?! She couldn't still be red about lil dude? That shit happened ages ago. He could understand her feeling some kinda way about being kicked out of Fleming's but to hold onto that shit for 2 whole weeks was just absurd!!!

Slipping his phone inside the pocket of his Nike joggers, Pharaoh turned to catch the attention of the bartender. Angel's grin was wide as she sauntered over to him.

"Another one?" she asked. Her smooth, dark skin glowed, beautifully laced with tons of melanin.

"Yeah, that's cool…..make it a round Babes," Pharaoh confirmed. "And pour yourself one."

"Thanks Crush," Angel smiled, using the nickname she had long ago given him before she turned to focus on refreshing the drinks. Angel was always accommodating when he walked in. He knew that she wished that she could accommodate him in other ways as well. But knowing that his guy Reg had already hit that, he dared not toe step.

Pharaoh was used to receiving loads of special attention most everywhere he went. With his forever swagged out, stylish, well groomed B-Boy good looks and deep, edgy Brooklyn accent, he stood out like a sore thumb in any crowd.

Sitting at the bar in his favorite spot, 100 West, the Thursday Ladies Night crowd was in full swing. Ladies were flowing in from all directions. The warm weather brought along with it the beautiful sight of long legs and fat asses that were revealed in mini skirts and the shortest shorts. He and his Trues, Tremaine and Reggie, were enjoying the fabulous view over drinks.

Pharaoh had lived in Milwaukee since his Dad had relocated with his job when he was just a teen. It had truly been a rough adjustment for him being that the city was much slower and much smaller than what he had been used to, with living in Brooklyn for the first fourteen years of his life. It took time, maturity, along with several satisfying trips back and forth to his hometown, before being able to see the perks of living in laid back Milwaukee over the hustle and bustle in the extremely fast moving city of NYC. The cost of living topped the list of perks. It was much less expensive residing in Milwaukee where real estate ran astoundingly less in cost for a space much larger in size in comparison to the costs to purchase in New York. This was extremely important as this is what his business was primarily based upon.

His Dad had relocated to accept a Managerial role with the manufacturing company that he had worked with for several years. When the opportunity opened at the Milwaukee plant, his Dad had took a chance and applied, not really expecting to be seriously considered for the position. Imagine his surprise when he had received a call inviting him to schedule a phone interview for the following week. He was offered the position just a few weeks later.

Dropping the news on Pharaoh didn't go over so well. Pharaoh had protested the entire way and given his Dad the hardest of time. He did not want to relocate to a city that he knew nothing about, better yet, had never even heard of. What about school?

What about his friends? What about their family? He would be leaving them all behind.

His Dad had tried to comfort him in his agony with the symptoms associated with having Big City Withdrawal Syndrome by spoiling him to no end, spending and throwing money non stop. Whatever Pharaoh asked for, Pharaoh had received. The latest kicks. The latest game systems. Large allowances. Freedom to roam. He had even received his very first car just a few months after they had arrived, and a whole year before he received his driver's license after turning sixteen.

His Mom wasn't in the picture during his upbringing. She had lost her way in the rough streets of Brooklyn just after Pharaoh was born. Instead of offering motherly love, she opted to pursue her first love which comforted her and left her in a lifted state of delusion, one that she had spent the last of her days pining after until her last breath of life was sucked from her lungs by the metal prick that had ultimately lifted her so high that she wasn't able to return back to Earth. Pharaoh had attended her funeral at the age of 2. Needless to say, he had no memory of his mom whatsoever. The only proof of her existence was by photograph that his Dad had given him on his 13th Birthday. A photograph of his Dad and his Mom, sitting at a dining table, smiling at one another over one of her notorious soul food dinners that everyone always talked about being so phenomenal, but he had never had the opportunity to experience. In that picture, she was beautiful, healthy and glowing with pregnancy, hand on her huge stomach. Hand on him, as he developed within her womb for the last 28 days before his birth and arrival into this world. He looked like a splitting image of her in male form.

His Dad did the best that he could in raising him. For assistance, he had moved in his Great Old Man from Mississippi after his

Grandmother had passed. Having his Great Old Man as a constant in his life was the best blessing he could ever have hoped for. Three generations of men, all living under one roof. The many lessons and the abundance of wisdom that he had received from being the youngest in this remarkable set-up was incomparable. Together, these wise men taught him not only how to be a stand up provider, but also about the beauty of the black race, his African roots and the practices of the Kemets (Ancient Egyptians). Here he learned the importance of following the 42 Laws of Maat for a record of daily accountability, and as a spiritual way of living life. The Ancient Egyptians served many Gods and Goddesses and did not believe in there being just one male dominated deity that rigidly controlled the daily functions of all human beings. They believed in one being accountable for oneself. They started the day in stating the Laws of Maat with honest intentions to hold true to the affirmations, then ended the day giving an account, checking themselves to ensure that no harm was committed on their behalf. Start of day =I WILL NOT/ End of day=I HAVE NOT. The Deities were forever watchful and in every living matter on the planet including the elements of Air, Fire, Water, Minerals & Earth. Since we as human beings are made of these elements, that meant the deities also lived within us. The belief is that some deities show up more prominent in one than in others. Pharaoh knew without a shadow of doubt, that he was Son of Amun, in every sense of his make-up and every sense of his being. No doubt this strong, fearless God was reincarnated within his essence.

"On the tab, Crush?" Angel asked when she returned, placing the drinks down on the bartop in front of the gentlemen.

Pharaoh nodded in agreement. Angel picked up her glass, waiting for the guys. Altogether, they raised their goblets in salute of the moment before taking the shot. Tossing the warm liquor back, the fluid burned going down. Pharaoh immediately chased behind the burn with a swallow of his favorite beer, Miller Genuine Draft (MGD).

Pharaoh spent around in his stool watching the group of ladies who had just walked in past security. All four ladies were quite attractive and scantily dressed with tops revealing their mid- riffs, breasts and asses. All of the ladies flirtatiously smiled as they passed.

"Ayy, Pha, I think they want you Playboy," Tremaine Hoskins had also turned making sure that he didn't miss the scene that the ladies had created entering into the lounge.

Pharaoh ran a hand across his chin and down the length of his thick, neat, well groomed beard. He noticed that the ladies had stopped around the opposite side of the bar to order drinks. The whole while whispering and grinning over in his direction. Licking his lips, he knowingly took a sip of his beer. It was always the same, he looked, they jumped. No challenge whatsoever. No chase whatsoever. One thousand watt smile crossed his lips and panties dropped. He was King with the ladies. He was Pharaoh in every sense. He could literally make a selective check list of which females he thought worthy of having his dick shoved down their throats and without any fuss, bless them with the duty within a week of rounding them up. Thirsty ass ducks with watered down pussies and soggy ass dreams.

Since being in Milwaukee, he had probably ran across a handful of women who were actually about something. Who wanted something out of life. Who had bigger dreams than just wiping asses for a living. Who wanted more than to just be some lazy ass nigga's Baby Mama…..who cared about themselves more…who valued themselves more…..

Z was one of those women. Now Z was a BEAST!!!! Beautiful, educated, chill, witty, intelligent....there wasn't any way possible that some wack ass nigga would run up on her sideways. She held her own and didn't require any assistance from anyone. Girls like that, he would give the world too. Why weren't there more women like Z? This city was polluted with the same ole government supported, hood celebrated bitches. The shit was disheartening. Asses hanging, hands out...never thinking that real niggas required more. Demanded more.

In his eyes, these women weren't worth more than what their pussies offered. Because of this, he made it a point not to ever set up situations where they could ever feel as if more could be a possibility. Following certain guidelines, he had managed to eliminate issues and to keep trouble down. They always knew what it was from the start. He had never been one to mislead them into believing that they stood a chance as his Queen. His Queen would be radiant, damn near Supernova luminant, from the start, not dull, scarred and used up the way that most of the chics he had run into were. Simple rules, made for simple exits. He had followed these to the letter.

NEVER allow women to sleep over in his bed. EVER!!!!
NEVER fuck a woman more than once in a night.
NEVER spend too much time showering attention on just one woman.

He had never experienced a trip up or had any type of misstep thus far.

Pharaoh was cut from an entirely different cloth. In this dead end city with even deader opportunities, his father had paved the way. After 5 years on his new job, his father had recognized the need for better housing options in the most impoverished areas of the city. He purchased the first 4 unit building, remodeled the entire construction and enlisted his first tenants. Every year after until his retirement, he had purchased another. Now, at the well ripened age of 35, Pharaoh had learned the ins and outs of the business enough to take over ownership of the company. And he took business serious. Never half-assed in his dealings. Pharaoh had learned from the best. Smart purchases along with an eye and a passion for providing the best service to each and every tenant, he was a notable and profitable businessman.

Pharaoh nodded in recognition before addressing Tre. "Man, typical broads. I'm cool on them."

Tre was well aware of Pharaoh's views of the women that the city produced. Never a hater, he actually agreed with his friend's opinion that options were limited within the town. Tre himself wasn't one to be overlooked. Partnering with Pharaoh in business, he provided the reconstructive services needed to repair the buildings to top notch condition. Tre was amazing with the artistic work that he produced. Standing at six feet two inches in height, with brown sugar coated skin, a clean shaven head and a more laid back personality, Tre was also known to pull in the ladies. Earlier in the night he had reeled in a young lady who seemed to be a decent catch in the form of what looked to be a career woman clad in a business suit with the ability to formulate an articulate sentence.

"Hey man, there are some legit chics out here," Tre spoke encouragingly. "You attract what you put out my guy."

Pharaoh gave what was a cross between a snort and a laugh. "Now that's your biggest lie to date. These chics ain't leveling up enough for me to even consider them past one round." He took another sip from the half emptied bottle.

"Stop worrying so much about Z and checking up behind her and you'll be aight." Tre said matter of factly. "Hell, you might as well go on and link up with her. You so busy trying to find chics JUST like her."

Pharaoh shot Tre a fake evil glare over the top of his bottle. "Now, you looking to get fucked up."

Tre laughed. Noone really knew how deep the dynamics of Pharaoh and Z's friendship were. Most just assumed that there was more between the two of them. Their love ran so strong for one another. Noone dared even step to Z knowing that Pharaoh would pop off with just the slightest thought that someone, especially one of his boys, could be interested in a possible pursuit. Because of this, Tre steered clear. Z was definitely a major catch and being in her presence was enough to note just how attractive she truly was. But Tre valued his friendship with Pharaoh and would never cross the line into what he just knew would eventually be just a matter of time before the two aimed for more. Now Z's cousin Kai, that was an entirely different story.

Tre eyes narrowed as the gorgeous, honey colored girl with matching honey colored eyes walked through the door. Her large, thick, coily, Afro pulled up into a style resembling a Pineapple, stuck out, wild and unruly around her head, demanding that everyone take notice . She gazed around the room knowing that she was the center of attention. Seemed as if every guy in the room had stopped mid-sentence to take a look at her thick curves covered in a thin sundress that served no justice in it's attempt to provide coverage. Her ass was perfectly round and firm. Her waist was trim and clinched in comparison to her hips. Her face was smug, and naturally beautiful with her Creole ethnicity. Just gloss, green eye liner matching her dress and mascara completed her look.

Catching Tre's eye, Kaimery Thompson smiled and walked over wrapping her arms around his neck. "Hey Boo." her pet name had Tre grinning like she had revealed to him the winning lottery numbers.

"Hey Beautiful." Tre responded like a groupie. Her light golden brown eyes, twinkling in the flashing lights of the bar, were breathtakingly seductive. "You gonna be here for a while?"

"Yeah, I'm meeting a friend here." she replied in her soft, creamy, extremely feminine, Southern accented voice yet the words caused Tre's heart to drop.

"Okay cool." Tre knew that some undeserving nigga would be walking through the door shortly behind. "Can I get you a drink until he gets here?"

"Wow. You just auto assumed it's a guy, huh?" Kai laughed acknowledging the disappointed look on his face. "Yea a drink would be cool Hon."

Tre ordered her signature Ciroc and Pineapple juice as she took the seat next to him, ensuring to place her purse on the vacant chair beside her to save the seat for her guest.

Seconds later, Reggie Morton appeared, returning from his conversation with a few girls he had known across the bar..

"I guess you can have my seat Young Lady."

"Hey Reg!" Kai wrapped him up in the same style of hug she had given to Tre moments ago.

"Wus goin on Lil Lady?" Kai had always been one of Reg's favorites to see. Her Country bold persona and southern accent dripping in honey was soothing to his ears. Not to mention the fact that she was one cool, kick ass kinda sistah who said what she meant and meant what she said.

"Stopping down for a drink with a friend." she offered as explanation for her appearance."Speaking of which, this negro better c'mon. I ain't got all night." she glanced at her watch.

Pharaoh turned to place an order for another round of drinks with Angel. The crowd was picking up in numbers and the DJ had arrived to get the night crackin. Feeling his phone buzzing in his pocket, he removed the device expecting Z's reply.

"Hey handsome. Wus on tonight?"

The text had come from Dana, one of his fans.

Disappointed and concerned that it had not come from Z, Pharaoh responded.
"Out and about right now. Sup witchu?"

Angel placed the drinks in front of Pharaoh. With a lowered voice she asked, "Are you ordering one for Kai too?"

Pharaoh responded with no words and a fully blank stare.

Angel laughed knowingly. Throwing her hands up, and slowly shaking her head side to side she replied "Hey, just thought I'd ask."

Pharaoh sent his attention back to the text conversation. Although Z's first cousin, the whole city had to have known by now that he did NOT fuck with that dusty ass, rusty colored tramp AT ALL. Their beef was infamous. It wasn't often that they could even sit in the same room without some near physical dispute occuring.

"Wanna swing through after you wrap up where you are?" Dana's text was loud and clear.

Pharaoh thought back to his last episode with Dana. Tall, sexy with legs for days, she had great skill with that mouth of hers. Hooking up with her would not be a total waste of time, that's for sure.

Pharaoh replied "Yeah, I can make that happen. I'll hit you when I leave here."

Placing his phone back in his pocket, he ran his hands around his head to straighten his New York Yankees cap and to sweep his long, waist length locs to the back. Tre was still engrossed in some sucka'ish" ass conversation with Kai, while Reg had exited, back across to the chics he was speaking with earlier.

Taking the shot down in one swallow, Pharaoh rapped along to the lyrics of Jay-Z's Already Home, feeling the words to his core. The song was like a life motto for him. Nothing hit closer home than the arrogant, true yet precisely direct bars recorded within this track.

Pharaoh's attention was obviously being summoned by one of the chics that walked in with the group earlier. He could feel her eyes burning the side of his face like a laser. He opted to ignore her. Since they had walked in, they had already been bombarded by flocks of niggas and the last thing he had time for was for some green ass cat to roll up on him in a fit of jealous rage. He wasn't with the shits tonight.

Standing to his full six feet three inch frame, he handed Angel his credit card to close out his tab.

"You outta here Boss," Tre turned abandoning his conversation with Kai who sucked her teeth and rolled her eyes heavenward. Rude bitch.

"Yeah, I'm headed on. Got an early day tomorrow," Pharaoh handed Angel a thirty dollar tip upon the return of his card. Autographing the receipt, he placed it in her hand.

"Thanks Crush. Have a good night." she blew a kiss at her favorite customer. Pharaoh winked, causing her to blush.

Catching Reg's attention, Pharaoh used his index and middle fingers, touching his forehead in a salute to his guy.

"Everyday is an early day for you man, who you fooling?" Tre laughed. "Gon' get it."

Pharaoh smirked as he made his way to the door. "Mind ya business Playa." He shook Ron, the bouncer's hand and stepped out into the coolness of the night. Temperatures had dropped being that the warmth was only temporary and not quite ready for a permanent stay in what should be a cool season.

"You outta here?" His barber, Dee, had just made it to the door.
"Yeah, I'm headed out. I'll holla at you tomorrow My Guy."
"Aiight Pha. See you tomorrow Boss."

Pharaoh hit the locks on the remote for his Jet Black on Jet Black Jaguar XJ. The machine sat laced with 22" Chrome and Black Forgiato rims. The personalized Wisconsin license plates read "T'Challa" after his favorite Marvel Comic Book Superhero, Black Panther.

Speeding out into traffic, Pharaoh headed to the nearest gas station to fill up. One task that he would not have to worry about completing tomorrow morning. After topping off the tank in premium fuel, he dipped out into traffic again heading South and East and into the inner city.

It took him fifteen minutes to arrive in front of Dana's duplex apartment. He sent a text to notify her of his arrival outside.

Opening the arm rest, he reached inside and sparked one of his favorite Cohiba brand Cuban cigars to life. Letting all four windows down halfway and cracking the moon roof, he rested his head on the leather headrest, enjoying the sweet flavor of the smoky tobacco. Glancing over to the right as the front door opened, Pharaoh watched Dana as she headed up to the passenger door. Popping the locks, the pretty, brown girl jumped in with a wide smile.

"Hey Handsome."

Pharaoh took another puff and tossed her a megawatt smile. "Hey you."

She stared at him for a moment, taking him in before reaching for the cigar that was stuck between his lips, placing it between hers. Pharaoh watched as she inhaled, never allowing her eyes to leave his. Her lips wrapped around the thickness of the blunt, purposefully giving him a show.

"That's what we doing?" Pharaoh's dick was standing at attention, full well knowing the girl's capabilities. She didn't answer, just took another puff, wrapping her lips tight around the "prop" she was using to perform in her show.

Pharaoh watched her a bit longer before asking in a low voice, "So when do I become as lucky as that blunt is right now?"

Dana loved his accent. His question in that deeply eastern tongue was enough for her to slowly remove the blunt from her mouth and place it back in between his lips. She reached over to let his seat back. Reaching down into his joggers, she wrapped her hands around his thick, long, hard meat and used her hand to relax him even further. Leaning over, taking in and loving the scent of his Yves St. Laurent Y cologne, she used her tongue in a circular motion around the tip of his hardened piece. Slowly, using her lips as suctioning device, she slid her mouth down the shaft until her bottom lip touched the sack of his balls, engulfing his entire dick in the confines of her sloppy, wet mouth. Pharaoh, leaned back in the seat as far as he could, looking out the moon roof directly into the pinkish tint of the glowing planet directly above. Mars was bright and prevalent in the sky as if it's very presence along with it's known association with Male dominance was a sure sign intended particularly for him and him alone. It felt great to be the man.

Chapter Three- Zaire (Living My Best Life)

Smile/Living My Best Life- Lil Duval & Snoop Dog

Zaire exited the elevator shaft into the front lobby with the young man that she had just completed interviewing, walking behind on her heels.

"Thanks so much for coming in. After your background check is completed, you should be hearing from us shortly after." she smiled and shook his hand.

"Alright cool." the young man thankfully took her hand in his own. "It was a pleasure meeting with you Miss Jefferson. I look forward to receiving the call."

Zaire nodded and made her way back to the elevator. The door opened immediately. Pressing the button to the 4th floor, she glanced at her Chanel watch. 11:03am. She had made great time.

Feeling excited about the response from the job ads and the candidates who had come through the door that morning, she mentally patted herself on the back. Progress was always rewarding.

Zaire stepped off the elevator. The sound of her pumps clicking against the tiled floor notified her supervisor of her return back from walking the last candidate out.

"Hey Zaire, come see me hon."

Zaire had made it a few steps passed the cluttered office but back tracked to the open doorway.

Naomi Lopez sat behind her desk, plucking away at the keys on the board that was connected to her PC. She wore a wide smile on her tanned brown, native Mexican face. Her glasses sat just on the tip of her thin nose.

Glancing around the office, Zaire made note of the many files that sat in tall piles on top of the cabinets.

"My God, you need to hire a temp to come in and get you right," Zaire teased, knowing this would probably never happen with Naomi being so strict with the departmental budget.

"I wish." Naomi sighed. "These are all of the terminated files that need to be boxed and put away in storage." Shaking her head, she reached over and removed a pile from one of the chairs that sat in front of her desk, clearing a space for Zaire to sit. "Have a seat, Superwoman."

Zaire laughed and took the space that Naomi had cleared. "Now, I don't know about being Superwoman but hell, I try."

Naomi laughed along with her.

"Well I applaud your effort Young Lady."

It had been a long week after placing the ads the Thursday before. The response has been amazing. It was just Wednesday and they had already interviewed 40 plus candidates for the open positions. The roles consisted of CNC Machine Operators, Assembly Workers and Material Handlers for all shifts. Zaire was stoked to see many people of the darker race walk through the doors, including a few women. She couldn't have asked for a better turn out.

"Going at this rate, you need a vacation Z."

Zaire frowned and shook her head from side to side. "Nah, no vacay for me. I got entirely too much work to do in order to meet this deadline. You think 45 candidates, half will either not make it through or have some sort of fall off." her voice trailed out. "We will still spend the entire summer recruiting, extending offers and completing New Hire Orientations." she knew the game all too well. "Vacation is the last thing on my mind."

Naomi studied the younger woman closely. She couldn't remember Zaire taking vacation anytime in the last year in a half which was concerning. Zaire sometimes stayed and worked long nights and arrived early mornings, always trying hard to stay ahead of demand. This work ethic, although admirable was just not healthy in Naomi's eyes.

"Z, you have to take care of you sometimes Lady. The show will go on without you Dear. Don't work yourself into an early grave."

Zaire was used to the backlash that she regularly received from Naomi. She meant well. Since starting her employment with Narvo Corporation, Naomi had been like a Big Sister to her. Their working relationship was one of the best that an employee could ask for in a subordinate role. Naomi was super cool, laid back and very easy to talk too. Everyone at the office loved her as the departmental head.

"I know and I do," Zaire responded, tucking a loose strand of her coily hair behind her ear.

"So you mean to tell me that you haven't considered putting your feet up on a lounge chair that sits in the sand on a beach in let's say…Miami, at any point?" Naomi watched and waited for Zaire's response.

"I mean, yeah I have considered but it is just not in the plans at the time." Zaire offered to the awaiting older lady who again frowned with concern.

"I truly believe that a little R&R would do wonders for you. You can not forget to live life My Dear." Naomi leaned forward in her chair ensuring that her words got across. "You are young, vibrant, beautiful and hell, frankly, you deserve it!!!"

Zaire considered what she was conveying with her words. As always, she was right, and she would possibly make plans for later in the year, but for now, lounging on a beach, although it sounded wonderful, it would have to wait.

"Maybe later in the year. Just not now."

Naomi leaned back in her chair, a mischievous smirk crossed her face. "Well, it just so happens that your calling won't come so later in the year."

Zaire squinted, not sure what Naomi had up her sleeve but listened intently. "Oooookay. Come again."

Naomi smile was bursting from her face. "The new plant is weeks away from Grand Opening in Miami. They are starting the recruiting efforts to staff the North Warehouse." Naomi paused watching the expression on Zaire's face. After a few seconds, she continued. "During the Leadership call yesterday, the Plant Manager asked if there was someone who could help in starting the process who had a good grasp of the entire recruiting cycle and ...." she paused again for emphasize.."...I immediately thought of and volunteered you."

Zaire blinked several times before her mouth was able to move. "Huh? Why would you do that?"

"Because you are the obvious choice to give them full effort and to hit the ground running without needing any immediate assistance." Naomi said matter of factly. "Come on Z!!! You will do an amazing job at the Miami site."

Zaire continued blinking with an incredulous stare. "Are you serious right now?"

"Yes. I couldn't be more serious. This is an amazing opportunity and no one deserves it more than you!!!"

Zaire sat silently, letting the impact of what exactly Naomi was saying set in. Miami?!? What the hell!?!?

"During this time, you will work under the title of Director of Recruiting. We are offering you an additional $30,000 annually on top of what you are currently receiving. The position will last in duration of 3 months." Naomi made note of the look of uncertainty on Zaire's face. "Z, this is an amazing opportunity. Upon return, we will keep your salary as the same. I know that it seems abrupt and random, but believe me, we will look out for you and compensate you for your trouble."

Zaire had many questions. Who would keep her apartment while she was gone? Who would watch Nala? Where will she stay? What would she do for 3 whole months away?

"How soon are they expecting me to arrive?" Zaire managed to get one question of importance to move from her head to her mouth.

"We will be putting you up in one of the finest hotels and covering all costs from rooming, meals, uniforms , laundry...whatever you need." Naomi skimmed past Zaire's original question which in Zaire's eyes made it even more of a pressing one.

"How soon Naomi?"

Naomi braced herself for the objections that she knew would come with delivering the answer to her question. "You leave as soon as Saturday?" her reply came out more so posed as a question of her own rather than an answer.

"SATURDAY!!!!" Zaire hopped up nearly flipping the chair over. "As in THIS Saturday?"

Naomi chewed the side of her lip. "Uhhh ...yes. This Saturday."

Zaire paced back and forth in front of the desk, taking time to allow the news of her departure to sink in. Naomi watched her every move.

"I know that this is short notice." Naomi started, but was immediately cut off by the killer dagger that Zaire shot her way.

"Short notice? You think!!!" Zaire was now fuming.

"I know Sweetie and I wish that I was able to deliver this news to you with more time to prepare." Her response was sincere. "But this all came to me so suddenly along with the request. I apologize for the short notice, but yes honey, this is happening and it is happening fast." Naomi reached for a document that sat fresh on her desktop printer. "This has all of the details you will need including flight and hotel reservations along with a daily meals and necessities budget." Opening the top drawer to the file cabinet, Naomi removed a sealed envelope. "This contains a company credit card for expenses. And a few copies of the Expense Reporting Form. The hotel has a transport service which is available for your use at anytime but if you'd like, I can reserve you a rental."

Zaire reluctantly retrieved the items from her hands. She felt as if she had just been completely bamboozled. What exactly had happened? She never expected this as being a part of her work day when pulling into the parking lot that morning.

"Yay or Nay to the rental?"

"Nay." Zaire managed to choke out knowing that all arrangements had been made prior to her arriving into Naomi's office and even in protest, she would be fighting a losing battle.

"Don't look so defeated hon!!!" Naomi spoke from some invisible bright side that only she could see in the blinding moment. "It's MIA!!! Get out, get some sun, have a load of fun and enjoy yourself while you are there. I put some extra in your budget just for this purpose."

Shoulders slumped, Zaire continued down the hall to her own office. Much neater in appearance and very well decorated, the wooden door was a welcome sight as she made no hesitation in closing it upon crossing the threshold.

Miami. For 3 whole months!!! What in the entire hell!!!

She needed consultation.

Reaching for the phone, she pressed in the 7 digits that dialed out to Pharaoh's number.

"Z!!!!! How's my favorite girl?"

"Uhhhh, lunch. 15 minutes. Mo's Irish Pub." she hung up the phone and collected her purse. Dropping her cell phone inside the bag, she grabbed her keys from the front pocket and headed out of the office.

"Marcella, I am taking a long lunch and will be back within the next hour and a half." she announced to the receptionist on her way out.

Stepping from the elevator shaft, she headed out the back door to the employee lot. Again, it was yet another beautiful May day with temperatures well into the 80s. Hopping into her car, she pushed the buttons that would allow the fresh air to seep in as she headed to her destination.

Parking in the lot, she realized that Pharaoh had beaten her to the restaurant. His car was freshly waxed and immaculate as usual. She pulled in the vacant space next to him. Stepping out and making her way through the front door, her bestie sat on the guest bench in the lobby with the most concerned expression on his face.

"Z, what's wrong?" he asked rising from his sitting position at the sight of her.

Zaire stepped into his arms for a long needed hug. "How long is the wait?"

A young lady stepped forward at that moment and ushered them to follow her to be seated.

After ordering a glass of wine to sip with her lunch and to calm her nerves, Zaire looked into Pharaoh waiting face.

"Lawd, Naomi just tried to murder me." Zaire put her head in her hands and rubbed her temples for a minute. After receiving no response from Pharaoh, she looked up and laughed at the dangerously confused expression on his dark chocolate face.

"Okay, that was a bit dramatic." she admitted causing his expression to relax.

"Listen, unless you want me to go and blow that muthafucka up, I suggest you never start with that shit again."

Zaire laughed and enjoyed the feeling. Pharaoh was such a character. Somehow, he always knew how to bring her storm back to a normal calm.

"No, what I mean to say is that she called me into her office and literally sent me away on a 3 month "adventure" to Miami." she watched Pharaoh's expression switch to one of shock. Continuing, she explained, "I am to go to Miami to head the recruiting department in an effort to hire staff for the new facility." She continued on, giving him the details as Naomi had relayed them to her.

Pharaoh didn't say anything immediately. He seemed to also need time to allow her news to set in. "Three months!!! Wow."

"I know right. What am I supposed to do there for THREE whole months?"

Pharaoh, knowing that she needed a session that consisted of upliftment, swept his own selfish thoughts away and opted to take a more positive approach.

"What to do? Well I can think of a million things for you to do. After all it is Miami Z."

Zaire looked at him skeptically and sighed. "But 3 WHOLE months!!!" she whined in defeat.

The waitress approached, setting the glass of wine in front of Zaire and a glass of water with lemon in front of Pharaoh. Zaire ordered the Shepherd's Pie and a side Caesar salad. Pharaoh ordered the Citrus glazed Salmon with roasted potatoes and seasonal veggies, the Spinach Tapenade as an appetizer.

"Awww Boo, it will breeze by before you know it." Pharaoh offered after the waitress left to submit their order. "And don't sleep on the MIA Baby Girl!!! There is a shit ton of things to do. Truth be told, I must say that I'm a little jealous that you get to go and not me."

"But see it's different for you because you at least have friends there. I have no one. I don't know a single soul residing in Miami. I can see a few weeks but a few months is a completely different story!"

"I really believe that you are making it out to be worse than it actually is Z." Pharaoh sipped his water before continuing. "This is an amazing opportunity for you to step into a role that will ultimately take you higher up that ladder that you have been so desperate to climb. This is your chance! Take it and run with it like your last name is fuckin Gump."

"You sound like Naomi." Zaire sipped her own Chardonnay frowning at her friend.

"Nah, Naomi sound like me." Pharaoh teased drawing a sarcastic expression from Zaire, who flipped him off with her hand.

"Boy, bye."

Pharaoh laughed causing her to join in.

"But seriously, I have so many plans to make being that I am expected to leave out on Saturday." Zaire's mind was racing. "My flight leaves in the evening. I have to pay up my bills, find a sitter for Nala, get a ride to the airport, find someone to apartment sit…."

Pharaoh cut her off pulling his phone from his pocket. "Listen Z, one thing at a time. Worrying about how you will get to the airport is the last thing you should be worrying about, you know I got you on that. As for Nala, reach out to Tre, you know that he loves cats and will not have a problem taking her in. Do you really need an apartment sitter?"

Zaire considered his question. Okay so maybe she didn't need an apartment sitter but a cleaning service to come through while she was away. Yes!

"Well, a cleaning service to keep it tidy while I am away."

"Cool. I will holla at Niecy and Yolanda and have them to stop through once a week to keep it on point. They do great work in cleaning my apartments after tenants move out."

"Alright, let me know how much they will charge for the service. I can cut them a check before I go." Zaire mentally placed the task on the growing list of duties that needed to be performed before her leaving out.

"Nah, I got that covered. Don't worry about the cost." Pharaoh took another sip of his water, placing his phone back into his pocket.

"No. I appreciate you wanting to help but I will cover my own cleaning costs."

Pharaoh shut her down with a wave of his hand.

"I said don't worry 'bout it. I got it Z. So cross that off your little list along with the rental payments. I got that as well."

"Okay, Now you trippin. I can handle my own expenses Pharaoh. I know you mean well but I'm cool. I will pay my own bills."

Pharaoh watched as the waitress made her way from the kitchen to their table. "Too late. It's already paid."

Zaire's mouth fell open before she started to protest but was quieted by the waitress who arrived to place their meals in front of them. That explained what he had done on his cell phone while he had it out.

"Is there anything else that I can get for you right away?" the young lady's eyes rested on Pharaoh's face. Her smile was extra wide.

"We're good. Thanks." Pharaoh picked up his fork digging into his fish and completely ignoring the young girl's obvious flirtation.

Zaire shook her head. Good thing she wasn't on a date with him or there would have been some real problems. She watched as the waitress made her way over to the bar where another waitress sat. She placed a hand over her heart and mouthed an "Oh My God" to the second young girl and they both giggled. Wow. Zaire chuckled. The Pharaoh Effect was on the move.

"What?" Pharaoh was wolfing down his food oblivious to the scene that played out behind him.

"Seems you have a little fan club over by the bar." Zaire smirked taking a fork full of her Shepherd's Pie. Delicious.

Pharaoh turned around and spotted the waitresses giggling at the bar. He turned back around and took another fork full of his fish.

"What are they? Like two years old?" Pharaoh sipped his water to wash the food down. "They are fucking babies. And I ain't FUCKING babies."

Zaire rolled her eyes and laughed. Taking a moment to appreciate the humor, the caring nature, the raw and realness of her best friend. Just moments ago, she felt like her world was falling from underneath her and now in the company of her human blankie, she felt as if her feet had been planted solidly on leveled ground once again. She loved him for having this effect, always.

They lightly chatted over the rest of their meal. Pharaoh filled her in on his latest purchase of an apartment building that he had been eyeing and his latest conversations with his family over in New York. Zaire put claim to at least paying the bill to show her appreciation for his forever having availability and just forever having her back.

She stepped into the Ladies Room to wash her hands. Her attention was immediately pulled to the conversation that was taking place in the handicap stall.

"Girlllll, I would eat ALL of his chocolate up. He is too damn fine!!!"
"Yes honey, he is EVERYTHING!!! And you can tell he ain't from here. What is he Jamaican or something? Maybe African. I don't know but they don't make 'em like that here."
"AT ALL!!!"

The two waitresses giggled.

Zaire smirked and turned the faucet on in the sink, startling the girls. Moments later, the door opened and the two girls walked out freezing at the sight of Zaire. Their frightened looks were comical.

Zaire laughed as she reached for paper towel to dry her hands. "It's okay. He's a friend. But remember to be careful with the way that you two are carrying on. This could have easily been a situation of a different outcome. Control your hormones and never allow inappropriate behavior to jeopardize your employment Little Queens." Zaire put on a serious face. "And I say that because you are. So always conduct yourselves as such."

Zaire exited the bathroom and returned to the table. Pharaoh had once again beat her to the punch.

"Come on Pharaoh!!! I said that I was paying the bill!!!"

"Well, while you were in the restroom I caught one of the waitresses passing by." He shrugged. "I was looking for ours but I couldn't find her anywhere."

Zaire shook her head and thought to herself. "If only you knew."

Zaire's last half of the day at the office was completely uneventful. She took it that maybe it was God's way of cutting her a break, knowing that she had been the recipient of enough excitement for one day if not a whole damn year. Leaving at exactly 4:30pm sharp, she locked her office door and headed home for the day.

After speaking with Tre to confirm that he would be willing to take in Nala in her absence, Zaire called her parents who were absolutely elated with the news. Their baby girl was moving up in the world which is all they could ever hope for. They were so ecstatic with the accomplishment.

Ending her conversation with them, Zaire made her last call of the night to her cousin Kai.

"Hey Pooh," Kai's Southern drawl answered on the third ring.

"You are going to have to come and visit me in Miami." Zaire blurted out after hearing her younger cousin, by 2 years, voice.

"Sure. But why would I have to do that?" Kai asked, her voice laced with concern.

"Because Naomi is sending me away for 3 months, that's why." Zaire went on to fill Kai in on the details of her day.

After hearing the story, Kai fell silent. For the past few years since she had traveled to Milwaukee from her hometown of Mansura, Louisiana to obtain her Master's in Education from Marquette University, her Big Cousin had been her lifeline. She knew that in spending her days without having her around, even if for just a few months, would be torture.

"Well of course I will swing down and visit you Cuz. We can make a fun time out of it. Get out in the sun, holla at some cuties and get White girl wasted!!!"

Zaire laughed, fully expecting her cousin to turn what was an unofficial trip into a turn up session. Kai was all about sights and being seen. The girl was always down for a good time. Her total opposite, Kai loved hanging out and was a certified social butterfly. She was forever searching for opportunities to party and knew of all the happenings around town, which was always quite funny to Zaire being that she wasn't originally from the city and knew more than Zaire did who was. Kai was bold, tough, funny and wild in her country girl kind of style and super protective of her mild mannered cousin.

"Just promise me that you will not spend the entire time lying around in the hotel moping. Please get out and enjoy the obvious blessing that the Lord has placed at your feet. This is the perfect

opportunity for you to start working on living your best life Babes."
Kai knew her cousin all too well.

"That would be easier to commit to if I actually knew someone who would be there with me." Zaire pouted.

"Okay, well let's do this, " Kai started in her attempt to pull Zaire out of her funk. "I will search for some tickets online this weekend. I have vacation that I need to use up anyways. If I find some that aren't too pricey, I will purchase them to fly down and spend a weekend with you."

"Thanks Kai, you are a complete gem in everyway Luv." Zaire really appreciated her cousin going out of her way.

"Hey, I'm not leaving my Cuz out to drown. And anyways, we can make a real Girl's trip out of it. So, I expect you to know what's what by the time I make it down. Understood?"

Zaire laughed, knowing not to make any promises. "I will do my best."

"Okay, that's that. Now, let's make plans to celebrate that salary increase this weekend before you head out Chica." Kai's excitement for her cousin was noted."They got you ballin' outta control over there at Narvo! Hell, loan me five dollars when you get that first big check."

Zaire laughed at her animated look-a-like. After, making plans for a Saturday morning spa day, Zaire ended her call with Kai. She was feeling much better about the upcoming endeavor after speaking with her favorite four: her parents, her bestie and her little cousin.

After packing most of her clothes, Zaire jumped in the shower and snuggled in her bed next to Nala. She was much less stressed as the silence of the night engulfed her into a dreamless sleep.

Chapter Four- Pharaoh (Classic Man)

Classic Man- Jidenna (Wondaland Presents- The Eephus)

TGIF!!!!

The week had been a beast!!!

It seemed as if there had been non stop, appointment after appointment. Brookfield to meet with the Real Estate agent. South side to meet with the attorney. North side to make sure all was going well and according to schedule with the contractors. West Allis to connect with the construction company responsible for providing and surfacing the cement that would lay the foundation for the new parking lot that would be installed in the back of the new 8 family building that Pharaoh had purchased. From one side of the city to the opposite, he had accumulated many miles on T'Challa throughout the duration of the last 7 days.

Now in traffic, speeding down I-94, he made his way to scoop Reg in route to Tre's house who had invited the fellas over in honor of his lighting the grill. He looked forward to having the night to unwind.

Turning, headed West on the connecting ramp for I-43, it took minutes before he exited at Capitol Drive and pulled in front of Reg's home that he shared with his child's mom. She sat on the front porch surrounded by three of her girlfriends. Puffing on the joint, that sat between her two fingers, she waved as Pharaoh parked.

"Hey Pha," she shouted from the top step.

"Wus good Lady?" Pharaoh yelled back. Aleisha was all smiles in a baseball cap the displayed the words "Smoke Somethin" across the front. It wasn't often that she was in a good mood, especially anytime that Reg was preparing to leave the house. Reg had made sure to save himself from what would have been one of her fiery tantrums by providing her with her favorite treat. A few puffs was all she needed to calm her usually off the chart and completely out of whack emotions.

"He should be down in a sec." She assured Pharaoh who nodded in return.

Surveying the block, there were many kids out running around and screaming at the top of their lungs. Loud music blasted from the top porch of the corner house on the opposite side of the street. A few neighborhood teens stood directly in the middle of the street chopping it up while eyeing the clean make, model and body of his vehicle. The warm pre-summer was in full swing.

Reaching in his arm rest, he grabbed his own favorite treat. Sparking life into the Cohiba, he waited patiently for his guy to make his appearance. Minutes later, his debut arrived.

Reg kissed Aleisha on top of her head and handed her the squirming young prince that he had securely placed upon his hip.

"Ayy, tell your friend to get at me. He's a cutie." One of the girls sitting beside Aleisha called out to Reg as he made his way to the passenger side door.

Although, Pharaoh had heard the girl loud and clear, he continued to puff on the blunt, choosing to ignore her comment.

Inside the car, Reg pursed his lips. Knowing his friend would have zero interest, he waved off the girls advances.

"Yeah, well Renee ain't worth mentioning."

"Then why mention her?" Pharaoh gave his homie the side eye before pulling off from the curb.

Reg smirked and reached into the arm rest to light himself a cigar. "Hey, you get no argument here my guy." He pulled the thick smoke into his mouth. "But, I did see Naya Morris the other day at Target. Had ran up there to pick up Little Reg some pampers. Remember her from school? Have you seen her lately? She getting thick as shit!!!" Reg forever had a story on who he had seen from the high school they attended together.

Pharaoh, Zaire, Tre and Reg had all attended John Marshall High School for senior studies. He had met both Reg and Tre as his squad mates on the basketball team. They were all star players during their years with the sport. Those days had been fun times that kept them as close friends ever since. Tre was the cool, laid back guy that everyone loved. Reg was the tell it like it is unintentional class clown who keep his holster stocked with details about everyone's personal business that he could fire off at any minute. Pharaoh was the ladies man. The three together formed the makeup of what became the most popular trio for the entire time that they had attended. They were the life of the party and were first on everyone's guest list.

"Nah, I haven't seen her since high school. She was nice even back then," Pharaoh remembered that he had the opportunity to take the pretty young girl to Junior Prom but after finding out the Z had accepted a date with Will Davidson, his nemesis at that time, he had instead decided to rescue Z from total reputation destruction, by taking her as his date. Of course she had put up a huge fuss, but he wouldn't dare have his Sister Friend out here bad, stooping as low as to show up to prom with Wil'lin Will who had a reputation of exposing his many rendezvous with the ladies through vividly shared details, pictures and violation of privacy.

Naya had been upset and had pulled many antics out of jealousy at the dance, trying to humiliate Z. But Z, being mature and well above petty schemes, was too smooth to feed into her bullshit.

"Yeah, she asked if I still rock witchu." Reg turned, flirting with a young lady waiting at the bus stop at the light where they currently sat. "I told her ass, shit, of course I do. This fam for life right here." Reg turned back to Pharaoh giving him a fist pound.

"Yo that's wussup." Pharaoh pulled off once the light turned green. "Decades and counting, My Nig."

Parking in front of Tre's house. They made their way to the back deck, daring not to step on the well manicured lawn. Tre was anal about the beautiful work that he had put into his yard and his home in general. Passing the brand new Cadillac Escalade that sat in the driveway on the side of the house, Tre was sitting at the patio table, sipping on a glass of Hennessy.

"Whaddup y'all?" he greeted them both with "homie hugs" as they stepped up onto the wooden deck. The barrel style grill was smoking with the aroma of burning Applewood and deliciousness permeating the air. The double glass doors provided the sight of various liquors, an ice bucket and clean glasses sitting on a large tray in the center of the pub style kitchen table. He was always a great host whose preparation rivaled many women Pharaoh knew. "Help yourselves Homeboys."

"Say less," Reg was already inside and at the kitchen table before the last word left Tre's lips.

Pharaoh opted to claim his favorite seat, a soft, reclining lounge chair first. After the week he had, relaxation was in order. His priorities was on point, knowing that the comfort of the chair was one that he and Reg usually fought over.

The darkness of night was falling upon them fast. Pharaoh made note of the many errands that he would need to complete the next day. A visit with his barber was first assigned. Afterwards he would run down to Kenosha to hit the outlet mall to check out the sales. He then needed to swing by to check on Mr. Robinson, an older tenant whom was a friend of his Dad's and one whom he had grown extremely fond of. He of course needed to get Z to the airport in time for her flight. His hot date with the new chic, Lacey, whom he had met a day before would end his night.

After Reg had given him the evil eye and settled securely in another seat, Pharaoh, stepped inside to pour himself troubles in a glass of Remy Martin 1738, no mixer tossed on rocks. Returning to his seat, he took the first swallow as Tre pulled a slab of ribs from the grill.

"I'm truly hoping that you got more than just that swine coming off that grill." Pharaoh spoke disapprovingly.

"Yeah I got a Red Snapper going on last for your extra bourgeois ass." Tre and Reg laughed, knowing that Pharaoh was a Pescatarian and didn't eat the meat of any land animals as a part of his diet.

"Preciate it, God." Pharaoh responded with a smirk. "Guess you really do have love for ya boy."

Yeah, I got you homie." Tre spoke in an airy voice. And that he did. And they had come to expect this from him. Tre had always looked out for his closest guys who he viewed as his "brothers." Gatherings at his bungalow meant that everyone would have exactly what they liked, and he knew his brothers like the back of his hand. Knowing that Pharaoh also loaded up on tons of veggies, he made one of his favorite Grilled Brussel Sprout dishes as a side, along with Reg's favorite smoke gouda, cheddar and colby jack mac n' cheese. Pharaoh would also partake in his share of 1738 while Reg drink his regular Belvidere with a back-up stock secure behind the bar in his basement.

Tre's home was his pride and joy. He had purchased the Foreclosed home for a little of nothing after Pharaoh's recommendation and had spent years working to construct it up to his satisfaction, bringing it to its current state of beauty. The four bedroom, one and a half bath tri-level, (including the rec basement) was purchased with family in mind, which ended up being a dream deferred after his unexpected break-up with his fiancee the year before. Pharaoh had never felt that the woman in which he had proposed to was right for his friend. Stuck up, needy and self centered, the girl had given zero effort in terms of helping with finances but expected to be given everything. Having that entitled attitude along with her sneaky infidelities, is what ultimately did her in. Although truly devastated that his guy had to endure the level of heartache associated with the split, Pharaoh was elated when Tre had finally sent the chic kicking rocks. Since then, Tre was finding it hard to trust in another female again and Pharaoh still sensed the hurt in him till this day. Pharaoh knew that Tre was a good guy who would one day make a lucky woman extremely happy and prayed for him many nights. Now Tre was one who he could definitely see living a wonderful family centered kind of life, but for himself on the other hand, he couldn't see that far into the future and had yet to run across a prospect that he would even consider having to play a regular starring role within his home.

"What's Z up to tonight?" Tre asked sticking a few bratwursts on the grill. "She could swing thru if she feels up to it"

"Nah, I doubt that she would. Z is busy with packing and handling her last minute duties before heading out," Pharaoh sipped his Remy and took a pull from a newly lit cigar. "I know she's not gonna be game tonight. When I spoke with her earlier she kept mentioning the many things that she still had to do."

"I'm so happy for her. She truly deserve that promo man," Reg said to the gentlemen who nodded in agreement. "She been doing her thing since graduation!!! So glad to hear about the pay-off finally being handed her."

"Yeah, she wasn't feelin' having to travel for it, though." Pharaoh disclosed to the guys. "But I believe she is going to kill it down in MIA. That shit's perfect for her. New plant. New place. New space. Yeah, the trip will definitely do her some good."

Both Tre and Reg turned to look at Pharaoh incredulously. Both were amazed with what Pharaoh had just stated.

"Whoa!!! Stop the muthafuckin' press!!!!" Reg would not ever bite his tongue. "You mean to tell me that you are cool with Z being away in Miami for 3 months My Nig?"

Pharaoh scowled. "Why wouldn't I be? It's no secret that I want what's best for huh. And this is huh opportunity to shine." He took a long pull from the blunt. "I'm supportin' huh fa'sure wit' this. His accent fell thick, knowing full well what his friends were getting at.

Reg exchanged a look with Tre and they both shook their heads with a smile.

"Okay, I must say that I am proud of you, Pha." Tre said before stepping inside to refresh his own drink. "You can be really over-protective of her at times."

"Shee-it ALL the time." Reg stated matter of factly. "Call that shit what the fuck it is."

Pharaoh waved them both off. "Listen, Z is my True from top tuh bottom. I fucks wit huh harder than I fucks with chics in my own fam. That's SIS and there's NOTHING I won't do for huh. I would go above and beyond to make sure she's straight. Damn right!!!"

Reg gave Tre the look. They both knew it was time to leave it alone. They had traveled down that lane several times with Pharaoh and knew that it would end the exact same way, with Pharaoh proclaiming that his feelings for Z were strictly platonic no matter how overly weird their relationship was in the eyes of others.

Pharaoh could give two shits about what everyone had been trying to insinuate for years regarding his love for Z. He and Z knew what it was. That's all that mattered to him. Z was his sister and that was that. His thoughts about her were of the highest. She was special and deserved one who was just as special as she. Many had tried to get a sample of her offerings but only one had ever been special enough to gain his approval. And that was a devastatingly horrible story in itself.

Tre grabbed his flashing phone from the table and took a call inside. Pharaoh checked his own phone. He had several notifications, mostly from miscellaneous apps. He chose to ignore the text that had come through from Dana, but he did welcome the text that he had received from Lacey.

Lacey would be a treat. Her body was incredible and was the first thing that he noticed when she had come galloping into the store the day before. Her skin tight leggings left nothing to the imagination. He had let her skip him in line just so he could take full advantage of having a good long view. Smiling and introducing himself, she had bitten right away. They had exchanged numbers and spent the majority of last night back and forth in an "interesting" text conversation. The kind that placed her at priority in receiving responses from him. At least for now.

Tre made his way back outside and stopped in front of Pharaoh.

"Heads up, Kai is pulling up out front to pick up a book that I am loaning out to her." Tre watched the expression on Pharaoh's face knowing that he would not be happy about her arrival. "She's stopping in and leaving out. She's not staying."

Although irritated, Pharaoh nodded, appreciating the warning that he guy took time to give to him. Just so long as she steered clear of him, all would be well.

Tre walked around front to greet her. Hell he could have just walked the book out to her if he were going to meet her in the front, Pharaoh thought to himself but decided to let the thought go. This was not his home when it was all said and done. He was chillin and relaxing and he would keep it that way.

After taking a swig of his drink, Pharaoh noticed that Tre had returned, holding Kai's hand as if she were fragile.

"Careful stepping up," he spoke as her eyes scanned the guests. She lit up at the sight of Reg.

"Hey Reg!!!" she ran over to where he sat, plopping down on his lap and throwing her arms around his neck. Her southern accent was drippy and overly sweet, almost factitious sounding to Pharaoh's ears. Her voice reminded him of First Lady Tasha Spanks from the show Greenleaf.

Just like a THOT, walk up holding one nigga hand and running over to plop down in the next nigga lap. Pharaoh shook his head at the foolery.

"Hey Pretty Lady," Reg stood from his sitting position, lifting her in the air. She screamed out with her known phobia of heights.

"Sorry, I just gotta do it when I see you." Reg laughed placing her down, squealing on the deck. "I have always been told that angels belong in the air."

She giggled and hit Reg on the arm. "Oh, Stop it now."

Yes Please!!! Pharaoh silently agreed, his soul was becoming more and more irritated by the second. The girl could damn near be Z's twin, minus her lighter skin, eyes and lighter sandy colored hair, she and Z shared damn near the same exact facial features. But that was where the similarities stopped. From the very first day that he had met her when she had come to Milwaukee in order to attend school, they had bumped heads. She had some issue with the way that he had advised Z, or said something to Z or who really gave a fuck? The majority of their disputes spinned from some way that she felt about how he had addressed Z or felt about his attitude. Hell, he couldn't help that he was Don ass nigga sitting a level wayyyy above the typical Average Joe. But this chic was forever on bullshit!!! In his eyes, she was a certified country bumpkin who needed to be seen and was always heard. A hood rat of the worst kind being that she had no clue that this is exactly what she was!!!. She always needed to receive some type of attention from some sucka ass nigga, no disrespect to his homies. She was the type of chic that he hated with a passion, loud, overly social and gutter trash. Hailing from the Bayou, she was Creole in every sense. Not like a smooth Beyonce kinda Creole but more some kinda fucked up Creole mix that the Gods probably needed to throw away instead of giving the go ahead and placing life into what was obviously a flawed creation.

Pharaoh pulled out his phone and continued his conversation with Miss Lacey. He wasn't sure what he would plan for his night with her. He just hoped that in any case, it would end with him bussin that pussy open with that pretty ass in the air.

"Hey Pharaoh."

The voice sounded forced. Looking up, Kai stood with her hand on her hip and a bored look on her face. Really? This is where she had the balls to go? Just weeks ago, she had called him every fucked up name under the sun during one of their infamous disputes and now she had the nerve to try to engage in niceties with him. Not just niceties, but pleasantries with a whole entire attitude.

"Tuh." Pharaoh laughed inwardly and looked back down to his phone. She could miss him with all of that bullshit. One thing that he didn't do was the phonies.. She could keep that fake ass greeting to herself no doubt.

Kai laughed wickedly, rolling her eyes."See Tre, I did that shit for you. Don't ask me to speak to that muthafucka ever again!!! That's a wrap. Rude ass."

Pharaoh looked up from his phone. Folding his bottom lip tightly under his top to keep from saying what he really wanted to, he stood and stretched his legs with his arms over his head. Stepping off the porch, he looked back at Tre.

"I'll be back when this little girl is gone."

"LITTLE GIRL!!!! Boy, don't get me started!!!" she yelled to Pharaoh's back as he walked off.

"Too late Little Mama," Pharaoh called over his shoulder. "You STARTED, with having the audacity to speak my name."

Tre held the yelling girl back as Pharaoh continued to his car. Inside, he let the seat back and resumed pulling on his half smoked blunt.

Looking into the now dark sky, the visible stars twinkle bright. He thought about his Great Old Man and sent a puff of smoke into the air and out through the cracked moonroof in honor. His Grandfather had passed just days before Christmas not surviving long enough to bring in the new year. Although his death was not considered sudden, being that his old age had long ago worked overtime deteriorating the organs within his body, in particular his heart, the sudden vacancy that plagued his life was one that he was still desperately trying to find some kind of solace in. Some means of adjustment. It felt as if a part of his very spirit had lost its connection to its universal antenna and all reception had been static ever since.

The universe, it's makeup and its functions had been of most importance to his Grandfather. The older man had always been interested in the study of the stars. He never had the chance to pursue his career of choice as an Astronomer being that he had to work starting at a very young age in order to help support his family. Unfortunately, too many from his generation could recite this exact same story. Never finishing high school, he was completely self taught in his understanding of the cosmos. Since being in grade school, he had saved every penny that he could in order to buy every book that he could regarding his favorite topic. All of the knowledge that he had consumed over the years was passed down through his son and lastly onto his Grandson. Pharaoh had soaked up the information like a never completely saturated sponge.

He had enjoyed everyone of his "teaching moments" with his Great Old Man. His kind, loving, prideful Great Old Man.

It took just minutes in order for Tre to turn the corner on the side of his home making an appearance with Kai. Tre walked her to her car and lingered there in the driver side door, rapping up some type of conversation with her.

Pharaoh waited patiently until her car pulled from the curb and sped down the street before he emerged from his vehicle. He had not come at ALL for any form of drama.

"Man, why does it always have to go there with y'all?" Tre asked with a disappointed look upon his face.

"I don't fuck wit huh. PERIOD!!!" Pharaoh offered with finality. "No other details or discussion is required. If y'all good wit huh, then leave it there."

"Boy you be wil'lin," Tre shook his head knowing his friend. If Pharaoh was irritated, accent strong and abrupt with his reply, then pressing would get him nowhere. Tre decided to let the tense moment that had occurred pass.

Back seated in his comfy spot, Pharaoh had a fresh glass of 1738, a plate full of Red Snapper with Brussel sprouts and a better attitude. The laughs continued into the wee hours of the morning. After dropping Reg off back at home, Pharaoh took a drive down to the Lakefront. Illegally parking on the side street by Big Bay Park, he took the short trek through the private owned property surrounded by trees until he reached the destined clearing. The mass of water seemed to go on forever and seamlessly blended into the darkness of the night sky. This was his absolute favorite spot in the city. The natural beauty was unmatched. He had affectionately named this area The Palisades after the name of the street in which he had parked. This is the one place where he could come to free his mind and gather his thoughts. The one place where he could truly unwind all while nurturing his relationship with the beautifully magnificent Mother of Nature. He could hear the waves splashing upon the shoreline. Walking out further he made his way to the end of the cliff, knowing that here is where he would be able to actually see the naturally moon controlled wrinkles of H2O meet with the rocky and sandy beach that lay just below. He stood still, admiring the beauty.

By habit, he gazed up into the night sky. Most of the stars had been covered by the fast movement of storm clouds marching in from the Southwest. Closing his eyes, he inhaled the extra oxygenated air. The scent of the fresh water rushed into his nostrils. Here he silently gave thanks to the Sun God Ra for allowing him the opportunity to be in the presence of so much beauty. He ran through his account of daily actions using the Laws of Maat, knowing that he had missed the mark with many, he promised the Deities that he would work harder to do better each and everyday. Lastly, he touched the Ankh pendant that was dangling around his neck in recognition of the precious gift of life. Ashe'

He ended his dedication and accountability session by inhaling one last deep breath into his lungs. He held it for a count of ten before exhaling slowly with a matching count of ten. Opening his eyes, he headed back to his car, popped the locks and hopped inside. He could now see the lightning in the distance. He wasn't a bit worried about being trapped in the oncoming rain as he was turning his key in the lock leading to his apartment within 10 minutes after leaving his open confessional, knowing that Lake Michigan would hold onto his secrets, and deepest desires for all of existence.

Chapter Five- Zaire (Keep On Moving)

Keep On Moving- Soul II Soul (Album: Soul Jams)

Zaire turned into the salon and spa parking lot and exited her vehicle. Stepping out into the cool air, the gray morning greeted her with the promise of a misty and gloomy day. Last night's rain had done a depressing number on what had been a great stretch of weather for two weeks running.

Walking up to the receptionist desk to check in, the lobby had revealed her company for the scheduled spa date. Kai stood and greeted her cousin with a warm and enduring hug. Yonica Travis and Tasha Quinn weren't far behind, both offering Zaire love in the form of an affectionate gesture.

"Miss Z!!!" Tasha smiled. "Congrats Beautiful Lady!!!" Zaire responded with appreciation in returning a long hug and kiss on the cheek.

Yonica, in her typical, nose to the air fashion, was a bit more standoffish than the other girls. "Yeah girl, congrats."

Zaire was pretty sure that her happiness was forced with her delivery obviously lacking in genuine excitement.

"Thanks ladies!!!" Zaire, as always, kept it moving and didn't spend much time trying to decipher Yonica's coding.

Zaire had come to spend girl time with her cousin first and foremost. The other two girls were more so friends of Kai's than they had ever been actual friends of her own. Although, Zaire and Yonica had attended the same high school together, Yonica had been known as a party girl and of course, because of this had made an instant connection with Kai, another known party girl, from their very first interaction. Now Tasha was more settled than that of the other two girls. She was a great mother to her two children and a contented wife to a fabulous, hard working husband. She spent her time ensuring that her family were taken care of and well provided for. Partying was the last thing on Tasha's mind. She had worked hard and graduated with honors from the same program that Kai had chosen for her own studies. She was now an elementary/grade school teacher with the Milwaukee Public School System.

Taking the seat that Kai had saved for her, Zaire was immediately bombarded by news from her chatty cousin.

"So, I was able to find some tickets as promised. It's cheaper to fly into Ft Lauderdale than it is to fly into Miami, Sis. The good thing is that there is a shuttle that would be able to take me from the airport in Ft Lauderdale to the airport in Miami. So, I will of course need the info for the hotel Z. I can book both the flights and hotel accommodations tonight." Kai paused only when a talented naturalista with a beautifully styled mohawk walked up to greet them.

"Both of you can come on back ladies," Trish had been both Zaire and Kai's beautician for a number of years. Zaire and Kai collected their belongings, accepted the hug that young lady offered and followed her to the back of the salon.

It was a traditional Saturday morning at the shop. Every chair held the body of a customer who were using the time to beautify their appearance. The salon was sectioned by the customized service provided. In the far right corner sat six chairs specifically reserved for weaving services, the far left housed regular styling services, the middle housed the braiding stations and in the very center was where the shampooing bowls were located. Shelves were installed around the entire salon showcasing the various products from top professional lines. Zaire followed the beautician and her cousin, heading left.

Trish decided to start with Zaire first, leaving Kai's longer, thicker hair, the obviously tougher project, to deal with last. The wash and deep conditioner felt amazing as Trish worked her wonders massaging it into Zaire's scalp. Afterwards, her coils were extra soft and much more manageable. Using her own homemade 9 oil mixture as a treatment, Trish coated Zaire's hair with the solution, placed a plastic cap over her locks and sat her under the dryer a bit, allowing her some time to get started with Kai's long, thick, lioness mane.

While Trish repeated the same steps with Kai, Zaire removed the latest novel by Joccity Phenix, a local author who had been causing a huge stir with his Frienemies series from her bag. Everyone had been raving in reviews about his 2 part work. Any time that she could, she tried her best to support the many talented local artists that the city regularly produced. Milwaukee, being a city where the platform for creative arts wasn't mainstream, she felt that it was her (along with other residents) duty to let these mega talented individuals shine through, with the unwavering support of community. Especially those of the darker race. If we don't support our own, then who will?

Zaire's concentration was broken from her read when Trish walked Kai over to sit under the dryer next to the one that she occupied. Switching out between her two clients, she motioned to Zaire to follow her back to the sink, Trish worked quickly in rinsing the oil mixture from her hair, clipping dead ends and lightly coating her hair with a Curling Cream that was heavily scented with Lavender and Lemongrass.

"What are we doing with all this loveliness today?" Trish asked a well relaxed Zaire, who had always relished in having her hair handled by someone with a light professional touch and Trish was amazingly gifted.

"Hmm, let's try a twisted updo of some sort," Zaire had recently seen a few of the intricately placed styles while browsing Pinterest and had made a vow right then and there to find out how her hair would look in one of these beautiful creations.

"Gotcha hon." Trish started detangling and working through Zaire's strands with a wide tooth rake. After removing all of the tangles, Trish relieved Kai from underneath the steaming heat of the dryer, asked one of the Salon Assistants to rinse the penetrating oils from her scalp, before making her way back to Z.

Zaire was overall in better spirits about her trip to Miami. She had never been to the gorgeous, tropical city even though it had sat at the top of her list of ones that she needed to visit for several years. This would allow her the opportunity to remove it from its placement. She had never seen an actual palm tree up close, had never frolicked around in a tropical climate, had never been further than the Central Southern part of the nation, and had never took a dip in any one of the oceans. With Miami being located in the Southeast, visiting that area of the country would definitely be a welcomed first. With Kai promising to make arrangements to join her for an upcoming weekend, her mood derived earlier in the week when receiving the news had performed a complete about face. But that was her Babygirl Kai. Sweet, thoughtful, ridiculously caring and a Certified Aquarius, always wanting better for others than she wanted for herself. Always true, real and probably the most genuinely caring and wholeheartedly giving person she had ever had the pleasure of having in her life. Kai was her Sweet Southern Pecan Praline, her Baby Cousin, her Ride or Die.

Once Trish finished placing the last open toothed bobby pin in place, Zaire marveled at the creative and artistic finished look. She had done an absolutely amazing job with arranging the beautiful loose two strand twists that now adorned Zaire's head in a way where the twists actually looked like an elegantly crafted bun, and the perfect protective style. After thanking Trish, Zaire moved over to the side of the salon which offered various body spa services, Zaire signed in to receive her scheduled waxing. She spotted Tasha sitting in the corner, contently receiving a pedicure. Tasha waved her over.

"Where's Yonica?" Zaire looked around and asked, to the response of Tasha rolling her eyes.

"Away from me is most important," Tasha shook her head and laughed. "That girl is a whole entire mess. Mugging and gossiping about everybody who walked through the damn door. It doesn't make any sense why she is always so worried about how every other person is looking or what they are doing."

Zaire joined in on her laughter. She knew Yonica all to well. She only tolerated her because of her friendship with Kai. The girl had a way of taking the calmest person to a whole different type of hell.

Zaire looked forward to receiving her much needed pedicure, which she was sure would come immediately following the wax job. She would have to request the same esthetician that was working her magic on Tasha's feet, She meticulously took her time with each step, not rushing at all.

Zaire was called in the private room for her waxing. After 30 minutes, she walked out completely bare and void of hair from the neck down. Sitting next to both Kai and Yonica, her pedi got underway. She did not receive the same esthetician, but the one that was assigned was equally careful in her work.

Kai had opted to have her thick, sandy brown mane straightened by Silk Press leaving it swinging and hanging long. Her hair was glossy, healthy looking and absolutely gorgeous. Yonica appeared with a fresh weave sewn in. The wavy texture looked great with the shape of her pretty brown face.

"I can't wait to visit you in Miami Cuz!!!" Kai gushed. "We are going to have so much fun, just us girls!!!"

"Yes we are." Zaire smiled, matching her cousin's excitement. "Thank you so much for your future booking. I love you Chica!!!"

Kai tossed kisses over towards Zaire's way.

Yonica scowled. "Miami is sooooo overrated. I went last year and was more than ready to come back home after only a couple of days. It rained the entire time and the men are mediocre."

"Well, that was YOUR experience," Kai interjected. "When I get there, me and Z are taking over, you heard!!!!" She twerked in her chair, causing Zaire and those around them to laugh. All besides Yonica.

Pursing her lips, Yonica continued. "I'm just saying don't be surprised if the trip turns out to be a total flop. South Beach was just okay. Nothing but tourists looking for a quick out of state come up. It won't be a good trip."

"But why would you say that?" Kai frowned in irritation. "Girl just wish for the best and stop being such a Negative Nancy your whole damn life."

Yonica rolled her eyes, put her hand up to silence Kai, who in turn laughed at her silliness, then turned her attention solely on Zaire. "What I am surprised about is not hearing that Pharaoh's breaking his neck to get down next to you." she smirked. "What y'all do, break up?" her voice was laced with sarcasm.

Zaire opted to play along with Yonica's little game. "No, but when we do, I will let you know first as I know you would LOVE to have one more chance with him, Yonie Boo." Zaire winked. "I gotcha girl."

The comment sent Yonica on her defensive rampage. "Girl please!!! Been there, done that YEARS ago!!! I ain't thinking about Pharaoh's Punk Ass!!! Muthafucka ain't got enough dick for me!!! Tall ass nigga with no dick!!! How the fuck is that even possible?!?! Trust me, you good with all of that." Yonica turned to Kai who giggled along with her. The one thing that they both had in common was their obvious dislike of Pharaoh. Kai had her reason: being that she wasn't fond of his arrogance and Yonica's being: that she had at one time (and even still) wanted to be with Pharaoh back in high school. Used to getting what she wanted with the guys and thought to have been a great catch with her pretty looks, popularity and her being Captain of the Cheerleaders, Yonica was humiliated when Pharaoh had taken her up on her offering of herself, screwed with her mind a bit and left her hanging high and dry, in a public scene that had left the entire school gossiping for weeks.

Seeing the look on Z's face, Kai immediately stopped her laughing. "Okay, Yonni, let's chill out and enjoy the day." Kai tried to diffuse the situation, but Zaire was already pushed into her pre-livid state.

"What you're not going to do is sit here in my face, trying to defame him with your petty ass lies. Now that is uncalled for." Zaire had no hesitation in defending her friend. "He is not here to defend himself and what you are stating right now is utter bullshit."

"Listen, I give zero fucks about how you feel about what the fuck I am saying about that foul ass negro that you call your friend or that you are fucking or whateva the fuck y'all are doing!!!" Yonica snapped back, causing Zaire to pull her purse from the table next to the chair. Zaire felt her blood pressure going up and in order to calm herself before exploding, she pulled out her earbuds, plugged them into her phone and tuned into the sounds from her playlist. The first song was Soul II Soul's "Keep on Moving" which was the perfect song needed in order to calm her temper in that moment. Taking a deep breath, closing her eyes and leaning back in the massage chair, she relaxed her mind, knowing that the jealous, petty ass girl wasn't even remotely close in proximity when it came to level comparison and because of that fact, going back and forth with her was not worth it. Besides, she knew that Kai was probably chewing her out Big time under the sound of the music flowing into her eardrums.

Zaire kept her earbuds in the entire duration of receiving her pedicure. A manicure was the last scheduled service of the day. Tasha, finished with her scheduled services, walked up and placed her arms around Zaire's neck in her exit from the salon. "You are a Queen, and Queens don't entertain peasants. I love how you shut her down and kept it moving. Oh and PS, you will KILL IT in MIA!!!!" she whispered in Z's ear, planted a kiss on her cheek, waving her goodbye.

"Thanks." Zaire turned and mouthed before Tasha made her exit.

Kai was right behind, checking to ensure that her cousin was okay. Yonica had already left the building after what Zaire was sure had been a pretty explosive exchange with Kai.

"I'm sorry Cuz. If I would have known that Yonica was going to be on bullshit then I wouldn't have invited her."

"Honey listen, you gotta know that I am NOT trippin on her AT all." Z hugged her concerned twin cousin. "So long as I was able to spend time with you, my day has been fantabulous!!!"

Back in the comfort of her home for the last time before heading to the airport and away for three months, Tre had stopped by to pick up Nala who fought tooth and nail, literally, going into her crate. She had always hated the cage ever since she was a kitten. She whined angrily, walking around in circles inside the solitary style kitty prison. Zaire had kissed the top of her head before placing her inside. Even still she was fussing up a storm and scratching at the sides in her attempt to make an escape.

Tre laughed at the overly fussy kitty. "She get it from her Mama," he teased, warranting a light elbow nudge to the ribs from Zaire.

"Ouch!!" he faked being hurt. "See exactly, feisty little ladies."

"One more time Tre," Z warned with a pointed finger in his direction. "One more time."

They both laughed.

"How are you managing with the news Babygirl?" Tre asked with concern. "Last I had heard from Pha, you weren't too gung ho about going away to Miami."

Yeah but I'm cool now. It was rough at first, but I just had to remember that I would only be gone for 3 months and I forced myself to find the silver lining. This could truly become a lucrative experience that I won't ever forget."

"Wow Z. Just know that I am so proud of you. You really deserve this. You have always been so driven and so unstoppable. You are amazing in my eyes. You will do an extraordinary job in this new role."

"Awww Tre." Z went misty eyed." Thanks so much. That means the world to me."

"Come here Sweetie," Tre took her in his arms and kissed the top of her head. "Don't get to going all misty on me," he joked.

"That's like the sweetest thing you ever said to me," Z wiped a tear from her cheek that had escaped.

"Love you girl!!! We go back decades and don't think that I haven't watched you do you thing the entire time. Remember, you are our Ashanti to our Murder Inc.," he teased using the old reference from high school. "Your light is beautifully blinding. Don't you ever forget that." He picked up the carrier with Nala inside and headed for the door.

After thanking him for agreeing to care for Nala in her absence, Zaire let Pharaoh up as Tre walked out.

Pharaoh greeted her with a hug.

Dressed from head to toe in New York Mets gear and orange and blue Nike Huaraches, he was New NEW fresh from the outlets. Locs twisted in some zig zagged plaited style down his back, face neatly lined and groomed, a matching cap sat on his head. The scent of his signature YSL filled the entire front room.

"Hmm.…...hot date?" Zaire gave him the once over with an eyebrow raised.

"Yeah, I got a lil dessert added to my menu for the night." Pharaoh plopped down on the sofa picking up the latest Essence magazine from the coffee table. "But shit, you know I stays flyy to death E'erDAY Miss!!!!" he ran a hand down his beard for emphasize.

Zaire rolled her eyes. Even still she had to applaud his fashion sense.
"Nice Sir. I like the get up." Zaire winked in approval of his very well coordinated gear.

"Glad to have your approval, Ma," Pharaoh looked up from his task of flipping pages. He squinting at Zaire's hair from his spot in the Living Room and to her spot in the kitchen."You pretty fuckin' flyy yaself there Young Lady. Loving the hair. Trish did her thing."

"Thanks Luv," Zaire blew a kiss in his direction. She washed the dishes in the kitchen sink and disinfected her countertops. Officially closing her kitchen for business, she flipped the switch that turned off the room's LED lighting and made her last round through her apartment.

"Is this all of the luggage?" Pharaoh was standing at the front door when she had returned. She pulled two larger travel bags behind her. Reaching on the kitchen counter, she grabbed her diamond ring, hooking the chain around her neck.

"Along with these, this is all of it." Zaire grabbed her jacket that was hanging from the back of the barstool and headed out of the front door that Pharaoh graciously held open for her. All of a sudden, Pharaoh went into his playful tirade.

"Awwww nawww my Z is leaving!!! Lawd take me now!!!!" Pharaoh joked pretending to pass out in the hallway as Z locked the door behind herself. "That's not rain coming down outside, those are my salty ass tears!!! When I cry, the whole damn city suffers!!!!!"

"Boy getcho ass up before you ruin your new fit!!!"

Pharaoh rose from his place on the floor with a huge smirk on his face. He walked up behind Zaire taking her in his arms and lifting her from the floor, spinning her around.

"Phaaaaarrraooooooohhhhh stopppppppp!!! Put me down!!!" Zaire voice was a cross between a scream and a whine.

"I'm not letting you go." Pharaoh continued his teasing. "Call Naomi now and tell her ass that all bets are officially OFF!!!"

After finally setting her down, Zaire punched him hard in the chest.

"Oh shit, OUCH!!! Little Buster Douglas Junior!!!"

"Now you got me all dizzy, You Jerk!!!" Zaire stood still to allow her equilibrium to return to normal from it's wild spinning before attempting to bend to grab the handles of her bags. She shot a mean mug towards her friend.

"Well I got an extra key so I will be in your pad everyday, smelling throw pillows, taking loose hairs out of your brush and wiping my hands on your fuckin' bath towels, stalkin' this joint until you return." Pharaoh pouted.

Zaire laughed. "Awwww come here Babes," She called the sulking, pouty, playfully tearful young man over. Her arms were stretched out to him, welcoming him into a long, loving, hug. He sank his tall frame into her arms.

Although the exchange was a comical one, Zaire knew that she would miss him for sure. He played such a vital role in her everyday life that it would be hard going day to day without being able to see his face. Here they were, still outside of her front door and hadn't made it out of the building. Hell at this pace, they never would.

Zaire pushed him away, took the handles of the bags in her hands and made her way to the elevator shaft.

"Come on Pha, I gotta get to the airport Silly."

Pharaoh frowned when he caught up to her at the elevator door. "Well damn, just push me down at my weakest point and head for the exit? You changing already Ma…." Pharaoh shook his head still in his playful mood.

"Oh, stop being dramatic," Z pursed her lips. Picking a piece of lint from his T shirt, she placed it in his beard instead. "This represents you right now. A little squishy, puff of soft ass cotton."

Pharaoh laughed, taking the lint from his beard and tossing it at Z, who ducked.

The elevator arrived and took them to the lobby floor. Pharaoh had found parking out front on Water Street. Securely strapped inside of T'Challa, Pharaoh sped off down the expressway making record time.

On the way to the airport, Zaire filled Pharaoh in on the conversation that had taken place inside of the salon and the foul comments that Yonica had spoken. Pharaoh, being too smooth to be bothered, chuckled in recognition of where the feelings and lies were stemming from with Yonica. He knew the truth and so did she. He did not feel the need to harp on the antics performed by one of his past Rejects.

At the airport, Pharaoh walked Z in, made sure that all of her bags were checked and properly tagged. Following the signs pointing to the direction of the airline's concourse and the TSA Checkpoint, he walked her to the end of the line knowing that he could not go any further than where they were standing.

He reached down and took Zaire in his arms , lifting her in a huge hug. Placing her down, but ensuring not to drop his arms, he leaned down to speak directly into her ear. "Z, you got this!!! Noone believes in you more than me. Go kill it Sis!!! We will party hard when you return in celebration. That is a promise." He kissed her on the forehead and stepped back, allowing her the freedom to go and start the clearance process.

"Love you Pha. Thanks for everything and just being you." She mouthed as she worked her way around the strategically placed rails. Taking two fingers, she sent him a kiss. She had the best friend ever. Hands down.

Chapter Six- Pharaoh (Sky's The Limit)

Sky's The Limit- Notorious B.I.G./112 (Album: Life After Death)

What would the industry be if Biggie had never died? East Coast till the world explodes but the beef had been so unnecessary. The lives that were lost as a result were so irreplaceable. They, both Biggie and Pac, set the standard and controlled the entire country during their reign, not just in some bullshit description about who they were and what they brought to their many fans, but in genuine reference of just how powerful these men actually were. They were so powerful and so supreme to where they were able to bring an entire nation into a Civil War with the East Coast versus the West Coast going toe to toe, fist to fist. Deny it if you want but real is real. Now that was some real POWERFUL shit!!! Unfortunately, the bloodshed that came from the beef ended the lives of these national rulers before the first question could be answered.

Pharaoh lingered in this thought as he sped over the Hoan Bridge driving West on I-794 from dropping Z off at Mitchell International Airport. The bridge was a signature staple in the city. The extremely scenic drive hosted Lake Michigan and the Lakefront Henry Maier Festival Grounds directly out of his passenger side window, while tall skyscrapers serving as corporate offices for major banks, filled the view in his entire dash just up ahead. The sounds of Biggie and 112 blasted from the speakers playing one of Pharaoh favorite songs on the Life After Death album, "Sky Is The Limit."

And for Pharaoh, the sky had never been his limit, as he had always been taught to aim for outer galaxies. To know in the deepest regions of his heart that if only he believed, he could absolutely "HAVE what he wants" and "BE exactly who he wants. PeriodT"

Thinking of Z, he knew that she would call him upon her arrival to her destination. The pride that he had for that young Boss chic...unfortunately there weren't any words created that could describe how honored he was being a friend of hers, nor the level of respect that he possessed for such an amazingly disciplined creature.

Pharaoh exited off the highway and continued down the city streets. The cool air that came along with the rain seemed to have sucked the life from the entire city. Saturday night and traffic was limited. Well, it was still pretty early.

Thinking about his planned evening with Miss Lacey, Pharaoh had given her the option of either taking her out for dinner where they would be able to have conversation over light music or meeting at 100 West for forced conversation over loud music and of course, strong drinks. Lacey chose the latter. Pharaoh shook his head.

This was this issue. Women complained about how men weren't looking to offer real dating opportunities and how men were solely focused on just one particular thing, but women never wanted to take any bit of responsibility for their role in the lack of value placed upon actual courting. Lacey had failed the test miserably.

Pulling into the parking lot, Pharaoh greeted the regulars and took his normal spot at the bar. Angel spotted him and walked over to greet him.

"Hey Crush," she leaned across the bar to peck his cheek. "You just missed Reg. He just left after getting into an argument with his Baby Mama." Angel frowned. "The shit was wild."

This was not surprising to Pharaoh in the least. Reg had been back and forth and on and off again and again with Aleasha for a number of years now. Reg had spent many nights sleeping on Pharaoh's sofa in order to take breaks from the heated disputes that he regularly found himself a part of, in dealing with his child's mom.

Pharaoh shook his head, knowing that he would never speak ill of his friend or run discussions regarding his business with randoms out in the streets. Especially potentially petty ones like Angel who had at one time fucked with Reg herself. He changed the subject.

"Let me get the norm," he placed his order with Angel and pulled his phone from his jeans. Lacey had sent a message announcing that she was on her way to meet him.

Sitting patiently, Pharaoh scanned the room. There weren't many patrons in the lounge. He figured that the cooler temperatures were to blame. Those who were inside were in some way or another grooving to the sounds that the DJ was spinning or engaged in their individual conversations, doing their own thing.

Angel brought his drinks to him and Pharaoh went for the bottle of beer first. It didn't take long for Miss Lacey to make her appearance. Dressed in a mini skirt, stiletto heeled sandals and a leather cropped jacket, she looked good walking into the room. Pharaoh smiled as she took a seat next to him.

"Hello Lovely Lady," Pharaoh initiated as she removed her jacket revealing a fitted tube shirt underneath.

"Well hello there." Lacey tossed her long, waist length weave over her shoulder turning her full attention to her Chocolate companion. "How are you this night?"

"Great now that I have a Princess in my personal space."

Lacey blushed, giving him a beautiful dimpled smile. "I bet you say that to all of the ladies."

"Nah, just those whose name starts with L."

She giggled.

"What would you like to drink?"

Sucking her teeth, entranced by the smooth composure and amazingly handsome looks of her date, she responded, "an Apple Martini…...for now.

Loving the response, Pharaoh summoned Angel over once again to his side of the bar. After placing the order, Pharaoh turned his attention back toward the young lady and asked, "So, tell me a little bit about what makes you tick?"

"What makes me tick?" She repeated, considering his question. "Well, it depends on the moment and the mood. Whatever gets the juices flowing. It really all depends."

Pharaoh narrowed one eye at her bland answer to his question. He probed further.

"Let's try this again, what seriously makes you tick?" he offered a counter response to his own question in hopes of leading her in the direction that he had intended to go. "For me, nothing makes me tick faster than a sexy women with an even sexier attitude about herself, whose spiritually connected and knows exactly who she is and what she wants in life. Having a nice ass is an extra perk," Pharaoh winked and continued. "On a more personal level, I love spending time alone in deep thought. This is when I am fully in tune with those who are deemed most high. I love going for runs at the most sacred hours. This usually occurs in the wee morning hours when muthafuckas are dead ass sleep. I love patrolling the city searching for the dopest, most amazingly scenic spots. I am in love with the blessings that Mother Nature bestow upon us daily, all we need to use is our ability to look around. Listening to music helps me to stay attune to my most creative side. I record some of my most profound shit while listening to music. Now, I can groove with Hard Core Hip Hop, R&B, and many other genres but it's Jazz in particular that has an amazing ability to free my mind and get my imaginative juices flowing.The sounds of the various instruments, blending so seamlessly together, the high points versus the low, always creating the chillest of vibes. These are some of the things that give me life. Keep me on my shit." Pharaoh studied the young lady. "Those were simple basics. Now, you're on the clock."

Lacey shifted uncomfortably and followed up with another lame ass response about how after long days at work, she likes to go home, turn on the TV and sip a glass of wine or some feeble bullshit. The fact that she wasn't able to carry on a deeply interesting conversation, going into detail about what was most valuable to her regarding the time that she spent developing in life, something that would make him want to know more about her as a human being, posed an issue for him.

Noting that she wouldn't be intellectually ready to handle more of his deeply probing questions with the way that she had struggled with the first of the most simplistic level, he moved her to the Fuckable but not Considerable list.

And that is the direction that his conversation went.

"I'm loving these legs out Ma." He took his hand and placed it on her crossed thigh. "You out here in the rain, brightening the day for'sho."

Lacey sipped her Martini loving the compliment. "I figured I might as well bring a little show with me tonight. Rain, sleet or snow, no precipitation ever stopped me."

Pharaoh smiled but inside died a little. Same ole shit. Here's another one. Shallow and dull, believing that she was winning with just her looks alone. There were many guys whose only goal in meeting women was to find one with a huge ass and a cute face to look upon when rising in the morning, but in order to hold his attention, there would need to be a whole lot more cognitively developed meat on the plate, and his preference in this case, perfectly seasoned, tenderly aged and delivered well done.

He needed excitement. Not just in the form of bomb ass sexcapades. Hell, he could find that anywhere. But in the form of

85

deep, engaging conversation, new experiences, spontaneity, interesting debates and a fucking chase already. He was so used to women falling to their knees at the sight of him that he had long ago grown bored with the whole routine. If his life was a porno, it would be entitled: Pharaoh Does Milwaukee with the number of chics that he had ran through in past years who threw panties on his stage like he was the hottest star in the game during an era of lack luster talent. Not that he didn't enjoy the freedom to fuck damn near whoever he pleased, but it was just too damn simple, No receipt of mental or emotional stimulation whatsoever! It left him with a bad taste in his mouth along with fading hope.

As for Lacey, she would be the next simple victim. He would charm her into submission, which wouldn't be hard at all with the way that she way now touching and leaning into him.

An hour and a half later, he was at her home, in her bed, moving her thong to the side, having his way. Another hour and a half after that, he was standing on his own private balcony, puffing on his favorite, freshly showered and feeling mediocrely satisfied. To think that he had been looking forward to the night just earlier in the day was extremely disappointing to him.

Pharaoh was irritated beyond belief with the amount of times that Lacey had called and texted him into the following afternoon. WTF!!!!

He had responded by sending her an SMS reply message stating that he would connect with her later, but the chic absolutely did not believe in allowing him time to breath. Every 30 minutes or so, he had received some type of communication from her. It had become a bit stalkerish with it now being well into the 4 o'clock hour in the evening portion of the day. He was truly close to pulling up her contact page and sliding on the option that would allow him to set a block of communication against her phone number. It was Sunday for goodness sake!!! This was the day that he usually set aside to relax and catch up on the number of shows sitting unattended in his DVR or catch a sports game on TV.

The shit reminded him of a time a few years back when he made the mistake of screwing a crazy ass, hood chic from hell. The girl had stalked him so bad to where he had to get a restraining order placed in an attempt to keep her away from his office. It worked, up until 2 weeks after filing the order, when she, against restriction, showed up to 100 West with a pistol as a loyal companion in which she used to fire at Pharaoh & Reg as they exited the bar heading home that wild night. Long story short, she was arrested and sent to Taycheedah Correctional Facility for 18 months. Upon her release, she had gotten the approval from the Department of Corrections to relocate to somewhere in Alabama with family. Pharaoh hadn't heard from her since.

The last thing that he needed was another one of those deranged situations on his hands. He really had to stop inviting chics up to 100 West. He was in the spot way too often and there were too many head cases living in the city. He would need to be just a bit more careful in his dealings with randoms. Maybe he would need to start searching for a suitable duck off spot somewhere.

Taking his hand and digging in for a slice of cheese pizza, with the other hand, Pharaoh flipped through the channels using his remote. So many premium movie channels, so many basic cable channels but always the same ole programming. BET had a Top 20 list of movies and shows that they played several times within the course of one week. Not to mention that Iyanla was REALLY focused on fixing just a few folk's life, or you would think, with the regular 7 to 8 pre recorded shows that stayed in heavy rotation on The OWN Network. But Pharaoh wouldn't complain. He found a rerun episode of Game of Thrones on HBO and settled on watching it.

The highlight to his day had come at the sound of his Dad's voice coming from the other end of the phone circuit when he had accepted the call earlier that day. His Dad was enjoying his travels in Africa with his current location being a small village in Ghana. He had called to check in and to catch his son up on his many adventures since Pharaoh had last spoke with him a long month before. He truly looked forward to receiving the updating phone calls from his Pops. Proud of him and his accomplishments, his Dad's goal has always been to return back home to the Motherland after retirement. He was determined to have his body, full of his ancestors blood, returned to the soil in which it had originally derived. Although his body was forcefully born in the West, and definitely not by choice, he would not be subjected to having his body buried in the country where his oppressors have wreaked havoc upon his people for the last 400 years with continuous counting, still until this very day. The country where, Africanites were given the worst of welcomes. The country where Africanites were harshly judged solely on the sheer fact that the dazzling, sparkling black gold that was gifted, by the native Sun & biologically reflective within the skin was so gloriously royal and so amazingly valuable that in high levels, those carrying it were automatically deemed a threat, even when the only ones being threatened, were the Africanites.

He had been moving his way around Africa for the past 5 years. He started in Egypt, next to Nigeria, Kenya, The Congo and now Ghana. Next on his list would be the Island of Madagascar. No particular order. Just wherever he decided to be at whatever given time. It was in Kenya where he met whom he was now referring to as "The Love of His Life," a feisty Kenyan Queen who had fell widow when her husband passed on from his complications associated with a Bloodborne disease that eventually attacked every organ in his body, bringing upon his death. She had opted to do a bit of traveling herself after his departure and had met Pops after returning home from a trip. They both had been passengers on a train and had hit it off immediately. She and Pops had journeyed together ever since.

Pharaoh had his own plans to travel to Africa one day and soon. His Dad's tales were one thing but to have the actual experience of setting foot to the dirt of his blood native country would be another story all his own. After all, he was branded at time of birth as a Leo, sign of The Sphinx. It would be a shame to not witness the wonderess statue with his own eyes. He was more than sure that the Giza Plateau would welcome him, even when the Caucasians of the West wouldn't.

The day went by in a breeze. A much needed, uneventful day after a pretty demanding, overly eventful week. The night's devotion was one where no promises for better actions were needed. He confidently gave his account, knowing that he had succeeded in carrying through with his conduct as the Royal Court of NRT had intended.

Chapter Seven- Zaire (Soul Sistah)

Soul Sista- Bilal (Album: 1st Born Second)

Zaire stepped into the lobby of The Beachfront Chateau Resort Miami scratching the first full week from the mental calendar that she kept in her head to record her countdown until her return home. The first week at the new job had been pretty dull, consisting of an overkill of teleconferenced managerial meetings and her creation of a recruiting plan. Everyone on staff had been extremely helpful and receptive of her for the most part. Unfortunately, with the company being in the opening stages, the office staff consisted of only her and one other Director of Finance. Because of this, the office was dead silent and was in major need of liveliness. The good news was that she had hired a Personal Assistant, and a Recruiter for her team who both would be starting employment the following Monday morning, along with an Accounts Payable Clerk and Accounts Receivable Clerk for the Finance team who both would be starting the following Wednesday. The addition of the 4 new office staff would be a true welcome with the silently mundane vibe of the office.

The representative at the Front Desk of the hotel greeted her upon entering.

"Hello Miss Jefferson. Is there anything that you need right away?" The young Cuban girl's smile was wide.

"No hon. I'm good but thanks so much for checking." Zaire responded matching her expression.

In her room, she noticed Housekeeping had come through and tidied. They had so far done an amazing job with ensuring that her room was well taken care of and that items were restocked. Narvo had really pulled through with the accommodations. The hotel was magnificent. Friendly staff, fast service, great food and fabulous drinks. The location was right on the Beachfront where just walking out the back door led directly onto the property's private beach equipped with three Tiki bars (one being in the middle of one of the five outdoor pools), Bublr rentals, city tour reservations and water sport excursions right on site. Unfortunately, Zaire had not had the time to partake in any of the hotel's amenities so far. Tonight, she promised herself that she would slip on a bathing suit and make her way to the pool centered Tiki Bar by any means necessary. After all, it was Friday, and her first weekend in Miami had officially begin.

She made her way inside the vanity room to pull her hair into a ponytail puff atop her head. Grateful that the beautiful style in which Trish had created had lasted the majority of the week, Zaire had taken it down for a much needed wash and conditioning treatment the night before.

Glancing at her reflection in the mirror, she immediately saw that the sun had toasted her complexion beautifully. The tan had lifted the coloring in her skin at least two shades darker even though she had spent the majority of her time inside. She could only imagine how much darker and more deep of a tan she would have with being able to sit out and relax in the sunlight without interruption. She looked forward to finding out as soon as that evening.

Her five feet six inch frame was curvaceous. She had slipped on a pair of jeans, in honor of casual Friday, that hugged her form in all of the right places. The colorful tank underneath and equally colorful blazer completed her look. Her signature diamond ring hung around her neck.

Removing the faux strip lashes from her eyes, she turned on the faucet, and took a pinch of shaved Raw African Black Soap in her hand. Working up a lather, she rubbed the bubbles onto her face to remove all traces of her make-up. After rinsing off the residue, she patted her skin dry using an old white, cotton T Shirt and applied a thin coat of Raw African Shea Butter, followed by a fingertip size portion of Pond's Dry Skin cream. Lastly, she spritzed her face with Mario Badescu's Rose Water to complete her regimen.

Reaching for her toothbrush, she scrubbed away at her teeth with the bristles. Realizing that she was out of floss, she added it as an item to her list of products that she needed to obtain. Oh well, the pool would have to wait.

Calling down to Guest Services, Zaire scheduled a transport van to take her to the nearest store to retrieve the items. The representative advised her that the driver would arrive in fifteen minutes. Zaire removed her pumps and slipped her feet into a pair of Adidas flip flops, making her way back to the front lobby. As promised, the driver arrived in just under fifteen minutes.

Stepping into the Chevy Blazer, Zaire realized that the driver was not the same guy, Jose, who had been transporting her to and from work that week.

"Hello ma'am."
Zaire smiled and responded with a simple "Hi there."
"I'm Nyris and I will be your driver." He introduced himself. "Where will I be taking you today?"
"To any convenience or drug store that's close by thank you." Zaire answered. "What happened to Jose?"

The driver smiled. "Jose was only temporarily providing transportation for the guests at The Beachfront." He explained. "I am the regular driver for the hotel."

Zaire nodded as he pulled out onto the main street. Removing her phone from her pocket, she responded to a few text messages. Kai had sent her reservation details to her in screen shot format. Kai would be arriving in 2 weeks on that Tuesday evening. She had found the roundtrip itinerary for a steal. She was also able to book a room at the Beachfront Chateau in which Zaire was extremely excited about. She would be staying in Miami through the weekend leaving out that Sunday evening.

"Where are you from?" Nyris interrupted Zaire from her texting.
"I'm in town on business from Milwaukee, Wisconsin." Zaire replied.
"Milwaukee, huh? Home of the Bucks. Wow, they are having one helluva season!!!" he said.
"Yes, they are showing out." Zaire agreed. "Giannis is a beast!!! I am really hoping that he gets his well deserved MVP."
"I believe that he will." Nyris nodded. "If not him then who?"
"My sentiments exactly,"
"So are you enjoying your stay in Miami?" Nyris asked, turning into the lot of a strip mall.
"The city is absolutely beautiful, I must say. I haven't had the opportunity to make it out much with the demand of my employer but I have enjoyed the friendliness of the town's people since I have arrived." Zaire spoke sincerely of her trip so far.
"Well you must get out and enjoy. There's so much to see and to do." Nyris eyed her through the rearview mirror. Pulling into a parking spot out in front of the Target store, he released his seatbelt and turned to face Zaire directly. "First thing, may I suggest?" Zaire nodded giving him permission to state his suggestion. "Don't go into this Target for shopping purposes."

Zaire raised an inquisitive eyebrow before responding."No? Then where should I go?"

Nyris smiled, all perfectly white teeth, "Can I take you to a place that the locals along with most tourists love and that I am more than sure that you will as well?"

Zaire considered his offer for a moment. She trusted that an up top hotel such as the one in which she was staying would only allow extremely trust-worthy employees to chauffeur guests so she didn't believe that his intentions were ill. And furthermore, it was finally Friday after the first week of adjustment and she arrived at the hotel with thoughts of how she hadn't been able to enjoy her trip as much as she would have liked up until that time. Why not?

"Okay. I guess that's cool. But where are you taking me?"

"It's an open roof mall called Bayside Marketplace. There you will be able to shop department quality stores and find pretty much anything that you need." Nyris said matter of factly. "Are you game?"

Open roof mall. Sounded really interesting. On top of that, it was no secret that Zaire loved to shop. Winner winner.

Zaire agreed.

Nyris pulled from the parking space and headed onto the expressway for I-95 South. He made mention of the different sights as he passed by. He was an awesome tour guide and really seemed to know his way around the gorgeous tropical city.

It was a whopping 85 degrees in temperature for the day. Although she loved the warmth, her body had needed a total reboot to even begin to start the metamorphosis needed to be able to tolerate the level of heat that came along with being in the tropical climate this time of year. The weather back home was still in the struggling stages from it's cold wintery temperatures from just a month and a half ago. The blazing heat was a fabulous change that her mind was loving, but her body was in complete disarray trying to adapt.

"Do you have children back at home?" Nyris asked.

"If one with pointy ears and spotted fur counts as a child then yes."

Nyris laughed. "So I take it that you have a kitty. What's his name?"

"It's a she and her name is Nala."

"Like The Lion King." Nyris laughed. "Fitting."

Zaire smiled. "Yes that's my cat daughter. My little sweetie. I'm actually missing her like crazy. If I could have somehow brought her along with me, I would have."

"Who's taken care of her in your absence?"

"A friend of mine. He has always loved cats. He used to have a rescue kitty of his own but he recently passed from old age." Zaire thought of how much Tre had loved his four legged baby. He had rescued Buster from the Humane Society when he was a couple of years old. He had loved the cat until his dying day.

"That was really cool of him." Nyris nodded his approval. "At least you know that she is in good hands with an experienced owner."

"Yes. Tre is awesome. I can imagine that she is being spoiled rotten by him daily. I will probably have trouble on my hands when I return."

Nyris smiled at her through the rearview mirror.

Turning her gaze out at the passing landscape, palm trees seemed to line the entire highway and every city street. A waterway seemed to appear every few miles or so. It was almost as if the entire city sat upon a massive body of water. Oh yeah, right, it did!!! The massiveness of the Atlantic Ocean was all around, even in all of the man made canals that accommodated the major port city.

Beautiful, artistic deco style art was in the design of many of the pastel colored buildings. Instead of Miami, the town truly could have been called Easter Village and the name would have completely fit. Being in this part of the world, it seemed as if the sky was closer, as if it was truly "falling down." The fluffy cumulus clouds were like huge puffs of cotton balls, looking as if all it would take was an arm to be reached out far enough, and they could be grazed by fingertip. The sky: Clear, baby blue and stunning, it was a gorgeous day.

It was definitely no secret that she was closer to the equator but the change in landscape was absolutely phenomenal. Back home, in the plain states, the landscape was so flat, so plain and so dull in comparison. Milwaukee had its own northern beauty but colorfully architected Miami was a whole different beast.

Exiting the highway, it didn't take long before the scenic tour took them sailing in the truck along an even more scenic Biscayne Blvd. This downtown street hosted tall, artfully constructed hotels and major corporations. Riding past the American Airlines Arena, home of the Miami Heat, Zaire took out her phone to snap pictures. Just a couple blocks down, Nyris slowed and turned into a parking slab located directly in the center of the boulevard, he took out his cell phone and used an app to pay the parking fare. He exited the vehicle and walked around to open the door for Zaire's exit.

"Mind if I join you?" he asked. "I actually need to grab an item from here as well." Zaire readily agreed, appreciating having his company.

Crossing the busy boulevard, Zaire took more pictures of the massive open, outdoor structure standing directly in front of them. The huge Blue sign, displaying its name, was bold and proud. They walked up the walkway leading to the shopping palace. There were many entrances to the attraction. Nyris elected the wide open route which hosted Bubba Gump Shrimp Co., Hard Rock Cafe and Hooters as a few of the welcoming vendors. There were a number of kiosks up and functional in the wide open area.

"You didn't disappoint. This is a fabulous shopping venue." Zaire snapped more photos and a few selfies, thankful that she had changed into her more comfortable flip flops.

"Glad you like." Nyris gave a wide smile, patiently waiting for Zaire's photo shoot finish.

"I really appreciate you recommending this spot." she turned her attention to her tour guide after putting her phone away. They walked further into the area, giving her a full view of the backdrop, which was yet another beautiful waterway, a huge bay.

"Now this is Biscayne Bay, a major Miami staple. It is protected and hosts a wide variety of marine life, including dolphins. If you walk over and look out, you are likely to see one at the surface every once in a while, if the timing is right." Nyris explained.

Zaire lit up with excitement at the possibility. Almost childlike, she immediately started jumping up and down. "Oh my God!!! Are you serious? I want to see a dolphin. Let's move closer!!!"

Nyris laughed as she grabbed his hand, tugging him along as she moved over to the water's edge. She peered out hoping that the current timing was perfectly right and that one of the flippered guests would miraculously appear. Nyris watched her intently. Her face was glowingly flushed, wearing her excitement like a mask. He marveled at her natural beauty and trusting nature. She wasn't stuffy and self centered like most of the visitors that he frequently ran across. She was sweet natured, easy going and genuinely friendly. He had noticed first in the light conversation that they had carried on during the drive over. She was different. She was Sista Soul.

"So how will I know when one is ready to come to the surface? Do they make noises? Will I see it swimming underneath the water?" Zaire rattled of her questions waiting for Nyris to answer.

"Not sure how to answer as they usually appear when they want and how they want. One may leap out of the water, showing off for those who are watching. Another may just swim into the shallow portion and you will be able to see him there." Nyris shrugged, still smiling at her engrossed expression. "It truly depends. But I will say that most times that they are spotted, a yacht or ship is in the area. For some reason, they love following moving water vessels."

Zaire frowned noting that most of the vessels were located further out in deeper depths from the water's edge, which meant, unfortunately, further away from her eye's view. "Aww man," she responded, causing Nyris to burst into a fit of laughter.

"Oh wow, you are amazingly cute."

Zaire focused her attention from the water and into Nyris's face, truly taking him in for the first time. He wasn't the most attractive, but he had a casual attractiveness about him. Caramel complexion, full, soft looking lips, a wavy, low cut fade style underneath a cap with the transport company's emblem, relaxed eyes behind a pair of prescription glasses. He stood approximately five feet tenish in height with a solid looking build. He had an amazing smile, and a casualness about himself that naturally relaxed her.

"Well, you sit as long as your heart desires, my dear. I'm hoping that your dolphin shows face. But while you do that, do you mind if I run over into the Foot Locker? I need to purchase some new running sneakers for my morning jogs." he asked.

"Of course. Please go on. I am sure that I will be ready to make my way around when you return." She assured him.

"Cool. And when I return, I would like to take you up to the Food Court to grab one of the best Philly Cheesesteaks outside of Philadelphia. Have you eaten?"

Zaire had not eaten since breakfast and the fabulous aromas coming from the surrounding restaurants had forced her to make note.

"I haven't since this morning and I am definitely for taking you up on the Cheesesteak challenge." Cheesesteaks were one of her favorite treats.

Nyris nodded, knowing that the next destination would be just as big of a hit as his first. He walked off in search of the Foot Focker.

Zaire sat on one of the benches near the bay and applied a fresh coat of lip gloss from the tube that she had slipped into her jeans pocket earlier in the day. After snapping a few more selfies with the water being her background, she stepped over to one of the kiosked vendors that was selling swimsuits. After browsing the selection, she settled on a beautiful two piece made of Ankara printed fabric. She also purchased a matching Kimono wrap and beach bag.

As the seller bagged her items, Nyris made his appearance with a bag of his own.

"Please tell me that your dolphin showed up." he spoke sincerely hoping for her delivery of the great news.

Her responding expression told all. "I am going to have to chalk it up to not being the right time." her voice was sad.

For some reason, Nyris wanted to hug her in that moment and make it all better but the professional in him opted for otherwise. "Well, I know what will cheer you up in a flash."

"Cheesesteak. Let's go!!!" Zaire grabbed her card along with the bag from the vendor and followed Nyris back into the direction in which he had just come.

The entrance way took them into what was a typical mall set-up minus the fact that, yes, it had no roof. The corridor was still completely open. Many popular department stores along with local vendors occupied the shops. Zaire glanced around at the various different products offered, from clothing to handmade shoes to handcrafted household ceramics. Stopping in one of the convenience stores along the way, she grabbed the personal items that she needed. Further down the hall, passing a craftsman shop, she fell immediately in love with a huge, vintage style, hand-painted, wooden African mask and purchased it to hang on her wall upon her return home. Nyris graciously carried the bag for her as they made their way to the escalator.

Taking the ride to the upper level, the Food Court loomed in front of them. The restaurant " Great Philly Cheese Steak Sandwiches" had an employee out in front, offering samples to those who were passing. Zaire accepted one of the samples being held together by a toothpick. The first bite was all that she needed.

"This is incredible!!!" She raved. "Wow, two for two Nyris. I will definitely take one of these babies."

Nyris accepted the high five that she handed him, happy that she was thoroughly satisfied and really seemed to be enjoying her trip to the marketplace.

He ordered combos with fries and drinks for both him and the beautiful Ms Zaire.

Sitting at one of the vacant tables, they chatted over their meals.

"So tell me a bit about yourself and your living in this fabulous city?" Zaire started. "Have you lived here all of your life?"

"No but I have been here for most of my life. My mom is from Cuba and she had met my Dad on one of his service tours to the island. He is originally from Fort Lauderdale. He had been stationed in Cuba while on military duty and had fallen in love with my Mom almost instantaneously. Their love affair resulted in my being born. After 18 months on assignment, my Dad had to unfortunately leave us to return to the US with promises of gathering us up and moving us to be with him in his hometown. I'm sure you can imagine the hassle that came along with making that dream a reality. Immigation was an entire beast. We went through a lot before I was able to gain citizenship and the right of having my Dad as primary parent. Unfortunately, in the end, my Mom wasn't able to join us. They would not grant her citizenship. There was a ton of back and forth that my Dad and I went through several times yearly, with the both of us making every effort to maintain our close relationship with my Mom. The distance eventually fizzled the fire that had brought them together and they both opted to go their separate ways when I was a pre teen. I lived with my Dad, but still frequently visited my Mom throughout my entire upbringing."

"Is your Mom still in Cuba now?" Zaire asked wanting to know more.

"Yes. She still resides there. I go to check in on her as often as I can."

"How about your Dad? Is he still living here?"

"My Dad passed away a few years ago. He was a tough old man, but unfortunately cancer was a just a bit tougher."

"I'm so sorry for your loss." Zaire spoke sincerely. She rubbed the ring hanging from her neck in habit.

Nyris gave a soft chuckle. "Nah, it's okay. Dad lived an adventurous life. He was more than ready to move on to the next phase when he was given the honor. Just so long as he was good, I was good."

His strength amazed her. Spoke volumes regarding his character. Her own sadness plagued her.

Zaire was really appreciative of his feeling comfortable enough to share with her. She was sure that this was the story of many who resided in the city. How many had braved the waters hoping for a better chance at life? How many parents had sacrificed their children to the 200 plus miles of water that separates Cuba from Miami, handmade rafts set afloat to hellish waves, in hopes that in the Land of the free, their children would be able to find their own little piece of heaven. The Cuban population being the majority in Miami, told the story.

Zaire shared info about her own upbringing, her parents, her Southern Charm Kai, the Brooklyn Beast Pharaoh, Tre, Reg and her other friends back home in Milwaukee. Nyris listened intently seeming to be genuinely interested in learning more about the fascinating young lady who had brightened his otherwise dull evening. It was so easy being with her. Her midwestern charm was a true treat. He knew that her company was one that he wanted to experience again.

"So, since I am not running two for two, how bout I make it three for three?" He smiled brightly as Zaire sat back in her chair listening. "You can not have a true Miami experience without having one particular experience. Are you available tomorrow morning?"

Zaire pursed her lips and studied Nyris. She wondered what the guy had planned but the secretive smirk upon his face told her not to ask. Something about his friendly and easy going demeanor told her that she could trust him.

"Yeah. I have a pretty open day. And you have impressed thus far. I'm game." She replied, receiving a satisfied look from her companion.

"Alright. That's settled." Nyris rubbed his hands together before collecting their used items and discarding them in the nearby trash. "Well, let me get you back to the hotel so that you can get some rest." He handed her his cell phone. "Enter your number and I will call you before I arrive."

Zaire typed in her mobile number and returned the phone back to its owner.

Grabbing her bags, they walked toward the front of the mall and exited back out onto Biscayne Blvd. It was now late in the evening and the darkness was rapidly setting in. There goes her planned evening at the pool.

The drive back to the hotel didn't take too long. Upon arriving, the dark of the night was fully upon them.

Nyris offered to carry her bag with the mask in but Zaire saved him the trouble by carrying it herself.

Once settled in her room, she thought about her interesting evening with Nyris. He was such a great and knowledgeable host. So laid back and chill. She had to admit that she had really enjoyed their time together and truly looked forward to seeing him again the next morning.

Chapter Eight- Zaire (Beautiful Surprise)

Beautiful Surprise- India Irie (Album: Voyage To India)

Zaire moaned as her cell phone's LED light flashed in rhythm with the synchronized vibrations and annoying ringtone that interrupted her slumber. Looking at the clock on the nightstand, the red lit numbers announced that 4:47 was the current time of morning.

Who in the hell could possibly be calling so damn early. She considered allowing the call to roll over to her voicemail but thought better of it, knowing that it could be an honest emergency.

Sliding the her finger across the option that confirmed that the call would in fact be answered, she mumbled a sleepy "hello."

"Good morning beautiful. Rise and shine. It's your Saturday morning wake up." The male voice had an owner of Nyris.

"Huh? It's 4:48am." Zaire's voice was heavy from sleep. "You can't be serious right now."

Nyris laughed. Entirely too much energy was behind his voice for the given time. "Yes, my dear, I am serious. And if you don't rise, dress and meet me down in the lobby within the next 45 minutes, then you will miss the absolute best experience that Miami has to offer. And I am serious about this as well."

"Nyris really?" Zaire whined. "It's Saturday. Can we link up a bit later?"

"Come on you." Nyris pressed on. "I soooo promise that this will be completely worth it."

Zaire fake cried, causing Nyris to laugh again. When he asked to meet again in the morning, Zaire had not been expecting to receive his call so early in the am. What could he possibly have to show her at 5am?!?!? What could possibly be open besides breakfast spots at that hour. Food was the last thing on her mind.

"Where are you trying to take me?"

"It's a surprise that I guarantee you will love. You will be thanking me later. Now get up Sleeping Beauty. Time is ticking!!!" He wasn't letting up.

After a few more pressing attempts, Zaire reluctantly agreed to meet him in the lobby.

Thirty minutes later, she sat in one of the plush chairs, waiting on his arrival. Nyris's Chevy Blazer pulled to a stop in front of the building.

Dragging and mopey, Zaire climbed onto the passenger seat as Nyris closed the door behind her. This had better be an experience to write the fuck home about. Zaire thought to herself when he pulled out into traffic.

"Wow. You are a mesmerizing sight in the morning." He marveled at her fresh, natural beauty. She offered a small and tired smile, mouthing a quick "thanks."

Nyris allowed her the opportunity to relax and "thaw out" from her frozen state on the drive to the destination. And what a scenic drive it was. Passing the Port of Miami, Zaire was speechless seeing the huge gorgeous cruise ships that were pulling into dock from the Sea. The light of day was on the horizon and it seemed as if every Seagull in the city were flying above in search of a fresh meal.

Nyris pulled off onto a sandy road, just past the Port. He followed the road for a mile or so before coming to a stop, parking near the Bay. Exiting the vehicle, he headed around to open Zaire's door and held her hand ensuring that she was safely planted on the ground.

It was another scorching morning. Temperatures were expected to reach well into the 80s again that day. Continuing to hold onto her hand, Nyris lead her out closer toward the water. The beautiful liquid landscape stretched on for miles. He walked her out onto the sandy shore, stopping at an old wooden bench.

Nyris explained. "This is a lookout point that really, only the locals know about. This is the best place in the entire city to watch the sunrise at its full glory. All you have to do is look straight at the water's surface, it should appear in a few minutes."

Zaire turned her attention to the surface of the water. She sat still and with patience, not wanting to miss a single second. The whole while, Nyris watched her, happy that she was now wide awake and truly interested in the naturally amazing and wonderful scene that would occur in just minutes. Her soft and soulful vibe was hard not to admire.

As promised, the top of the sun appeared off in the distance, activating the entire sky surrounding it with an orange glow. Zaire was dazed by the beauty of the planet's power source, the native star, emerging slowly from what seemed to be beneath the depths of the water. It was her very first time actually viewing a sunrise with her own two eyes. Nothing could have prepared her for this dynamic experience. The warmth. The amazement. The glory. She somehow felt closer to God in that moment. Her entire spirit felt lifted. The sight was all that he had promised that it would be. Magnificent and memorable. Feeling completely relaxed by both the incredible beauty ascending before her eyes and the presence of her personal tour guide, she leaned her head onto his shoulder, captured completely by the movement of the celestial body. She could not take her eyes off of the incredible wonder. The surrounding scenic beauty was an added bonus. The sound of the seagulls calling to one another from flight. The sandy beach littered with various rocks and unoccupied shells. The pleasantness of no one else there to interrupt the moment.

Even after the Sun had completely risen, Zaire sat in her stunned state for several minutes continuing in her trance. Nyris sat without movement, holding her, leaning his face down atop her soft, sweet scented mane. They silently stayed. They silently sat. They silently stared. The moment was silently breathtaking. No words were required. The unspoken appreciation of one another's company was more than enough.

Back at the hotel, Zaire sat at a table on the outdoor patio area of one of the beachfront restaurants, still staring out at the now high risen sun. She munched on her Bagel loaded with Cream Cheese, Smoked Salmon and Capers. Her appreciation of Nyris and his incredible thoughtfulness had her mind going to places where she wasn't prepared for it to go. He was so different from the guys back home. He was such a gentleman in every sense. So polite. So proud of his native city. Such a fabulous host. In just a short day, she had met someone whom had touched her in ways that no one had ever been able to touch her in years. He had dug in his crates and effortlessly touch her soul through the creation of experience. Now that was fascinating during a time when guys

108

seemed to be so selfishly focused on their own personal pleasures. It wasn't always about how much was being spent but more about how much creativity were used in the planning.

He reminded her so much of Jordan in many ways. His cool, calm and mature nature.

Zaire hadn't been fascinated with a guy since her ex Jordan. Jordan was her everything. Her love of her life. Her soul mate. Her equal mesh. He was her fiancée, whose ring she still wore around her neck, reminding her of who he was and what could have been. It had taken her heart years to heal from the loss of him. Even till this day, she had many questions for the one most high. She just didn't understand why he was taken from her. Why was he fatally shot while attempting to leave a gas station late one night 10 years before in a robbery gone wrong? The thieves had made off with his car, his wallet, but most precious of all, his life and Zaire's heart, in which she had completely given to him to carry for eternity. A senseless crime. Zaire vowed to never love again. She had been so devastatingly hurt. The feeling was reminiscent of having her entire soul ripped from her very being slowly, torturously. She had gone through a stage of absolute depression, throwing herself into working ridiculously long hours in order to avoid the devilish pain that awaited her behind the closed doors of her home. It had taken the intervention of her bestie to pull her from her depths of non existence. The many nights that she had stayed at his apartment, coaxed to let the emotions flow free. To relieve herself of the demon that had latched itself onto her. The many prayers that he had lovingly spoke to the Gods at his beautifully constructed alter, while holding onto her tightly. Refusing to let her go. The tears that he had cried right along with her. Her hurt was his. Her triumph was his. His faith was indescribable. Pharaoh was her strength in her most trying moment. To him, she would forever be grateful.

Nyris seemed so humble. So loveable. Such a genuinely good guy. She wasn't sure why he was sent or what he had come to teach her but he was an amazingly beautiful surprise.

Sipping her coffee, she promised herself sun and relaxation that day!!! An hour later, she was dressed in the 2 piece Ankara printed bikini, straw visor on her head, sunglasses sat upon her nose, covering her eyes, skin protected by the power of SPF. The sun slowly baked away at her candy coated skin. She floated without a care on the balloon raft in the middle of the largest pool that the property possessed. She was able to read several chapters of the first book from the Frienemies series. Relaxing into a sleepy state, she pushed her raft back to the pool's edge and slipped from the floating device into the refreshingly cool water. She knew better than to stay out napping in the unforgivingly smothering rays of sun. Removing her hat and her shades, she dipped underneath, swimming around the bottom for several seconds before emerging. The water did wonders for cooling her skin and stopping the cooking process.

Exiting the pool, she grabbed her items and slipped into her flip flops before heading inside for a much needed nap. It had been an incredible morning. The smile that crossed her lips before drifting to sleep gave confirmation to her state of bliss.

It was late in the evening when she woke. While sleeping, she had received several text messages, one from Nyris who was sweetly checking in. A giddy smile crossed her face. Another text had come from Pharaoh who was also checking in on her. She decided to respond to Pharaoh with a phone call instead.

"Who the fuck are you?" Pharaoh answered on the second ring.

"Stop it!!!" Zaire laughed knowing that he would feel some kinda way by not not hearing from her the day before. "You are always so extra."

"Let me find out, some nigga got you distracted and forgettin' your priorities," he teased disapprovingly.

"As a matter of fact….." Zaire couldn't contain her excitement and went into her story of meeting Nyris and the adventures they had from the night before into the morning.

Pharaoh was unusually quiet upon hearing Zaire's story. If she could see the frown that he wore on his face while spilling her beans, she would have stopped the story before making it to the end. After hearing about Nyris picking her up and taking her to the beach, Pharaoh couldn't hold it any longer.

"Are you kidding me!?!?!?" He exclaimed. She was taken aback by the raised level of his voice. "You mean to tell me that you let some random ass, bullshit driver that you know absolutely NOTHING about take you to some secluded ass part of the bay where he could have easily slit your fuckin throat, tossed you in and no one would have known absolutely shit about your disappearance!?!?!?!? Z are you fuckin loosing it!?!?!?"

Zaire blinked rapidly with her mouth hanging open staring at the phone in her hand while Pharaoh went on his yelling rampage. What in the entire fuck.

"What are you on right now!?!?" He continued. "That has to be the most dumbest shit you've ever fuckin pulled!!!! Z wake the fuck up!!!!! People come up missing every damn day!!!!! Are you trying to make the evening news? Why would you do that?!?!?

Her anger was uncontrollable and in her attempt to try controlling it, her eyes rimmed in tears. She knew that he had always been very protective of her but her emotions were running rampant with everything that had occurred from the day before into the current morning, and she didn't have any patience for his bullshit spazz session in that moment.

He was still yelling and cursing her when she placed the phone back onto her ear. Her voice was direct and straight to the point.

"Let me tell your ass something. You have no fucking say so in what the fuck I chose to do with my life!!!! Do you understand me?!?" The sound of her shaky, angry, teary voice stopped his verbal weaponry immediately. "I am a GROWN ass woman and I do whatever the fuck I please with whoever the fuck I please!!!! Last I checked, your name is not Mr. Jefferson!!! So miss me with all of this foul and extra bullshit!!!" Zaire punched the button to end his call so hard she damn near cracked the screen.

It took several deep breaths to gain some control over the anger that was spilling from her core. Needing to consult with someone and quick, she punched in Kai's phone number.

"Hey Pooh," Kai's voice was a welcomed sound.

"Please stop me from purchasing a ticket for the next flight out so that I can fly home and slap the shit outta Pharaoh." Zaire choked out sending Kai into beast mode.

"What the fuck did he do?!?!?" Kai sat straight up from her lying position across her bed.

Zaire filled her in on the discussion that had occurred just minutes before. Kai was red by the time Zaire had finished speaking. And again, here this sickening muthafucka was coming hard at her cousin like he took some type of claim on the decisions that she made. Why lawd? Why did this muthafucka keep putting himself in a position where she would need to fuck him up?!?!? Why?

"Calm down Cuz. You told him right." Kai put her own anger with the situation to the side in order to focus on her fragile cousin. "That's what it is. He needs to hear that from you more. He needs to know that it is not cool to keep carrying on the way that he does." Her southern twang was showing through.

Zaire used the back of her hand to wipe her tears.

While Kai was trying to calm her down, her phone vibrated. Looking at the display, she sent the call to voicemail after realizing that it was Pharaoh trying to call her back. He could kick rocks!!!! The last thing that she wanted to hear was the voice of the one who had ruined what had been a perfect day.

"If he calls, don't answer." Kai spoke as if she had been cued that his call had just come through. "Fuck him. You go on and head down to that bar, grab you a nice strong drink and forget that Pharaoh fuckin exists. Don't sit around crying over that stupid ass negro. You go on and enjoy the rest of your Saturday honey."

Zaire considered what she was saying. A drink would be the perfect salve to soothe the hurting that a Pharaoh had performed on her ego. She agreed to Kai's suggestion, disconnected the call and pulled herself together enough to head down to the bar.

Kai sat on her bed after her conversation with Zaire had ended. The hurt in her cousin's voice had upset her to no end. Not one to bite her tongue, she dialed Pharaoh's number. He answered before the completion of the first ring.

"Z??" He asked obviously and hopefully expecting Zaire call.

"Nope. It's Kai." She announced matter of factly. Pharaoh didn't respond so she continued. "Why are you so pressed about what Z does?" Her voice was strained trying desperately to keep from snapping.

There was a long pause before he responded. "I really don't have time for this. I'm not discussing anything with you. Is Z cool?"

"Is Z cool?" Kai laughed evilly. "What the fuck do you think?!?!?" Not being able to hold it together a second longer, she yelled angrily. Unfortunately, her response caused the display on her phone to light up, indicating that the call had been ended.

She dialed his number again but was immediately sent to voicemail. She squinted, staring at the screen of her phone growing angrier by the minute.

Chapter Nine: Pharaoh (All The Stars)

Kendrick Lamar/SZA -All The Stars (Black Panther Soundtrack)

Nothing feels better after a long stressful day than a hot shower. Shutting off the water valve, Pharaoh pulled the curtain back and stepped out onto the jet black, fluffy, plush rug. Warm water drops ran down his back, his thighs, calves and finally to the floor. Grabbing his dry towel from the rack hanging from the door, he wrapped it around his waist, tucking the ends.

He did not understand what it was about being in a tropical climate that caused chics to all of a sudden try to reclaim some lost ass groove. Seemed as if all that they needed to see was a damn palm tree and that was enough to cause them to lose their fucking minds. A little sun get to shining down on them and all of a sudden they are extra hot in the ass and need to cool off by spreading their damn legs.

Plopping on the bed, he placed the pair of joggers and boxer briefs that he had removed from the dresser drawer down beside him. After rubbing Raw African Shea Butter on his skin, he lightly patted Frankincense Oil on his neck and chest.

It just wasn't like Z to run so wild and mindless. Fuck was she thinking rolling around in a city that she knew absolutely nothing about with some random Cassanova ass nigga whose job was to drive a fuckin taxi?!?! Ole' fake ass Uber driving ass nigga!!!! Fuck outta here!!!

Pharaoh shook his head in disapproval. Z had no reason for desperation. Her whole make up was On Point: smart, sexy, beautiful, educated, sweet, soft spoken, caring.......... He could go on and on. The girl was a rare gem. He refused to hear about her running around in Miami tossing pussy out all down I-95. Get mad if she want, mattered none to him. Hated that he had to bust her down to tears in order for her to get the point but, oh well, she'll get past it.

Calling Kai and bringing her into it was a bad move on Z's part. She knew he didn't fuck with her like that. And for her to think for two seconds that she did have it to where she could call his phone with her bullshit tantrum, he laughed out loud. He killed that jazz immediately. Throw the whole bitch in the garbage!!! Hell, truth be told, Zaire hanging with her was probably the reason why she was down there thinking that being Thotiana was some new type of cool. Nah. Pharaoh wasn't having it. He made the decision right then and there to search for plane tickets first thing in the morning. He'd fly down there and get her ass right. It would also give him the opportunity to drop in on some the homies and restock on Cohibas. Even he could use a little South Beach in his life for multiple reasons. It had been too long of a while since his last visit. Yeah. That settles it. MIA on deck.

Standing to full length, he pulled on his garments. He observed his reflection in the mirror that sat on top of his dresser. He noticed his dreads looking a bit dull. He made a note to get one of his fans over to run a little Jamaican Black Castor Oil across his scalp. Maybe tomorrow. Yeah that would work, he thought as he picked up his Rolex from the nightstand, strapped it on his wrist and headed out of the bedroom. Putting shit off was a necessary requirement. Tonight would be focused on kicking back, chillin, poppin the top off a beer, sparking up a cigar and watching Giannis commit a mass murder on the Indiana Pacers.

Pharaoh walked into the kitchen to grab an MGD from the fridge. He took a swig before closing the door. He lifted his phone from the kitchen table to check his notifications. He had received a couple of text messages from Lacey asking why she hadn't heard from him, a text alert from his bank notifying him that a deposit of some kind had posted to his business account, a few Snap and Facebook notifications. Nothing pressing.

Taking another swig, Pharaoh noticed a knock at his front door.

What the fuck? Who the fuck? He wasn't expecting anyone and did not want to be bothered. He wanted to watch the game in peace!!! He was really hoping that Reggie had not decided to pop up uninvited after yet another dispute with his son's mom. He just really wasn't in no shape to deal with someone else's personal shit tonight.

Taking the last swig and emptying the bottle, Pharaoh tossed it into the trash basket and made his way to the front door. He mentally noted to have Tre come and install a new door equipped with a peep hole as soon as possible. The missing feature would have come in handy in the moment. Hoping that it was just a tenant with a question or request of some sort, he sent up a silent prayer.

His entire prayer was intercepted.
Unfortunately when he pulled it open, the devil had already made it to his front door.

"Shit!!!!" Pharaoh threw his hands up. "C'mon Gods!!!"

"Why did you hang up on me?" Kai stood, arms crossed in the doorway wearing a scowl. Her southern drawl sharp. She looked all drama and ready for war.

"Dafuq????" Pharaoh's entire soul was at full irritation. "Listen, why are you here Kai?" Pharaoh didn't have the time for any of her foolery today and his patience was paper thin. The nerve of her, of all people, to show up unannounced. Scratch that, the nerve of her to even show up at all!!! This was one ballsy ass chic. After shutting her down on the phone, now here she was bringing the shit to his home. What type of foul bullshit was she on?

"You are going to hear me out whether you want to or not. Stay the fuck out of Z's life!!! Not sure what makes you believe that you were assigned some level of authority over the decisions that she makes and what she does, but I can assure you that is not the case Playboy!!! I'm trying to keep it calm, but you already know where this could go. So you've been warned." Kai was speaking in a tight, strained voice that gave indication to Pharaoh that she was still struggling to keep it together and ready to pop off in an instant if she needed to.

Pharaoh laughed out loud at the audacity of this girl. This little chic was looney tunes. The whole sight of her was comical. Hair up, flip flops on, dressed down as if she was "bloody gang." She was forever pushing limits. Why? He understood her wanting to defend her cousin and thought it to be honorable that she had Z's back, but what was being misunderstood was that he had Z's back as well. And even with that, he didn't owe her any explanation whatsoever. Not this Country, gutter garbage ass chic!!!

"I already told you that I am not discussing my conversation that I had specifically with Z to entertain the likes of you," Pharaoh yawned, in a clear indication of his boredom.

The arrogant way that he was attempting to dismiss her sent Kai's blood pressure up. That egotistical edge that he had always possessed. That better than thou New Yorker persona. The shit made her skin itch!!! This muthafucka really thought that the sun rose and set purely on his ass!!! He had to be right and never admitted wrongs. Always had a mouthful of advice that he himself never thought to follow. This attitude is what drove Kai mad!!!

"Nigga, you could neva in life entertain the LIKES of me!!! My level is out of your league." Kai folded her arms and looked Pharaoh up and down as if his very existence was a mistake.

"Yeah, you are damn sure right with that," he smirked wickedly shaking his head." Your low ass gutter rat level is wayyyy out of my league." he loved watching the smug look on her face dissipate. "Take it down a notch Lil Mama, don't want you thinking that you're prime porcelain when you ain't shit but damaged goods."

Kai's response was quick fire. "Said the muthafucka WITH damaged goods!!!" Her reference to the rumors that were being spread by Yonica was well received. "Little Boy, find the rest of your dick before trying to come for me."

Pharaoh wasn't phased one bit. He knew what it was with Yonica. Yonica was ran on, ran thru and wrote off. Her rumors were the result of her feeling rejected to receiving what she really wanted which was more with him. Even years later she was still obviously carrying the bitterness from the way that he had publicly humiliated her when he checked out on her ass.

"Look," his laughed again looking at his wrist and checking the time. "Don't you got some meaningless ass fuck boy's house you need to scurry along too or something? I don't care where yo' ass go, just get the fuck off my doorstep."

"You know what Pharaoh, FUCK YOU!!!!" Kai screamed, her soft southern accent increasing in levels. Her proclaimed "calm" had been replaced with high winds and forecasted hail. "I tried it!!!! I tried again with having a decent conversation with you but I should have known from what occurred over by Tre's that I can't have a decent conversation with an indecent individual!!!!"

"Fuq outta here!!!!" Pharaoh's hearty laugh carried down the hall. "A DECENT conversation?!?! This was your attempt at that?!?!" he laughed again a bit louder. "If this is your attempt at having a DECENT conversation, then you for sure need meds."

Standing back looking at Pharaoh in his act of hysterics, laughing as if everything about her was a complete joke, his indignant nature, shirt off in all his glory truly believing that his shit had absolutely zero odor, the sound of his arrogant East Coast accent and the fact that he had insulted her yet again, created the recipe that caused Kai to spass.

"You are a NOTHING Ass Nigga!!! Let me be the one to set the Muthafuckin' Record STRAIGHT!!!! You think you are HOT shit but YOU are NOT!!!!" Kai was fuming. Her entire face had gone flush.

"Shhhh...Kai, quiet down," Pharaoh tried reaching for her arm while surveying the scene, hoping that none of his neighbors were disturbed by the noise, but she quickly snatched away.

"Don't tell me to QUIET DOWN!!!! FUCK YOU!!!" she continued on her tantrum. "My cousin called me crying over some FOUL ASS shit you spoke to her!!! Damn right I'm at your doorstep NIGGA!!!! AND I WILL FUCK ALL YO' SHIT UP!!!"

Her voice carried through the entire building. A building in which he himself owned and was required to keep a low profile to set an example for his tenants who occupied the other 3 units. Now she was fucking with his business and that was unacceptable.

The stress of what had unfolded within the course of his day, the fact that he had only wanted to watch the game, relax, chill and not be bothered, his early conversation that went South with Z and ultimately, him just being over Kai's loud, slick ass mouth and disrespectful presence had taken Pharaoh to the point of no return.

Needing to get her out of the hallway fast, in one swift and precise movement, he reached for Kai's arm, grabbed her and snatched her through the threshold of the door and inside the confines of his apartment. He then pushed the door shut with one mighty shove strong enough to shake all of the walls in his living room. Kai's facial expressions went through full metamorphosis from total surprise, to total shock, to measuring Pharaoh up, to complete fight or flight with fight being the obvious choice present in the final look that crossed her face, reminiscent of a wild banshee, it took control of her features before all hell broke loose.

"YOU MUTHAFUCKA!!!!" Were the last words she spoke before the first slap connected to the side of Pharaoh's face causing his entire head to jerk back and his locs to swing free from the loose banded bun that sat atop his head. Holy shit! This chic pack power in a punch, Pharaoh thought to himself before blocking the next blow using one hand as a shield and allowing the other to pin her for control as he walked her flailing body back against the wall nearest the once open door to confine her.

"Kai, calm the fuck down." Pharaoh spoke through gritted teeth trying desperately to get some control over the wild swinging girl. But he knew that it would be hell attempting to control her, especially with her next move that nearly connected, being a hard knee that lightly grazed past his balls.

"Oh shit, KAI, CHILL!!!" He pushed himself directly in front of her and quickly lifted her up so that her legs wrapped around his waist and pressed her hard into the wall.

"DON'T YOU EVER PUT YOUR MUTHAFUCKIN HANDS ON ME!!!!" Kai struggled to move but freeing herself from Pharaoh's strong pin wasn't an option. "PUNK ASS NIGGA, LET ME GO!!!"

Pharaoh wasn't sure if it was just him being exhausted and sick of hearing her yelling, the stinging from her hand that had connected to the side of his face, his needing to quickly think the situation through and make a move fast, the sexual nature of the position in which he had her pinned or what caused his next action, but he felt the need to kiss her and before he could process this thought, his mouth slid over hers causing yet another full metamorphosis of Kai's expressions. Mostly shock before changing to disbelief and finally softening, taking in what had actually happened.

"Wh…..what are you doing?" She spoke breathlessly against Pharaoh's lips that were pressed against her own. After breaking the trance that his soft kiss had created, she pulled her lips back exposing her teeth, took a part of Pharaoh's lower lip into her mouth biting down hard enough to draw blood to the surface.

Pharaoh quickly responded by pulling back just far enough to lock in on Kai's eyes. "DON'T." In a low, controlled voice, he warned with finality. "STOP IT. NOW." If looks could kill, Kai would have known that she was dead and that the battle was lost. Within Pharaoh's eyes was the coldest, most dangerous, yet sultriest glare that Kai had ever seen. A look that immediately evaporated all fight within her. Her white flag was waving in defeat.

Pharaoh was lost as to where the emotions were stemming from. He felt angry, almost predatory, yet poised, yet turned on to the highest level staring into Kai's beautifully flushed, now frightened face. Not frightened with fear, but by the unknown that she had never experienced with Pharaoh before. He was overly aware of all of his senses suddenly. He could smell the light, sweet scent of her fruity perfume. He could hear the soft shallowness of her short breaths and the increased beating of her heart. He could still taste the lingering sweetness of her lips and the drawn blood on his. He could feel the heat from her center being pressed against the now rock hardness of his own. Even her wild feistiness had turned him on which was definitely a first. He knew from the relaxed state of her body that she was equally as turned on as he was.

Looking deep into her eyes, he slowly leaned forward, carefully ensuring that he was reading her signals correctly. She didn't pull away and that told him everything that he needed to know. He allowed his lips to touch hers as if time had stood still and they were now in a mutual game played in the slowest of motion. Her reaction was receptive, wanting. He moved his full bottom lip in place and clamped over, taking her top lip between his two, suckling. A light gasp escaped from her throat. He went in for the kill, lightly sucking on her lips for a few moments before satisfying his need for more, sending his tongue on a personal, probing journey into her mouth.

Kai wrapped her arms tighter around Pharaoh's neck. Her hands grabbed a fistful of his locs at the nape and performed a sensual massage. Their rhythm switched from the initial slow and enticing into a now desperate and all physical connection. His hands explored the soft, perfect curviness of her form. Pressing her further into the wall for balance, he used his palms to cup the fullness of her butt. Her soft moans were turning him on to no end.

Kai ran her hands over Pharaoh's hard chiseled chest. He felt so warm to her touch. The thin Pink brand biker shorts that she had on along with the cotton joggers that he wore offered no protection as a barrier to the brick hard probe that was attached to his body, yet pushing through fabric, fighting to get inside hers.

She wasn't sure of the exact moment that Pharaoh carried her over to the chaise, but she made note of how effortless it was. He balanced all 170 pounds of her without a single sign of struggle. She also wasn't sure of the exact moment that her t-shirt was pulled over her head but what she did remember was that when his hands smoothly traced the outline of her bare waist and next, over her equally bare stomach resting into the elastic of her bikers, she shot up, as if being struck by the strongest of current, into sitting position stopping Pharaoh in his exploratory tracks.

"Wait!!! What are we doing?" she asked, shaking her head in disbelief. She turned to Pharaoh who seemed to also be slowly coming into realization with the moment. He took several seconds to size her up. Here he was kissing Kaimery. Fucking Kaimery of all chics?!?! Holy shit, what WERE they doing? Kaimery Thompson, who just moments before clobbered him upside the head as if she her name was more so fitting of Kaimery Tyson. Kaimery Thompson who was the exact representation of everything that he disliked about rat ass females with fucked up attitudes. Kaimery who now sat in a red lace bra with Cappuccino colored flesh spilling from the top. Kaimery whom he had just moments ago hated the entire sight of standing at his doorstep, smug with a fucked up agenda. Kaimery who now looked absolutely gorgeous displaying swollen, well kissed, moist pink lips and those seductive, light brown, inward slanted eyes. Kaimery who had his dick bout ready to burst through the whole damn ceiling. Whoa.

He raised a hand up to her face sweeping a loose lock of hair from her eye. "You call it. What do you want to do?" his east coast drawl now seemed relaxed, caring, and sincere. The same accent that made her ass itch moments before.

Kai was shocked at how much her body responded to the simple touch of his hand against her face. How gentle he was being with her. She was seeing him in a completely different light and the way that her heart was pounding at the realization of what was occurring and with whom, downright scared her to death. She was suddenly so turned on to him. She tightened her legs together in hopes that the movement would help to slow the flow that was causing her panties to soak.

He took her hand in his and pulled himself up to her eye level. "It's whateva you want?" He kissed her softly on her lips.

"I don't know." Her innocence was adorable. "What do you want?" She cowardly passed the ball into his court.

Pharaoh smiled, licking his lips causing her to melt. He was amused with the fact that she actually DID possessed that sweet, timid southern femininity that his boys seemed so mesmerized by. His gaze then changed instantly to one of raw and pure desire. The way that he intensely and confidently eyed her before responding, caused her heart to beat even faster in terror. She squirmed under the heat of his eyes and adjusted her legs a second time. Squeezing them together wasn't providing any justice for the throbbing occuring deep within her center. The dam was completely broken and beyond repair.

"You want the truth?" He paused for emphasis. Kai was still and unresponsive, waiting for his next statement with anticipation. "I want to you. BAD!!!"

His response was so matter of fact. It was so raw. So genuine.

Kai made the decision right then and there to put everything on the line. To sacrifice it all. She was so sure yet so scared. The moment just felt so right. Her body was calling and she had to allow him to answer.

"Okay……ummmmm okay. Yes." Her voice was shaky and not absolute.

Pharaoh pulled her down flat onto the chaise and took her face in his hands. The shakiness in her voice raised red flags causing him to sense something else that he couldn't place his finger on. "Are you sure? We don't have too. I don't want you to feel pressured in any way."

Kai closed her eyes and a few seconds passed. Pharaoh studied her face waiting patiently. She softly sighed and opened her pretty browns.

"Yes. I want you too."

Pharaoh continued tracing the sides of her face. He made his way up to where the dark brown clip held her silky straightened hair in place. Gently removing the clip, he watched as the pile of hair free fell in a waterfall onto the cushion around her head. He kept his eyes locked into hers the entire time. The moment was so simple yet so intense. Pharaoh played a while in the softness her hair sending tingles down her spine from the sensations his fingers caused against her sensitive scalp as he almost lovingly admired the beauty of her natural length. Her sweet innocence was all of a sudden extremely sexy to him. She responded to his every touch. Wanting more. Needing more. He wondered just how long she had wanted him? Was this sexual energy the cause of all the tension between them? Had he been wanting her as well? When her eyes closed for one last time and reopened accompanied by the softest, almost kitten purr-like moan, it was decided. Oh well, he would have to catch the game on DVR. He knew for sure that whether or not he had been wanting her in past was irrelevant, because right then he had to have her.

Pharaoh moved his body over the top of hers, bent at the knees. He placed his fingers into the folds of the elastic waist of her bikers and tugged the material away from her soft, smooth flesh. He pulled the shorts away from her feet and tossed them on the floor. He took some time to admire the matching lace panties that gave off an almost lethal effect against her brick house curves. He next unhooked the latch on the front of the crimson colored bra revealing the full mounds with perfect Hershey kisses directly in the center of each. The intensity of his gaze caused Kai to cover her breasts with both hands, a reaction that Pharaoh wasn't expecting. Why was she acting so shy? This couldn't possibly be the same chic that was just screaming and cursing him out.

Pharaoh smiled again to reassure her and removed her hands one at a time from over her beauty. He kissed each hand and placed them at her sides. Kai twitched in obvious discomfort as he lastly reached for her panties.

"Uhhhh.....wait...." she mumbled. Pharaoh sat onto the back of his calves and again studied her face.

"Wussup Lil Mama? Wus wrong?"

Kai bit her lip. Once. Twice. The look on her face brought Pharaoh immediate concern.
"Wus the matter Kai?" he stroked the side of her face in hopes of calming her once again.

"Pharaoh, I…...I'm a virgin."

Pharaoh almost laughed aloud at the ridiculous confession. Chics were known to call bullshit ass bluffs that claimed virginity. But in past dealings with her, he knew that she wasn't known to bluff and the look in her eyes stopped him dead in his tracks. She looked terrified, waiting on his response. He knew her well enough to know that she was telling the honest truth.

What?
How?
But she had been with so many niggas.
It couldn't be possible.
But her worried eyes said it all.

Pharaoh raked a hand through his own locs while processing the revelation. Wow. If she was a virgin, then why would she choose him?
Why him as her first?
Nothing made sense anymore.
The whole damn night just didn't make any bit of sense.

Her twitching and reaching for her clothes brought him outside of his head and back to the moment. She was unsuccessfully trying to blink away an accumulation of tears.

"Wait a second Kai" Pharaoh collected her hands in his. "I got you Lil Mama, it's okay."
He pulled her to him in a gentle hug that enveloped her fragile frame.

She leaned her weight into Pharaoh. She wasn't quite sure how or when his opinion of her started to matter so much but in this moment his approval meant everything.

For the life of him he just couldn't understand. Why would she be willing to give her innocence to him, someone whom she couldn't stand the sight of? Someone who couldn't stand the sight of her? What was happening right now??? How is it that here he was holding her half naked in his arms? He was convinced that Hell had to have without a doubt frozen over.

Although confused, he still felt that it was his duty to comfort her. He rocked her side to side for a moment and kissed the top of her head.

What THE FUCK was going on? The fact that he felt this overwhelming need to care for her and make her all better. Needing to pacify her and to kiss her uncertainty away. Wanting her more now than even before her confession. Feeling a sense of entitlement or belonging or whatever the fuck he was feeling…..It was Kai and it wasn't right!!!!

He turned her face up to his and kissed her trail of tears away. Damn even in tears, why was she so damn beautiful all of a sudden??? Her gorgeous brown eyes interrogated his. She wanted to know what he thought? How he now felt knowing her deepest secret? What he now thought of her?

"I told you that I got you Lil Mama." He replied. "I GOT you."

The response answered all of her questions. There had never been a time before that Kai had enjoyed when he had referred to her with the name "Lil Mama." The negative connotations associated with his past usage of it, flipped her stomach. Hearing the affectionate way in which Pharaoh was making use of it now meant the world to her and gave her a new appreciation for hearing it roll off his tongue.

She reached a hand up to his face and pulled his mouth down onto hers. Her kiss was so sweet. Cherries. She tasted like Cherry flavored Now and Laters. Or was it Starburst? Whatever it was, Cherry had always been his favorite flavor. He pulled her into his lap facing him. Forcing her to straddle him. Right then and there, he made the unspoken promise to give her the most memorable experience that she would ever have.

He traced kisses down her neck, loving the scent of her fruity perfume. His mouth slowly made its way to the start of her supple mounds. Taking the perfect grapefruit sized lumps in his hands, he flicked his thumbs across the hardened chocolate drops. He watched as her head fell back. She licked her lips in anticipation. He teased her a while until he could feel the winding of her hips as she rocked onto the hardness that poked up from his pants.

"You want it Lil Mama? Tell me you want it." he whispered into her ear allowing his lips to softly linger, teasing the lobe, all while rubbing her nipples a bit faster, sending her damn near over the edge. He made note of the unmistakably soaking state of her panties. The juices had seeped through, causing wet spots to appear on his own grey sweats.

Pharaoh let out a light chuckle. "Nevermind. Your dripping pussy says it all."

Pharaoh sucked a nipple into his mouth receiving a deep moan of pleasure from her as a response. Using his tongue and mouth in combination, the licking and sucking sent Kai's rocking rhythm from a slow, majestic Waltz into a now steamy, provocative Tango.

Lifting her from his lap, he lowered her body next to his on the chaise as he stood and removed his sweats and boxer briefs, loving how she watched his every move. He wanted her to watch him and with reason. Her beautiful eyes admired his body from head to toe, all six feet three inches of him. He stood motionless and smiled as her eyes traveled the length of his dark bittersweet chocolate build until they rested on the prize. Her eyes widened at the well endowed sight that greeted her. Holy hell!!!! A look of fear crossed her face which made Pharaoh laugh. Now there would be no mistaking the fact that Yonica and her bogus ass rumors were ALL lies.

"Don't worry. I told you that I got you. I won't hurt you."

He approached her and kissed her lips to settle her nerves. He chuckled at the thought that she was currently as quiet as he had ever known her to be. She was usually a woman of soooooo many unnecessary words. Looking at her now, it was as if looking at a completely different Kai than the one he had always known and argued with. This Kai was soft, sweet, innocent and incredibly sexy.

After he'd gotten her to relax, he slipped his fingers into the rim of her lace panties and tugged them down her hips and over her feet. Her legs were intentionally pressed together in her shyness but he could still see a neat thin landing strip at her triangle.

Leaning over, whispering in her ear while teasing her earlobe "I am going to make you open up for me. I'm not worried at all."

He started his trail of wet kisses down her neck across her breast and down her stomach savoring every part of her. He kissed her belly button making her squirm under the beating that she was receiving from his tickling and pleasurable tongue. Her moans were angelic to his ears. If at anytime he had ever hated the sound of her voice, he was loving the hell out of it now. Raising slightly he slid a knee between her tight pressed legs to pry them open slightly, enough to slide a finger down her slit until it reached it's destination. He took full advantage of her wetness allowing it to lube his finger as he slowly rubbed her center. Her moans increased in pitch and frequency. What were deep throated mumbles now gave way to open mouthed gasps accompanied by deep breaths of pleasure.

He kissed and sucked the tops of her thighs, rounding to the inner most part. As if on cue, her thighs opened, welcoming his mouth. There she goes, Pharaoh thought to himself when her thighs spread, allowing him access to her most private and most secret place. He rubbed his finger over her opening noting how tight the entrance was. Yes. No doubt. Her virgin status was confirmed. Somehow this confirmation made him happy. He couldn't explain why, it just did. Wow. And to think of all the names he had referred to her as being. All of the ill names that he had called her. This thought brought shame on his behalf. One day he would need to apologize. But now would not be the time.

He proudly admired the view of her perfect pinkness. Shining from the glaze of her natural biological river, he noticed that her clitoris was a perfect outie. Shaking his head, loving that she possessed this feature, he mentally thought "Boy is she in trouble".

Replacing his finger with his mouth, he spread her lips and began slowly swirling his tongue around her clit. Using his bearded chin, he pushed up against her opening, mimicking the sensation of his dick teasing her before full entry. Her gasps of pleasure and deep breaths now gave way to outright calls to the heavens.

"Oh my….oh my God. Ohhhhhhh…..ohhhhh…..Goodness. Oh my……"

He was determined to perform his best head job to date.

He lashed her bud with his tongue slow then fast flicking across the very tip then slow swirling then fast flicking yet again. He continued this for a while, bringing her close to the brink before pulling back and replacing his mouth with his finger applying just enough pressure to keep her at pre-climax.

"You like that?" he asked before receiving her mumbled reply. "Oh...my....God ...yes," she managed to choke out through shallow breaths.

"You ready to cum for me Lil Mama?"
"Oh shit.....oh my God."
"Are you ready to cum for me?"
"Uhh...ohh…"
"Just say yes Kai." Pharaoh's ego was on Level Ten.
"Yessss"

Pharaoh chuckled before returning his mouth to her clit, this time sucking her bud into his lips and into his mouth while still allowing his tongue to flick the tip along with the suction. This sent Kai into a wild frantic frenzy. She cursed every biblical name she knew. Her hands started grasping for items that were not visible. Her toes curled into the weirdest, most disjointed position he had ever seen.

It took him everything to keep from laughing at his own inside joke. "Damn, even her feet are able to make fists with her extra feisty ass."

It took seconds before she exploded in orgasmic bliss. The shaking along with the clamping of her thighs around his head was all the sign he needed to know that she had arrived.

Once he had pulled himself up into position, he was able to see how flushed and spent she was. Eyes closed, her mouth hung open in her attempt to catch her breath and slow her breathing.

Pharaoh smirked and silently patted himself on the back. Mission One accomplished. Check.

Now for mission two.

He lowered his lips to hers. "You good Lil Mama?"

"Yessssss" her response was breathless.

"You like me sucking your pussy like that?"

She opened her eyes and was immediately gazing into his own. The feelings. The sensations. The emotions. The thrill. All together the recipe created the most dangerously refreshing concoction that she had ever partaken in.

"It was amazing." Her reply was spoken slow and soft, almost whimsical in her southern tone.

Pharaoh softly removed the lock of hair that had returned from her forehead as he mischievously stared into her eyes. He knew that he possessed to power to destroy her entire world as she had known. Fuck her whole understanding up. His skill was impeccable enough to drive the most experienced to the looney bin. It would be effortless to take a virgin there. But this wasn't just any virgin. This was Kai. Even through it all, she was still Z's cousin which, in itself, had allowed him the opportunity to still care for her to a certain degree. Never would he have imagined that she would be lying here, on his chaise, in his apartment, fresh from wild'in out in the hallway. Thinking back to all the shit slinging contests they had engaged in: the blatant disrespect, the name calling, the anger, all of the unnecessary drama.....Shit he had the opportunity to pay her back OVERTIME!!! And shit did she deserve it!!! He could let loose, fuck the entire shit outta her, take all of the disgust he had felt for her out on her pussy with a vengeance. Show her just how much of a "NOTHING ass nigga" he really was. But looking into her trusting face, the pure passion in her eyes, he knew that he would stick with his promise. He would issue his payback in a different form. He would still have his fun, but just with waiting, until the right moment. Call him the devil and she would become his Ghost Rider. And with that......

Mission 2: Snatch her entire soul from her evil little body.

Holding her gaze, he slowly begin his entry by placing the tip of his dick at her opening. She quickly responded by spreading her legs wider. He was amazed at how trusting and willing she was with him. She was so ready.

Her hands were at the edges of the cushion belonging to the chaise. Already she had a good firm grip, heart pounding, awaiting what would come.

He moved the tip back and forth into her wetness, teasing her there for a few seconds, careful not to push in past her intact hymen. He guessed it to be true what they say about Aquarians. She was definitely a water bearer, her pussy was certified WET wet. Teasing her almost caused him to sacrifice his own composure. Shaking off the brief moment of weakness, he reminded himself that this punishment would be solely about her and her alone.

"Are you ready?" he asked watching her press and release her lips together. She nodded in response.

Pharaoh used his hand to control the pressure and he slowly guided his dick in. It took several tries before being able to break past her protective seal. He knew that he would need to give her time to adjust to every single inch of him being that every single inch would be accompanied by gerth. Her sharp draw of breath indicated his need to check in.

"Are you okay?" he studied her contorted expression. She nodded her head up then down while digging her nails into the unlucky cushion that was twisted into a death grip in her hands. He leaned down to reclaim her lips for the purpose of her relaxation as well as his own. Her super wet, tight, virgin pussy could easily throw his character off if he wasn't careful. While intertwining his tongue with hers, he pushed further into her well, capturing her loud moans and smothering them with his own mouth. He gave another slow deep push causing her to release her grip from the cushion, placing her hands on his back instead.

Oh Shit! He cursed to himself knowing that it would only be a matter of time before his back resembled that of freshly whipped slave. He had prayed that she would remain clutching the cushion. His prayer had obviously been rejected by everyone of the royal NRT.

His next push was a bit harder and deeper than the first few and caused a moan to escape from his own mouth. He immediately dismissed it to being a boomerang effect with her moans traveling into his mouth and somehow sailing out. Couldn't have been him. But the final push confirmed his lie, as his eyes closed in enjoyment of the sensation that her sinfully tight walls caused engulfing his steel.

"Oh shit, your pussy is so fucking tight." his broken down state was reflective in his need to lay his head on her shoulder like a newborn while he allowed some time so that they both could adjust. He hadn't had virgin pussy since his teen years and he had forgotten how lethal it could be. And Kai's pussy created a whole different level of the need for understanding with how warm and wet it was.

Kai planted soft kisses along the bridge of his nose. Her mouth searching out his, already addicted to his kisses and still tasting her own mild flavor on his lips. His kisses were amazing. The effect was as if they possessed properties of a sedative style drug. His kisses brought instant calm to her. She needed them desperately in this moment. Her pussy was on fire!

Pharaoh naturally accommodated her request. Her tenderness. Her trusting him with her grandest treasure. Her almost loving gaze. This girl was unknowingly in the process of performing her own unintentional soul snatching spell.

Sucking her bottom lip into his mouth and covering hers fully with his, he started a slow grind. Kai's gasps were deep and sensual. His own were low and vocal. "Damn......oh fuck this pussy is so good."

It seemed the more he moaned, the wider she opened, giving him more access and encouraging him to give her more, and that she could take on more. Accepting this reaction as permission, he picked up his pace, diving deeper and increasing his speed. Her nails dug deep into his shoulder blades, her throaty moans immediately caught voice. "Ohhhhhhhhhhhh Goodness......ohhhhhhhhh ohhhhhhhhhmygoddddd....." she was back to cursing Holy names.

Pharaoh fill every inch of her. There was no space between her walls and his hard steel-like pipe that was currently thrusting inside of her. He was so thick and so long.....her pussy screamed in an achy pain that was so pleasurable she wasn't sure if she needed to laugh or cry. How could something so painful make her feel the way that she was. Something deep in her core was being manipulated by the friction that his dick was causing by rubbing against it. In and out. The sensation was building with his momentum. The faster and deeper he dug, the more painful it became, yet, the more pressure built. The pressure sent her to a state of no return.

Pharaoh placed his hands under her ass for extra lift. This caused Kai to start yelling out. He knew that he had her at the place where he needed her to be in order to complete mission 2.
He could take her anywhere at this point and she would follow with no fuss whatsoever.

Leaning down and Brushing his lips against her ear, he started his mastery.
"Why are you here Kai?"
Her yells grew louder but she did not respond which caused Pharaoh to shake his head in disapproval. He punished her with one deep thrust that forced his entire dick deep into the depths of her pussy, ensuring that he tilted down in a way that the curved head rubbed solidly against her G Spot. She screamed out as a result. Nah...earlier she wanted to scream and create a scene, causing the neighbors to hear. Now, let her scream so that they can hear this shit too. No holds barred. Her nails dug into his shoulders causing him to flinch.
He collected her hands in his and cuffed them over her head, holding them there. Now she couldn't move even if she tried.
"I will ask you again, why are you here Kai?"

He wasn't expecting a clear response, just enough to rattle her completely.

"No…......I don't know……"

"Why are you here in my fuckin apartment?"

"Why am I fuckin you right now?

He pumped deeper with each question.

"All this time Kai!!!" He grinded into her faster. Her yells could be heard down the block by this point.

"Why me? Why did you give your virginity to me?"

"All this time you been wanting to fuck me!?!?" He was alarmed at the level of his own anger.

Releasing the cuffs, He placed a hand on her waist and slammed into her. He was careful not to hurt her but to keep her pinned in pleasure with just the right amount of thrusting against her G Spot. He used his other hand to stroke her clitoris.

"You like fucking me Kai? Tell me…..you like fucking me."

"Oh God yes…...I…….love…...fucking…….youuuuuu!!!" She once again connected with his back and dug her nails deep into his flesh. But that didn't stop Pharaoh. "Oh shit…..oh my Goddddddddd……..!!!"

Feeling her climax coming on with the sporadic, premature contractions of her vaginal muscles, he went in with the last of his answerless interrogation.

"All this fucking time!!! You wanted the dick all this fucking time?!?!" he kept a steady pace pounding into her. His accent was at an all time strong definition.. She was going crazy, again, reaching for shit that still wasn't there, wrapping her legs around his back and instantly unwrapping them. Calling out his name.

"Oh shit Phaaaaroooooooah!!! Ohhhhhhhhh myyyyy God!!!" She was at an all time loss. Her weakest moment she had ever known to date. So, this is why women went crazy over this shit. This was enough to put the most solid chic in a fucking straight jacket. Hell, she thought herself to be pretty solid, but this negro was on an entire mission to conquer. Literally. Her pussy was doing things that she had never imagined as a possibility. She'd heard stories, but had written them off as being mythical. She felt as if an evil spirit had invaded her body and taken full control. An evil spirit by the name of Pharaoh. He was the master and she was his helpless puppet.

The first wave caught her off guard. Uncontrollable contractions erupted from her very core. The vibrations were so intense, she thought she had seen Jesus. When the second wave hit, with even more intensity, she screamed as a stream of fluid shot out from her. Another stream flowed from her eyes, down her cheeks and onto the crushed cushion of the chaise. The back to back tightening of her vaginal muscles around his shaft sent Pharaoh drifting into his own climatic finish. "I'm bout to cum all in this pussy!!!" he announced before bursting, dumping all of his DNA into her deep, hollow well. He shouted out. She shouted out. Their synchronic climax left both of them completely and sincerely spent.

Pharaoh's body lie lifeless on top of her. His dick was still pulsated inside. Other than the rapid pace of his breathing which matched the racing pace of his heart beat, Kai would have thought he was dead. Her own legs were still wrapped comfortably around his back. She didn't trust her own movement, so she felt they would be best left as they were.

Kai felt as if her whole existence was in jeopardy. Something had to have gone wrong. This just couldn't be right. She was a bipolar ass disaster. A complete and utter hot ass mess. Caught between wanting to slap the shit out of Pharaoh and wanting to shove her tongue down his throat, she didn't know how to react. She opted to lie still, motionless, giving her brain time to recover.

Now minutes later and her pussy was still contracting.

What the fuck just happened? The first question that she asked herself when her brain had finally started receiving signals again. She had just fucked Pharaoh!!!! Or more he had just fucked her but either way….
SHE HAD JUST FUCKED Pharaoh!!!!
SHE HAD JUST GIVEN HER PRECIOUS VIRGINITY TO FUCKING Pharaoh!!!!

"Oh God No", she whined, unwrapping her thighs from around Pharaoh's back, pushing his shoulders, causing him to roll from on top of her.

Pharaoh wore a frown while he watched her.
Kai sat up and began collecting her garments. Where were her panties? And why the fuck was her pussy still contracting?!?!?

Pharaoh reached on the opposite side onto the floor to retrieve her panties.
He shook his head, raising his frame from the chaise. He knew that look in her eyes all too well. The look of shame.

He walked over to the double glass door, pulled on the handle to slide the door open, revealing the closed in balcony. He reached for the platinum cigar case that sat upon the mini bar next to the door. He pulled out a Cuban and gently set the case back in place. Grabbing his cigar cutter, he sliced away the tip before next reaching for the torch, sparking it to life. He inhaled, savoring the smoky flavor. He stepped barefoot on to the wooden balcony and rested on the edge. The night was rather warm but beautiful. He took another pull and looked up into the dark, clear sky. As a child, his grandfather had always taken him out at night, teaching him the importance of positioning, and being able to identify stars. "If you know the positions son, you will never be lost. Always look to the stars as your guide." He was such a wise old man. A true King in his own right.

Pharaoh turned and headed back to the door. Kai, with panties on, was crawling around on the floor trying to locate some other random item of hers. Calmly, Pharaoh called for her. "Come here."

Kai now had her hand underneath the chaise pulling what looked to be her lace bra out. "I need to go, to get out of here." she mumbled from her place on the floor.

"No......You don't......and the feeling will pass......Kai trust me, please...." he took another pull patiently from his cigar. "Come here Lil Mama."

His voice was gentle, stopping her in her tracks. She turned to him with a mix of vulnerability, regret, uncertainty and sadness all present in her face. Pharaoh held a hand out to her summoning her to him. She sat still for a long minute before reluctantly lifting herself from the floor holding her T-Shirt over her breast and slowly, walking over to him. She winced in pain and he quickly made note as to why. He was easily able to see her offbeat steps from the gap that had developed between her legs.

Up close, looking freshly fucked, her hair fell wild over her shoulders, her lips were a deep pink and swollen from being sucked and nibbled on. Her light browns were searching his own for a sign of acceptance, and again, of reassurance. Her took her by the hand and pulled her onto the porch.

"Nooooooo, won't someone be able to see?" she tried pulling back, whining with her child like innocence.

"They won't, it's covered. Trust me." He led her to the edge and turned her body facing front. He enjoyed the view of her trim waist, wide hips and extra well rounded cheeks swallowing the thong of the red, lace boy shorts before he placed his body behind her, wrapping his arms around her, holding her. Rocking her. Comforting her. His voice remained gentle. He held onto her for a while. His eyes locked onto the group of stars twinkling directly above.

"My Grandfather taught me about Astronomy and the stars when I was a young boy. We would go out back, lie in the grass and gaze up into the night sky. For hours he would teach me about the beliefs of the Egyptians, how they monitored and observed the movement of the stars, of the planets, of the moon.......and he would point out various constellations."

Pharaoh paused a few seconds before continuing, "On a good night, when the street lights were out, the sky would fall pitch black and we would then be able to see the arms of the galaxy." He laughed reminiscing.

"Now my Great Old Man loved when we could view the arms of the galaxy." his chuckle carried on, remembering the excitement his Great Old Man would have for what he called the "darkest" nights. "We would then play a game of trying to point out the empty spaces." his voice suddenly trailed off.

Kai turned her face toward him looking into his eyes. He seemed to be in a daze as if mesmerized by the beauty of the night sky. This whole while he kept rocking her back and forth. He raised the cigar to his lips and pulled. He turned to release the smoke upward, his routine: sending one off into the distance in honor of his Great Old Man. Kai could see the sadness in his eyes. It immediately made her realize that the stuff that she was carrying just wasn't of any importance. Pharaoh looked to be in a whirl of pain. The moment lasted a few long seconds before passing when in typical Pharaoh fashion, he laughed and continued, disguising, covering his pain.

"Funny thing is, there wasn't ever a winner between the two of us. Everytime we would look into the arm, there was never any empty spaces. The arm is completely full of life. Every corner, every crevice....." his voice trailed off again. "There is always so much life." he sat in that statement, knowing that his Great Old Man's life was no longer of Earth as his spirit had moved on, taking life from biological body, into eternal celestial body. "So much more than we are ready to accept.......how could we be so arrogant to believe there is just us...that the universe revolves around only us.... Trillions of stars, each with their own full solar systems....... How could it ever be.......just us?" Pharaoh's voice drifted again before puffing on his cigar once more, he continued quietly rocking her back and forth.

Sometimes Pharaoh could travel into some mysterious depths. Deep and laced with layers of pain. Those were the times that she had always, regardless of how much she had loathed him, admired and respected his deep and thoughtfully intelligent mind. Kai's heart broke for him. She knew that he still struggled with the loss of his Grand Dad, or his Great Old Man as he liked to call him. She could only imagine what pain he must be carrying and still coping with. The Aquarian in her wanted in that moment to kiss his pain away. To relieve him of the burden. To take it on herself. Or at least, to help him to carry the weight. Knowing that she couldn't do any of those things, she decided to do what she knew that she could.

Nothing else mattered to her in this moment. Didn't matter that she was just in the process of collecting her clothes, looking to run away from her own terrible self-judgement by making a quick exit. Didn't matter to her that the guy who stood directly behind was Pharaoh. Didn't matter to her that at the start of her night, he had never been written into her agenda. Didn't matter to her what the time or what the reason, all that did matter was that she needed to provide comfort to him as he had so graciously provided for her the entire night.

Interrupting his swaying, turning and fully facing him, she reached up and placed her arms around his neck. She allowed the T-Shirt that she used to cover her breast to fall to the floor of the porch, throwing all of her inhibition to the side. She first pecked softly at his lips before covering his mouth with hers. He welcomed her sweet kiss and took full advantage by allowing his tongue to go on a hike. He set the cigar in the ashtray on the balcony ledge and slid both arms around her waist, pulling her close. She could feel his rock hard weapon pressing against her belly. Pharaoh wanted her face closer to his so that he can look, without shifting, into her eyes.

"You trust me?" he asked waiting for her response.

"Right now...I guess ...I do...." she replied causing them both to chuckle.

Knowing that his action would catch her off guard and give her the fright that she deserved with her sarcastic ass response, he lifted her five foot four inch frame from being grounded and up onto the wooden balcony ledge. She shrieked out in horror trying to slide off to plant her feet back comfortably on the ground. In doing so, she tilted backwards, almost flipping over the ledge, causing her to shriek once again. "Pharaoh......nooooooooo....."

145

Pharaoh placed his arm firmly around her back to stabilize her. She wrapped her legs around his waist for dear life. She was freaking out with her known phobia.

"Kai, look at me and only at me," he took her chin in his loose hand, turning her face directly to him. "Look at me." She followed his command and looked into his face. "I told you before that I got you." His voice remained calm and light. "Do you really trust me?"

She paused a second to consider what exactly he was asking her. Following her first mind and knowing that even after all of the full fledged blow outs leading to their epic disputes, even with things going as far as they ever had with her actually getting physical with him tonight…...she somehow knew he would never harm her. She nodded and replied softly. "Yes, I trust you." Pharaoh sat a moment, taking in her spoken confession. The words spoke volumes to him and played at his heart strings.

Pharaoh took her chin and raised it up. "Look directly above you."

Kai focused her attention to the series of stars that were right above her head in the sky. Leaning his mouth against her ear, he whispered, "That is the Orion constellation." He kissed her ear and begin circling his tongue around the lobe, breaking her concentration. She moaned and tried turning her face back down toward him. He caught it in his hand and tilted it back upward. Keeping his mouth on her ear lobe so that every time that he spoke, his lips would tickle her ear, teasingly he whispered, "uhhh uhhh…...the only thing I need you to do is to focus and listen." He continued with his torturous lesson. "Orion is the most easily identifiable of all of the constellations because of those three stars there." He pointed to the three stars that were aligned in an almost see saw type of tilt. The first two were almost perfectly horizontal while the one on the right end sat back just far enough to break what could have otherwise been a perfectly straight line. "Those three are called the belt stars of the constellation because, well.…...they make up his belt." He dipped his tongue inside her ear almost again sending her flying backwards over the edge of the ledge. Needless to say, her concentration was again, completely broken. Steadying her, he chuckled inwardly. "I got you Lil Mama." When she relaxed, he tilted her head back upward. "The rest of the stars form the rest of him. See how those six stars on the far right come together in another broken line with the three in the center pointing outward to form a long triangle. Those are the stars that create his bow. The one in the very center aligns perfectly with the brightest one, above the right belt star that sits back awkwardly. You see that?" Kai nodded her head. "That very straight alignment creates his arrow. See the two that forms a triangle above the arrow?" she nodded yet again in agreement. He nibbled her lobe. She tried hard to keep her composure but was unsuccessful. The moan escaped her lips and set his teasing off. "Kai, concentrate!!!"

"What the hell Pharaoh, I'm trying.…." she was frustrated but genuinely turned on. Sore and banged up beyond belief, her "girl" still wanted him. What the fuck? It was over. She was a goner. And another one bites the dust.

"Those stars form the top of his chest plate." he continued. "Note the brightest of those stars on the left, that star is named Betelgeuse." Kai lingered a second on Betelgeuse. It was such a bright and beautiful sight. Pharaoh continued. "The three underneath the belt stars connect together to form his war kilt." He tenderly kissed her cheek."The five leading up from Betelgeuse forms his arm, raised in battle stance." he kissed her neck right under her ear. "And that completes his full body. The full constellation."

Kai lingered, studying the Orion constellation in fascination. "Do you know his story? Who was he and what did he do?"

Pharaoh kissed her on the lips and smiled. "Now that would be giving too much info out on the first date."

Kai chuckled and rolled her eyes "Boy, this ain't no date. This here, is a session."

"Oh really? A session huh?" Pharaoh smirked knowingly. "Well if this is a session…" he yanked her bottom to the edge of the ledge and moved her panties to the side. It took three pumps for him to enter halfway inside her. She gasped, throwing her head up, toward all the stars. "Then I want my monies worth."

Chapter Ten: Pharaoh (The Morning After)

The Morning After- Maze (Album: Back To Basics)

4:18am. Pharaoh glanced at the clock on his nightstand. Yawning he attempted to stretch his arms unsuccessfully. One had blockage. His upper right arm was pinned at the bicep with Kai sleeping peacefully snuggled next to him.

He slowly adjusted the weight of his body, turning toward her, keeping his right arm still, careful not to disturb her. Now able to see her full face, Pharaoh frowned, evaluating the situation as the memories of the prior night came flooding back in living color.

Whoa!

He had to accept the truth that he had indeed fucked Kai.
But how did this ever become possible?
And how is it that she was still at his home, lying in his bed?

So many rules had been broken, and that left Pharaoh struggling and truly upset with himself. What was going on with him? This shit was completely unacceptable!!! There was no way to explain how he could have made SO many mistakes in ONE damn night with ONE damn chic that he didn't even fucking like!!!!!

So many broken rules!!!

Since living in his apartment, the only woman who had EVER slept in his bed was Zaire, and he of course, had slept on the couch. NO woman was to ever spend the night and sleep in his bed!!! That was the Number One RULE!!!! How could he have been so careless? Why had he been so careless? Why was he acting so weak? And on top of that, why was he acting so weak over KAI!?!? Even after he smashed on the balcony, he could have sent her on her way then, but HE was the one who fed himself the lame ass excuses about how exhausted she looked, and how she just needed to get a little rest, and how it was his own fault that she was so damn tired. What type of backwards ass bullshit was that??? Not to mention that he fucked her TWICE in ONE night!!!!! Awwww man!!!! It was ALL bad for him. It did not look good at all. Another broken rule!!! Dammit he was smoother than that. Where were all of the missed steps coming from?

Yes Kai had always been gorgeous. Any man or woman with eyes could see that, but he had never been attracted to her. Had he?

He was so confused and the fact that he had fallen asleep with questions and now lay wide awake with the same questions, was just too damn much and was starting to torture his entire soul. He had never cracked over any chic!!! Always control, conquer, smash and dash. No sweat off his chest whatsoever. So what was his issue now?

Breaking him from his own mental beat down, Kai stirred, removing her thigh from over his and stretching it comfortably straight on top of her own, as if she could somehow hear the horrible thoughts swirling in Pharaoh's mind and no longer wanted to be close to him. The light from the street cast a thin stream through the blinds on the windows, into his room and across Kai's face. That pesky pile of hair was again partially covering her eyes and nose, falling diagonally across her forehead. Her mouth was slightly open with her breathing being heavy. Not quite snoring, but heavy with exhaustion. The light gave an almost mystic appearance to her face and skin. The loose sheet was wrapped tight around her naked body, pulling her in tight next to his. She was warm in temperature and extremely soft and supple.

Pharaoh admired her sleeping beauty a while, allowing his mind to settle enough to properly calculate his next move. He needed the time to be able to ensure that the decision would come from his brain and not his dick. Having his common sense intercepted by his dick is what got him into this mess to begin with. He needed to be sure that he was ready before he made another move.

The only problem was that in staring in her face, he found that his concentration was being tested to no end. All it would take is just one kiss and he would for sure be able to wake her up for Round 3. This time he could bend her over and take her from the back. He could just imagine fucking her while that infamous ass of hers was up in the air. How much fun would that be? How would her extra tight pussy hold up to that type of abuse? His dick twitched at the thought.

Pharaoh rubbed his free hand over his face in disdain and slowly pulled his arm from underneath her. Here he was thinking about a Round 3 when he already had fallen and hit his head at Round 2!!! This shit was ridiculous. He couldn't stop thinking of ways that he wanted to fuck her. He decided that he needed to get away from this chic and fast. Hopefully a long hot shower would do.

Pulling himself from the bed, he made his way to the bathroom. Turning on the water, he allowed steam to completely fill the entire room before stepping into the relaxing stream. The water felt almost therapeutic running down his back, especially being that he had war wounds, sore with missing skin that occupied the entire perimeter of his shoulder blades. He stood in the stream for quite some time before finally grabbing a sponge and lathering on Raw African Black Soap. Although causing major stinging to his open cuts, he used the thick lather to wash away what he could of the evidence of the previous night's rendezvous. His mind drifted again.

This shit was making him physically sick. He turned off the water after a good 30 minute rinse down and stepped out of the shower, onto the rug and into the fluffy towel that he had pulled from the linen closet. Opening the door, he made his way back to the bedroom. He needed to somehow get her out of his house so that he could just breathe. It seemed as if she had come through and polluted what used to be his very own fresh, clean air supply, and he needed it back purified asap.

Reaching the room, the first thing he was greeted with was an empty bed, sheets thrown back where she had been, her clothing no longer sat on the chair in the corner of the room. Turning on the light, he quickly scanned the confines of his sleeping quarters. No flip flops set underneath the chair. No Dear John note left on the nightstand. No sign of Kai anywhere.

He walked down the hallway into the living room. All was clear. Looking toward the back of the apartment, the kitchen was quiet and pitch black. Sliding the balcony door open, he stepped onto the porch, walked over to the ledge and peered over to where her car was earlier parked to find that it was no longer there. She had beaten him to the punch. With the swiftness of a Japanese Samurai, Kai had completely disappeared. His wish had been granted. Unfortunately, he didn't quite yet know how he should feel about her disappearance, especially with the fact that it was autonomic and he didn't play a single hand in causing it.

Back in the bedroom, Pharaoh went through his after shower routine. He next headed to the Altar room and knelt at the beautifully decorated shrine. Egyptian hieroglyphic art decals filled every inch of the four walls. A bookcase sat in the corner equipped with his collection of African literature from many different decades. A huge bean bag chair occupied one corner of the room.

Huge throw pillows sat in another. The alter table hosted many sacred items. Most were sent to him from his father and derived directly from Africa. A white table cloth made of fabric from Nigeria lined the table. A bowl of water sat atop with the goal of capturing all impure evil thoughts and spirits. Three quartz pyramids sat in the center of the table in exact alignment with those at the Giza Plateau. A small sphinx statue sat in front of the pyramids. The display was surrounded by small figurines of the deities: Thoth, Osiris, Isis, Hathor and Arubis. A bowl filled with dried leaves, a bowl filled with sacred stones and a third bowl filled with ash, covered the table. A beautifully colored feather stood from a vase on the end. Various colored candles along with an incense holder completed the items that were meticulously placed upon the table.

Lighting sage scented incense and selecting red candles, he called upon the Element of Fire for its purification abilities. He located a track from his favorite Spiritual Seas meditation album that he had saved in his iTunes. Taking a deep breath to calm his mind, he dedicated himself to a much needed 15 minutes of meditation.

Asking the God of Magic, Heka, for spiritual clarity and guidance in the realm of the unknown, he surrendered himself in sacred time and space. His calm came quickly. It seemed as if he had just settled in, but time seemed to have flown by. The sound of waves crashing against the shore ended abruptly, signaling the end of his cognitive, out of body exploration. He lastly recited The Laws of Maat. Blowing out the candles and allowing the final butt of the incense to burn out, he lifted himself from the floor and headed out the room to begin his day.

He settled on enjoying a light breakfast of oats, fruit and a few slices of Avocado on the side. While eating at the dining room table, he powered on his laptop and opened up a window to

Chrome. He checked a few sites for plane tickets to MIA and decided on reasonable priced straight trip tickets leaving out the Friday after next with United Airlines.

He would not give notice to Z regarding his plans. He would arrive and surprise her with his presence. He knew that is all that it would take to send her shrieking with excitement and to earn her forgiveness. She would be so ecstatic to see him. He smiled just thinking about her reaction to come.

Now 6:37am.

Grabbing his Beats earbuds and keys from the top of the minibar, he locked up his apartment and made his way across the street to the park. He turned on his phone's BlueTooth and found his favorite Old Skool Hip Hop playlist with iTunes. The first song put him in the exact headspace he needed to be. Stretching his thighs and calves while using the park bench for balance, he prepared for his morning workout. He broke into a slow paced jog, warming his muscles and raising his heart rate.

He smiled thinking about how well he had put it on Kai. Without a doubt, he knew that the rumors would cease and his skill would never be questioned again. He broke her in royally, thoroughly and unforgettably. Taking her on the balcony ledge had no doubt awaken the entire neighborhood. Her moans had to have carried for miles.

He had to admit that he was impressed with her ability to take dick. Being a virgin, she didn't give much push back. She took the pain, using her sharp nails to return punishment with the number that she'd done on his back. No doubt he had a MONSTA!! Most veteran puss struggled with adjusting to his length and girth. She cried, she yelled, but she took his dick like a champ. Kudos to Killa Kai!!! That's wussup. Touche'.

Boy was that pussy tight. And her juices seemed to have an endless flow. Had to have been the wettest, tightest, warmest he had ever had. And her appetite was insatiable. He could have gone on fucking her for hours longer and she would have been a willing participant. Wow. Amazing.

Picking up his pace, he broke into a run.

The day was promised to be another 75 degree beauty. It was still unseasonably consistently warm for Pre-Summer in Cream City. Known for having a 70 degree day here and there around this time of year, a full two week stretch equip with equally warm nights promised the arrival of an early warm season.

Taking in the natural beauty of the park, Pharaoh crossed the wooden bridge that provided mobile access across the rushing stream. Trees were in full bloom, nesting was being constructed in nearby bushes, ducks were swimming atop the pond that sourced the narrow water way that he had moments ago crossed. At any chance possible, he took the time to appreciate nature. His morning runs were a necessity. He always made it a point to take them in the early morning before the city woke. That was the best time to marvel the untouched and preserved nature, at least in his opinion.

How long had Kai been wanting to fuck him? Had he wanted to fuck her or was it just the heat of the moment? Why did he initially kiss her? Was it just that he needed to get control and to get control fast? The shit was just weird!!! He could never recall a time that he had wanted to be with her in the past. Yes he had noted her attractiveness on several occasions. Hell, she and Z could be twins they looked so much alike. Their faces were damn near identical. He had never been attracted to Z in that way, regardless of what others thought and not taking away from her actual attractiveness. That was his ONLY sister, blood or not!!!! So where did this overwhelming desire for Kai stem from?

What had he done? Unfortunately, he had opened the floodgates to some pure and raw passion in which he had not been ready for. That he knew. But in what form and to what level, he did not have a clue.

How would Z feel knowing that he had smashed her cousin? Tremaine would probably flip with him having wanted Kai for years now.

Pharaoh slowed his pace for a cool down after 40 minutes. Sweat had trickled from his head and soaked into his tank top. Coming to a full stop after the cool down, he pulled the buds from his ear and stopped the music from cranking on the app.

Back in his apartment, he took another shower and dressed for the day. Heading out, he hopped into T'Challa, who was awaiting a bath. He made a vow to himself that he would let the events of the night before dissipate. Aiding that accomplishment, he sent a text to Dana telling her that he would stop by later on so that she could oil his scalp. Dana's quick reply was expected and unexciting. He was doing her a favor.

It was what it was. He would expect Kai's call soon. Typical shit from typical females. Nothing ever changes. But in this case, somehow when the thought crossed his mind that she would call, it disturbed him that his heart skipped a beat.

Chapter Eleven: Zaire (That's My Main)

That's My Main- Mila J (Album: M.I.L.A)

Zaire pulled open the door to her room, allowing access, as Kai rushed in and plopped down on her bed. She had made it in from her workday just an hour before. Now sporting a one piece swimsuit and her straw visor, she was ready to head out for a day, or she should say evening of fun in the sun.

"C'mon slow poke. There's some cocktails with our names on it waiting at the bar." Kai had been patiently waiting on Z's return back to the hotel the entire day.

Shaking her head, Zaire smiled at the younger girl. She was so happy that Kai had joined her in Miami. Her presence had given her the little piece of home that she had been needing as of late. Her homesickness had been setting in within the last week. Granted, she enjoyed being able to hang with Nyris, whom had been a Godsend, spending every moment that he could with her, taking her to and from work and errand running. Some of those "errands" had included going on personal dates in the form of meals, tourism and walks through various parts of town. But she still had missed the comforts of being home on her own stomping ground.

Kai had arrived two nights before by way of the airport in Fort Lauderdale. Nyris had been so kind in offering his services, extending free transportation from the airport to their hotel in Miami. Zaire had enjoyed taking the ride with him into the neighboring city. Unfortunately, with it being late in the evening along with the fact, that in taking the fastest route of I-95, which brought them upon the airport just after crossing into the city limits, she wasn't able to take in the sights of what Ft Lauderdale had to offer. Because of this, Nyris had promised her a planned adventure in his hometown coming soon. But Zaire had opted to speak with him earlier in the day regarding a nice chill, type of attraction that she and her cousin could checkout. He recommended Beach Place.

"Did you bring your wallet? Because we actually have other plans." Zaire started. Kai raised an eyebrow." We're headed to Fort Lauderdale today. Nyris told me about a spot that he claims is much better than South Beach."

"Better than South Beach?" Kai was at full attention." I definitely wanna see what this place is about."

Zaire reached inside the closet pulling out a blood red wrap to tie around her waist. A pair of flop flops completed the look. Lastly grabbing her Louis Vuitton Canvas Clapton backpack, she was ready to head out of the door.

They sat patiently waiting in the lobby for Nyris. Catching her eye, Zaire waved at the Front Desk Clerk.

"Aunt Nae called me today to check in." Zaire spoke of Kai's mom. "She didn't sound too well. Is she doing okay?

Kai frowned. "Honestly I have been concerned about her for a while. She seems to really be struggling since having the surgery back in February. But you know Mom, she isn't going to say anything she believes will cause anyone to worry for her."

Zaire agreed. She knew her Auntie well. She would run herself looney worrying about the well being of those around her, but hated the idea of anyone extending that same form of concern for her. Boy was that familiar. The woes of being born during the astrological period of Cancer.

And for her Aunt, Zaire was already worried. The usually chipper voice of her Mom's younger sister had sounded really weak and forced earlier that morning when Zaire had received her call. She had heard about Zaire working on the project in Miami and wanted to check in regarding how things were moving along.

"My plan is to swing down to check on her next month. Spend some time with the fam. The last time that I had spoken with Javari, he had spent the day with her and made mention that Mom was up walking around and getting along just fine the entire time he had been there. She had even cooked a Gumbo while he was there." Kai spoke of her older brother's recent visit. He had traveled to their hometown from Baton Rouge to spend the day.

Although still concerned, the mention of one of her favorite Creole dishes sent her stomach to rumbling. "Gumbo huh? I bet that was absolutely delicious."

Kai smiled knowing that her mom made an incredible version of the roux based Seafood stew. Her mom's cooking had always been up top. Now, Kai wasn't one to frown at, knowing that she had major skills when it came to the task of throwin' down in the kitchen, but her mom was on an entirely different level, as were her Dad during the time that he was alive.

"I haven't been to Louisiana in so long." Zaire reminisced on her many childhood summers spent down in the Bayou when her Grandparents were still alive. She remembered that she could barely wait for school to let out knowing that it would only be days, after the last day, that she would find herself being shipped down to the country to stay with her favs. It was such a refreshing getaway from living in the forever moving environment of the city. And her Grandparents had a large 15 acre plot equip with fields of homegrown veggies, sugarcane and livestock. She remembered befriending all of the animals and later crying bloody murder when they had ended up on the dinner table. Zaire chuckled at the thought. Of course Kai was a regular on their grandparents farm as well. As soon as Zaire would arrive, she would have her bags packed, ready to spend her summer days playing and running around with her bestie-cousin.

Nyris pulled up in his blazer. The ladies climbed inside.

"You two are going to love BeachPlace. It's the same set up as South Beach with Sidewalk cafes, bars and shops. But, on the opposite side of the street is a direct view of the Atlantic Ocean. You can literally walk across the street and stick your feet right in the sand." Nyris was excited to take the girls to his hometown. He had already taken them to spend time in South Beach just the day before.

"Sounds like my kinda spot. The absolute best of both worlds." Kai reached inside her clutch to apply her favorite MAC gloss to her lips.

Zaire turned her attention to Nyris, leaning back into the passenger seat. She mouthed "Thank You," in appreciation of his sweet and caring nature. He smiled and winked with his simple response.

Arriving in Fort Lauderdale didn't take as long as Zaire had imagined that it would, especially during the rush hour of the day. Pulling off from the expressway and cruising along into the neighboring town, Fort Lauderdale was a twin of it's Big Sister Miami. Both cities on the sea were loaded with tourists and beach themed attractions along the road that shared the exact same name, only in Fort Lauderdale, it was called Ocean Blvd.

Beach Place was all that Nyris had promised. One side of the Boulevard hosted an entire strip with sidewalk cafes, lounges, various souvenirs and confectionery shops, while the other side hosted the scenically magnificent ocean. Pulling over to the curb so that the girls could hop out, Zaire thanked Nyris once again, confirming that he would visit with the family while in the city and return to pick them up when they were ready to leave.

Walking the strip and mutually deciding on Mexican cuisine, Zaire and Kai had decided to stop for dinner at The Drunken Taco.

"Welcome. I'm Pierre and I will be your server today. Just let me know what you need and I am here to take care of you ladies." The cute waiter was all flirtation and wide smiles. "Can I start you off with some of the 2 for 1 drink specials? We have 2 Fishbowl Goblet sized Mojitos and Margaritas for the price of 1."

"Uhhhhhh YES!!!" Kai looked at Z who nodded in agreement. "We definitely need parts!!! I will take an original Mojito."

Zaire laughed, shaking her head. "I will have a Pineapple Margarita. Thanks."

The waiter winked at both girls. "Great choices. Coming right up."

"Honey listen, I am trying to enjoy EVERY bit of my vacation." Kai said matter of factly. "In just a few days it will be back to the midwest, and back to the real world." She frowned just thinking about making the return home after visiting the tropical paradise.

"Well, that doesn't happen for a few days yet. So don't plan your return before you have even had an opportunity to enjoy yourself." Zaire warned. Not only were her words spoken in an attempt to lift Kai's suddenly sour mood, but also to give her own a much needed boost. She would definitely miss Kai once she headed back home. The very thought was saddening.

The vibration from Zaire's phone prompted her to pull it from her backpack due to the text message that had arrived. It was Pharaoh.

"Hey. Wus goin on witchu?"

She scowled.

"Okay, so that wasn't one that brought you good news." Kai wore a look of concern.

Zaire shook her head, mouthing his name. "Pharaoh." Her look was dreadful in response to the message that came in from the dreadhead.

"Oh." Kai reached for her own phone from her clutch.

Zaire was still not speaking with Pha. She was highly upset behind his snappy outburst from the last time they had talked. It was completely uncalled for. She loved him truly, but she was sick of him going to extreme levels when it came to matters of her life. Of course he felt that he was protecting her and so called keeping her safe, but as she could remember, she celebrated her 18th birthday 16 years earlier and that meant that she was free to move exactly as she wanted and how she wanted. She was not his damn child.

Kai made as if she was engrossed in her phone. The mentioning of his name had taken her to another place in time.

Pharaoh.

Her mind did the same as it had done since the sensual act had occurred. It begin racing out of control. She didn't quite understand what exactly had taken place between the two of them. But, what she was sure about was the fact that the act kept repeating over and over in her mind like a deja vu occurrence. It just would not allow her any peace of mind. She was so disappointed in herself. Of all people, why would she have given her precious gift to him?!?! She had never seen that coming in a million years, and she had no clear answer to the pressing question. She hadn't liked anything about him!!!

Okay, honestly, the boy was incredibly fine, but she had shaken those affects long ago!!!

She kept going back, replaying the scene. She was just so angry. He had taken her to such a bad place just before. But why was he able to? Why had she given him that much power? Why had she ALWAYS given him that much power?

Her body was lifted and pressed against the wall. Why had she been so turned on? She had felt his hardness before he had kissed her. Why had he been so turned on? Just thinking of what he had done to her with his mouth ...with his tool......everytime caused butterflies to hatch within her belly.

She had several opportunities to stop it from occurring. But she didn't. She had wanted him. So bad.

Why oh why had she gone there with HIM of all people? How would she ever be able to make sense of what had happened? The playboy of the century. She had given her virginity to the playboy of the century!!!! How could she have slipped up in that way?!?!?!?

The arrogance. The ego. The attitude. The fucked up views and nature of this foul individual.

Why did she do it?

She had many sleepless nights since that episode had aired. Visions of chocolate, his face leaned into her with his eyes closed, enjoying her. His cologne. She could still smell his cologne. Him touching her. Holding her. Fucking her. Him telling her how good her pussy felt. Him whispering in her ear. Orion. Him fucking her on the ledge. How she had called out his name to all who were public. Him kissing her until she fell asleep in his arms, across his hard, warm chest. Her feeling so comfortable there, as if she belonged.....her waking up, realizing that she was in his home. In his bed. Seeing him quietly leaving the room. Hearing the shower turn on just minutes later. Her lying in disbelief, having to live in her truth. Her panicking and quickly getting dressed before he could return. Her hopping in her car and speeding off, needing to get as far away and as fast and possible…

Being in Miami had helped her tremendously in controlling her chaotic thoughts. Until hearing his name.

Pharaoh.

The waiter returned to the table with their drinks. Zaire responded to Pharaoh's text message after placing her order.

"Hey." Simple enough.

Noticing Kai had fallen pretty quiet being engrossed in her phone, Zaire raised her glass in toast to their girls night. "To you Cuz, the real MVP who came down here, with perfect timing, saving me from losing my mind."

Kai smiled, happy for the distraction from her thoughts. She tapped Z's glass and blew her cousin a kiss across the table.

Zaire sipped. The Pineapple Margarita was delicious.

"How are things going at your job hon?" She asked.

Kai rolled her eyes heavenward. "Same ole' bullshit as always. Chiefs in charge that should no doubt be the Indians." She was currently working as a Kindergarten teacher at a Montessori school on Milwaukee's east side. Although she loved her students, she couldn't stand the constant disorder of her work environment. Those in leadership roles should not have been. She found herself questioning how they were ever offered their positions.

"Have you put in your application for the Montessori school that Tre told you about?" Z asked. Tre had given her information about a few open positions with one of the clients that he had recently contracted with, providing work updating an old bathroom.

"I have not but I will as soon as I return home from this trip." Kail responded, knowing that she needed to jump on completing the app as soon as she could.

The waiter brought their meals out. The tacos were authentic and very flavorful.

After paying the bill, they grabbed their remaining portions of their drinks which were poured into the foam cups provided by the restaurant. They crossed the busy boulevard and headed for some relaxation at the beach. Spreading a towel out in the sand to mark their selected area, they didn't hesitate in sticking their bodies into the cool ocean water. The waves felt incredible rushing in to shore against their skin.

After cooling off in the Atlantic, they were longing on their towels, in the sand, watching the sunset over the water.

"So Nyris seems pretty chill." Kai sipped on her straw waiting for Z's response.

"Yes. He is." Zaire agreed. "He's one of the sweetest guys I have ever met. Almost too sweet. Nothing like the guys back home who seem to have chips on their shoulders most of the time. No. With him, he's just genuinely a good guy. So sweet. So considerate."

"That's beautiful. It really it." Kai had a wishful look on her face. "And he seems so into you."

Zaire grinned at the observation.

"Have fun while you are here. Live life. Partake in some of Miami's goodies. I am not mad atcha."

Zaire laughed. "Not sure about the partaking portion of your statement but I'm having plenty of FUN with Nyris."

"Kisses yet?"

"Uhhhhhh no. Not yet." Zaire admitted. They had not crossed into that lane of traffic and she was cool where they were. Enjoying one another's company and taking it slow.

"Wow. Not even a peck on the lips?"

"No not even that." Zaire shook her head.

Kai looked at her cousin and could see that she was comfortable where she was. That, in itself, was enough for her.

"Okay" Kai threw her hands up. "Slow it is. Whatever you feel is right for you. Always remember that."

Kai nodded toward the flashing of her Zaire's phone, giving her notice to check it. Zaire saw that four messages had come through from Pharaoh since her last response.

"How's it going?"
"Are you enjoying yourself?'
"Hello?"
"It's like that?"

Feeling a bit irritated, Zaire responded. "I'm good." She was not having it with Pha.

Knowing that she needed to get back to the hotel to prepare for work the next day, she punched in Nyris's phone number. He answered on the second ring.

"Ready beautiful?"

"Yes. I gotta get back unfortunately." She sighed, wishing that she could spend more time lounging and enjoying her cousin's company.

"No problem. I will pick you two up in about fifteen minutes. Where will you be?"

"Directly across from The Drunken Taco restaurant."

"Okay cool. On my way."

Nyris arrived as promised.

Back at the hotel. Kai thanked Nyris for the ride and his kindness. She headed in towards the Tiki Bar in the back of the hotel.

Zaire spent a bit more time sitting in the truck with Nyris.

"So what did you think of Beach Place?"

"I loved it. I wish that we had more time. But, with it being a work night….." her voice trailed off.

Nyris nodded. "I know. There will be other times. Maybe I will personally take you back to have the experience my way."

"Hmmm sounds great. A definite plan." Zaire looked forward to the possibility. "How was your time with the family."

Nyris's face lit up at the mention of them. "It was good. They all are some really special people. Really SPECIAL." He laughed. "I was able to go to my old neighborhood and spend some time with a few friends of mine." He turned his full body towards her. "Speaking of which, if you are not going to be busy this Saturday night, I would love for you to accompany me to my boy's Anniversary party. Him and his wife are celebrating with a backyard barbecue kinda set up."

Zaire agreed contingent upon what her cousin had planned for her last full day of her visit.

Saying goodnight to Nyris, Zaire exited the vehicle and made her way inside. Kai waved to her and blew a kiss goodnight from her perch at the Tiki Bar as she pushed the button on the elevator that would take her up to her room.

Once inside, she wasted no time going through her motions and preparing for bed. She allowed the voices of the nightly newscasters to take her into her slumber.

Chapter Twelve: Pharaoh (I Can't)

I Can't- Lyfe Jennings (Album: 268-192)

Pharaoh stuck his key card in the electronic scanner to gain access to his room. Opening the door, the cool air blasting from the vents was a welcomed sensation against his overheated skin. Scanning the suite, he silently approved of the spacious, luxury accommodations. The huge King sized bed, the extra fluffy towels on the shelves in the bathroom, the jacuzzi tub, the flat screen TV mounted against the wall, the fully equipped service bar, the bright coloration throughout the room, and the beautiful, modernly artistic construction. Zaire hadn't lied, The Beachfront Chateau was a gorgeous hotel. Impressive.

Setting his luggage on the racks hooked to the wall by the closet, Pharaoh reached inside to grab a fresh fit to change into for the day. His homie, Everson had picked him up from the airport and dropped him off to check into the hotel. They had made plans to get together in South Beach later in the day. For now, Pharaoh had just one mandatory destination on his mind, and that was to get to Little Havana expeditiously!!!

Zaire had no clue that he was in Miami. He still hadn't spoken with her since she had her meltdown about Uber boy. Just a brief text conversation the night before that consisted of few words and a few responses on her part. He wasn't phased at all. He knew what the next day would bring and that his arrival would be all that she needed to completely forget about the little tantrum that she was currently fueling.

Just a smile and a compliment had gotten him what he needed from the cute little Cuban clerk at the front desk which was a bit disturbing. What he needed, was Zaire's room number. The ease of obtaining it was cause for concern.

After a fresh shower, Pharaoh had gotten dressed and was ready for that Miami ACTION!!! The plan was to grab Zaire, have her to accompany him to Little Havana all while using the time to catch up. It was now Friday evening, and the weather was absolutely perfect for a stroll down SW 8th Street.

Miami, Florida had always promised him a fantastic time and had delivered. He was not new to the scene by any means. A couple of his good childhood friends from New York, Everson and his brother DJ, had moved to the city after graduating high school. He had made several trips to the town since their relocation, each time attending what they had affectionately titled, planned "boys trips". Every time he had a blast. Beautiful people. Beautiful city. Beautiful memories.

Pharaoh put his plan of surprise in action by texting Z.

"Hey Baby Girl. I miss you. Are you still mad?"

It took a few minutes for Z to respond. "Hey. I'm cool." There were those limited word responses again.

"You sure? You are killing me with these short replies."

She responded a bit quicker with the second message. "I'm cool Pharaoh."

Slipping his wallet in his pocket and lastly grabbing his phone, Pharaoh made his way out the door and down a level to Zaire's room. Walking in the long hall, he sent another reply with the intention of getting her worked up.

"Well, get over it. I said what the fuck I said." He waited on her response, closing in on her door.

It appeared in all caps. "IF I WAS IN FRONT OF YOU, I WOULD SLAP THE ENTIRE SHIT OUTTA YOU!!! THAT'S WHAT I WOULD DO!!! GOODBYE!!!"

Pharaoh smirked, seeing that his plan had indeed worked. Moving in front of her door, he knocked. Waiting several moments, the door finally cracked open.

"WELL DO THE SHIT THEN!!!" He yelled, smiling in seeing her face.

"You ASSHOLE!!!! You play TOO DAMN much!!!! What are you doing here!?!?!?" She jumped into his arms, shrieking. It seemed as if he hadn't seen her in ages. His happiness matched her own beat for beat. In seeing her, he had to admit just how much her had missed his "better half."

Picking her up from the floor and into a huge hug, his gaze traveled past her shoulder, catching a sight that he wasn't prepared for. Their eyes locked.

Kai wore the expression of a deer in headlights. That was the first time that they had seen one another since "that night." Her mouth opened, then quickly closed, chewing her lip instead. She soon after, looked away and down at her nails.

What was she doing here? How long had she been in Miami? Many questions swirled around in his brain. Why hadn't she called? And again, what the hell was she doing HERE?

Pharaoh squinted, taking her in completely. The Miami sun had done wonders to her skin, toasting her complexion to a perfect, melted caramel hue. Her hair looked wet as if she had just come from the pool. A wrap covered her body and was held together with a tie around her neck.

She made a few uncomfortable movements, shifting her weight on the edge of the bed in which she sat. Her eyes stayed glued to her nails.

Setting Z down onto the floor, Pharaoh turned his attention back to his bestie.

"When did you get here? Why didn't you tell me that you were coming?" Zaire fired her questions off, going into full interrogation mode.

"I got in just a little bit ago. Are you surprised to see me?" Pharaoh smiled at his gleaming friend.

"Am I surprised? Negro, you almost gave me a heart attack!!!"

Pharaoh laughed. " Well I am going to need you to pull it together Z and quick because we got some places to get to."

"Slow down Pha!!! Let me recover first before you snatch me from the premises." She matched his laughter. "Come in. You still have some 'splainin to do partna."

Pharaoh walked through the door and over to a selected seat, plopping down into the comfort of the cushioned chair at the Executive desk. Again, Kai shifted but did not lift her gaze from what seemed to be her really fascinating nails.

"So you mean to tell me that your butt booked a flight here and didn't tell me? How long have you had tickets? How long are you staying?" Z kept on with her interrogation.

"Just here for the weekend." Pharaoh answered. "Booked a week or so ago. And no I wanted to surprise you, so of course I did not tell you. Had to get here to check on you and get you right." Zaire smacked her lips and frowned. Pharaoh continued. "You been out of fuckin' control Sis."

"Boy, don't start with it." Z warned, pointing a finger in his direction.

Pharaoh waved her off. "Go get dressed, I got a ride reserved that will be coming in a bit to take us over to Little Havana."

"I was just getting ready to hop in the shower so you will have to give me a sec." Z responded.

"Well hurry up. It'll be here in 20 minutes." Pharaoh looked at his watch to confirm.

"Okay okay!!!" Z made her way to the bathroom, cut on the water and closed the door.

Pharaoh turned to study Kai. She now had her phone in her hand, completely ignoring him. She looked amazing by the way. Delectable. Now seeing her in person after the many times that she had crossed his mind since their last encounter was almost surreal. The girl had set up permanent shelter in his mind's eye no matter how many times he had tried evicting her in the past couple weeks. He wasn't sure why she had affected him as she had. Even in the presence of his other fans, he couldn't shake the thoughts of her. Now, here she was. In the flesh.

She had not contacted him once after that night. It had frustrated him to no end. He didn't quite understand why she had stayed away. He assumed that it was due to her feeling uncertain about what had occurred between the two of them but even if that was the reason, the no contact was definitely a first that he was in no way fond of.

She cleared her throat and crossed her right thigh over her left, causing the wrap to fall open revealing her smooth, thick thighs. The thought of where those beautiful thighs had once been caused him to become a bit pleasantly bothered. She was truly uncomfortable and Pharaoh could feel her vibe from a mile away.

"If you don't want my attention, then definitely refrain from doing that." Pharaoh warned, causing her to look up from her phone and into his eyes. Her gaze was questioning, uncertain and sad. He saw sadness in her eyes. He held her gaze for what seemed to be a few long, breathless moments. Good God her eyes were fucking beautiful. Her artificially long but not too long lashes framed the slanted shape and added additional beauty to her light golden colored orbs. The long deep glare stopped his own heart for several beats. It was as if they were feeding from one another yet, trying to read one another. What was that look in her eyes? Where did the sadness stem from? What was she thinking? When had she arrived? None of his questions would receive answers at that time.

Kai raised herself from the bed and walked over to the door. No words. No response. No offering of an excuse whatsoever. Within a split second, she was gone. She had pulled yet another disappearing act but this time she was bold enough to perform it as he watched. The wrinkled sheets where her body sat was the only thing that gave indication that she was once there. Pharaoh sat silently and genuinely confused.

Pharaoh eyed "Mr Uber" as Zaire gave the introductions. He had not been aware that the Nyris guy was the hotel's 'designated driver'. Pharaoh nodded his greeting, sizing him up. So this was the nigga that had Z losing her fucking mind. Some mixed breed, Tiger Woods looking muthafucka. Really? And the nigga had the nerves to say, "So this is the infamous Pharaoh." Fuck was that supposed to mean? What the fuck had Z been saying to this nigga? Nah, he wasn't feeling him.

Z's whole face lit when dude pulled up. All giggly, trippin over herself and shit. The fuck? Sis was on one with this nigga. Here she was carrying on like he wasn't even there. He shook his head. He would keep his thoughts to himself, for now.

There was a jam on I-95. Traffic had come to a complete stop. Pharaoh suspected a pretty bad accident up ahead. All lanes of traffic including the Express Lanes were all at a stand still. Miami-Dade County Police was trying to cut through the unmoving cars to get up ahead to the culprit of the jam.

"It must be a really bad accident." Z put voice and concern to his and her thoughts.

"Yeah, I agree," Nyris looked through the rearview as 2 more flashing cop cars were attempting to push through. Moving to the far right lane, Nyris decided to take the next exit to detour around the traffic. After fifteen minutes or so, he was able to exit the out of service expressway. His goal was to take a cut through the inner city and far enough around to jump around the jam.

"I still wish that Kai would have come along." Z frowned. "You two have got to do better with getting along Pha. For her to have just left the room without at least saying goodbye was rude." Pharaoh couldn't have agreed more. Z had called Kai to ask her to join them in going to Little Havana but Kai had turned down the opportunity stating that she was in need of a nap. Z had pressed her further but Kai was not budging. Pharaoh noted that Zaire seemed oblivious to knowing about anything that had occurred between the two. Kai hadn't said anything and neither would he.

"Hey, I'm not the one back at the hotel napping. So you can't put that shit on me." Pharaoh said matter of factly. "If she wants to take a nap, then let her take a nap."

"Yeah but I honestly believe that she would have come if it weren't for you being the one who asked. And, she seemed a bit unhappy anyways when you knocked at the door. I love you both but feel caught in the middle all the time. I just need y'all to at least try to work on getting along." Z sighed and exchanged a look with Nyris who had empathy written on his face.

Pharaoh decided it to be best to ignore Z. Staring out the window his thoughts lingered on Kai. He wasn't sure how to read her or determine what was going on with her and he hated how much he was bothered by it. They had such a great night together and now she was acting as if she was upset with him that it actually happened. The manner in which she had exited Zaire's room, the look in her eyes. What the fuck was going on with her? He wanted to text her, to check on her. But in wanting to do so, he was worried about where the sensitive shit was stemming from. Fuck her. And that was that!!! He was in the muthafuckin MIA and he would be damned if he would be spending his time trying to figure out what some chic that he had smashed was feeling. Enough with that!!!

"What do you guys have planned for tomorrow?" Nyris asked taking Pharaoh from his thoughts.

"Not sure. I wasn't expecting Pha to even be here.' Z turned, rolling her eyes at her friend.

"Well may I suggest taking a cruise over to The Baha? There's a small ship that leaves out around 6am from the Port. It's about a 4 hour ride taking passengers to Nassau, Bahamas and back for reasonable prices. You'd have the entire day to spend enjoying the island and later in the evening, you just reboard the ship for the return trip. It's a great way to be able to explore Grand Bahama Island." Nyris explained.

Zaire looked back at Pharaoh who responded with a raised eyebrow. "Where would we go to purchase tickets?" Pharaoh asked.

"Easiest way is through the Viator app but they can also be purchased in various places throughout the city. Pretty much any place where city tours are sold."

"What you think Z?" Pharaoh typed the information into the Viator app that was already uploaded onto his phone.

Zaire looked back with a smile. "Sounds like fun. I'm definitely game."

Pharaoh located the info for the cruise, selected a quantity of 3 fares and used his credit card to purchase the tickets. Okay. Uber dude was good for something. He thanked Nyris for the plug. He copied Z's email as a second place to send the reservation details.

Nyris was finally pulling back onto the expressway when Z's inbox notification chimed.

Pharaoh leaned back, allowing his eyes to close for a few minutes. It seemed as soon as his closed his eyes, he felt a tap on his knee. Opening one eye, he looked into Z's beaming face. She mouth the words "Thank You." Pharaoh frowned and responded, mouthing the words, "For what?"

Z reached down into her lap and raised her cell phone showing the confirmation for the purchase on her display. Pharaoh gave her a wink and a thumbs up and closed his eyes again hoping to get a few minutes of sleep before the arrival in Little Havana.

After another 15 minutes on the expressway, they were pulling up at their destination. Nyris shook Pharaoh 's hand as he exited the vehicle while Z stayed behind for additional convo. Pharaoh walked over to a small souvenir shop to purchase a few shot glasses for his collection. Z walked in, all sashay and smiles.

Pharaoh smirked and rolled his eyes. "You look freshly caked."

Z returned his smirk. "Get up out of mines." She replied eyeing a beautifully crafted wind chime.

He studied his friend. She seemed to be glowing, which was not a look that he had seen from her since Jordan had passed. Seeing her in that way, played at his heart. There was still hope for someone so deserving of a happy ending. He grabbed her in his arms and hugged her.

"I'm sorry for upsetting you Babygirl. I just worry about you a lot. I want you to know you're worth, so that you never end up with some bum ass nigga who's undeserving of you. You are my Sis and I love you."

Zaire leaned into him soaking up the love for a few seconds before responding. It wasn't often that he apologized so she wanted to absorb as much of the vibe as she possibly could. "First off, WOW at the apology. That's so big of you Bro. Thanks. Secondly, you are forgiven. You know that I can't stay mad at you for too long. Third," she released herself from the hug, took his hands in hers and looked him square in the eyes. She needed for the point that she was getting ready to deliver to be received and received by an extremely attentive ear. "I really appreciate you Pha, there isn't ANYONE quite like you!!!! You are a KING Sir!!!! You are amazing!!!! You are stupid handsome, ridiculously intelligent, deeply spiritual, incredibly successful, your heart is so huge, you go HARD for those that you love, you are raw, real, true, genuine.....I can go on and on!!!! I promise that I can't wait until the day that you meet the one that will knock you off your feet. And when that happens, I will be there ten thousand percent in support of you. I need that same from you." She paused just a minute, making sure that her point had gotten through to him before continuing. "Besides, I will celebrate something serious when my Sis In Law finally steps in and shut all your bogus shit down."

Pharaoh pulled away, reflecting his playful hurt as if an electric shock had accompanied her last words. "Nothing bogus ever is to be associated with me." He placed his shot glasses on the counter to check out with the cashier. "And oh, bout your little speech, that's wussup." He winked.

Pharaoh handed the cashier a fifty dollar bill and waited for his change. What Z had said had touched him beyond belief. Wow. It was amazing that she actually viewed him in that way. Coming from her, he knew that she would never lie to him and completely entrusted in her spoken truth. Her words meant more to him than she could ever possibly know. His appreciation of her was on Cloud Nine.

"Now, you can be a cocky, arrogant, egotistical asshole from time to time but, I have learned how to regulate my blood pressure over the years to keep from smacking the black off of you. And that is a lot of damn BLACK Homie." The moment was ruined just that fast. Zaire laughed at the sour expression on Pharaoh's face.

"Damn Really Z? Can I have at least three seconds to bask in the glory of the compliment you extended before you rudely erase it from the record?"

"Why of course Babes. Have your three minutes while I check out the T-Shirts in the corner." Z teased making her way over to her mentioned destination.

Pharaoh took his phone from his pocket to look at the notification that had come through. Fucking Lacey. That was it. He would not deal with it any longer. He pulled up her contact and selected the option to block her correspondence. The constant text messages and phone calls hadn't ended but had instead, gotten worse. The chic acted as if she was obsessed. Damn, yes he had given her the same bomb ass dick that he used to bless all the ladies he dealt with, but she was acting like he now somehow belonged to her. Type shit is that? She had him fucked up.

After Z had purchased a few T-Shirts, they stepped out of the souvenir shop and into the blazing heat. The long street was loaded on that Friday evening with both tourists and natives alike. This area of town was primarily made up of those of Cuban ethnicity hence the name Little Havana. The area was in Pharaoh's opinion, the most culturally rich area of the entire city. It was as if being on the island of Cuba but within the territory of the US. Many restaurants, shops and cigar factories lined the avenue. SW 8th Street was lively and in full swing. On the corner across from his destination, tourists were lined up watching the Elders as they focused on a concentrated game of dominoes being played in the famous Maximo Gomez Domino Park. A tour bus occupied the corner next to the park. Crossing the busy street, he headed for the Little Havana Cigar Factory, made famous by its appearance in the movie Scarface.

Entering the front door, the strong aroma of Cuban espresso & sweet, fresh tobacco greeted them head on.

"Hey Sis, " Pharaoh pointed towards the front counter that hosted several pre filled sampler cups, "best coffee you will ever have. Hands down!!!"

The girl at the counter smiled. "Yes please. Have a sample. Fresh made just minutes ago."

Z headed for a cup of espresso while Pharaoh walked to the back towards the Cigars. He grabbed 10 boxes of the 100 quantity Cohibas. Stocked!!!!

Passing a display of cigar cutters, he picked out a few for himself and a few to give to the guys back home as souvenirs.

Zaire was sipping on her second cup of Espresso when Pharaoh returned to her side.

"You May want to make that your last." Pharaoh warned with a straight face. "One sample cup is equivalent to damn near half a 5 hour energy shot. Heads up."

"Oh damn. Now you tell me." Z frowned. "This flavor is so pure and delicious."

"Yeah, it's on point. First time I had it, they got me for 5 bags."

"I definitely want a bag to go."

"Give her three. And add it onto my total."

Z knew better than to object. When Pharaoh went on a spending spree, she knew to just roll with it. Her objections had never worked in the past and she was more than sure that it would not work in that moment.

Pharaoh and Z walked the strip, stopping next inside of D'Cary's jewelry design shop. The beautiful handmade jewelry surrounding gorgeous, fresh, natural slate cut gem pieces were to die for. Many necklaces, bracelets, rings and other items occupied the displays throughout the entire store. Pharaoh picked out an Onyx and Tiger's Eye skull bracelet and a Deep colored Ruby set that consisted of a necklace and bracelet for Z. It was her birthstone. She had found a matching set constructed with Amethyst birthstones for Kai. Pharaoh pulled out his card and purchased all of the items. Z's excitement was through the roof.

"Wow. Must be something amazing in the Miami air to get you to agree to buy items for Kai." Z teased. "Maybe we should pack up and move here for good. The extra Vitamin D intake is causing you to grow a heart."

Pharaoh shot her an evil glare. "I can always take it back inside. Or how bout just yours?"

Z threw her hands up. "Nope. I'm good Sir. I don't want no problems."

They made their way back in the direction that they came, waiting patiently on the bench in front of the Domino Park for Nyris's Return.

"So, tell me about this guy who got you so amped." Pharaoh asked. "What's his story?"

Z's smile was bright. "He is just genuinely a good guy. Very easy going, thoughtful ...we have just started really hanging out so trust me I know to be careful. I just need you to trust that I got this as well."

"I do trust you Z. I just don't want you going outside of yourself for this cat. Remember to always be smart." Pharaoh touched a finger to his head for emphasis. "That's the rule."

"You and your damn rules." Z frowned. "Just remember that I am only one year younger than you so I am not new to this. I'm good Pha. Thanks but I'm cool."

"Okay well, just remember to have fun for now but don't go in too hard. You will be returning home in just a couple months."

"I know."

Pharaoh watched as the expression of realization crossed Z's face. She fell silent. He thought it to be best to leave her in her current situational assessment. Exactly where she needed to be in that moment.

He took in the scene, watching the dancers in front of one of the lounges down the street. A salsa band played flamenco music from the inside. The beat was catchy with a Latin spin combined with a jazzy West African Soukous rhythm.

Everyone seemed happy and free of worry. He enjoyed stopping in the richly cultured area of town. The shopping. The dancing. The music. The food. The mindset. Everything about the area reminded him that in other areas of the world, they truly lived by the motto of "Don't worry. Be happy." And the citizens knew this well. Their home country was in turmoil. Many of their families were still stuck in the midst of it all. It truly could be a lot worse.

Nyris pulled up to the curb allowing the two to hop in. Taking the now clear expressway back without any hiccups, they arrived at the hotel in record time.

Walking into the lobby, Z stopped at the front desk to check in regarding some issue with her room. Pharaoh waited for her, by the elevator, to conclude her discussion with the clerk. Scanning the lobby, visitors were moving around, in and out of the restaurants and throughout the entire resort. It was crowded and busy, which was expected for a Friday evening. A set of visitors which had stood blocking the back door decided to move aside, heading out toward the water. This allowed a full view of the Tiki bar near the door. That's when he spotted her.

Kai was sitting at the bar, all wide smiles, sipping on a cocktail of some sort. Her attention was being held and entertained by the guy sitting next to her. He was leaning in and whispering something in her ear. She then giggled like a teenager with some type of kiddy ass crush.

Pharaoh wasn't sure why, but an ill feeling hit him in the pit of his stomach. Here it was that she hadn't spoken to him or even acknowledged him at all. She had literally ran away from him like he had the fucking plague but yet here was some random sitting at the bar receiving giggly-googly eyes and shit. Dafuq!?!?

Z walked up in that moment, derailing his twisted train of thought.

"Okay so, I am going to head up to the room and relax a bit before this night that you have planned." She rubbed her temples. "Y'all please just go easy on me tonight."

"I'll call Everson in an hour or so and check in on him. He mentioned some spot in South Beach. I figure we stop at one of the Sidewalk Cafes for dinner and meet him a little afterwards."

"Sounds good." She confirmed as the elevator arrived. "I'll call Kai and let her in on the plan."

Before stepping onto the elevator and at the mention of Kai's name, Pharaoh took a second glance through the back door. She was still laughing and having her Grand Old time. Shaking his head, he stepped into the elevator car. Why was he buggin out so much with this chic? So what she was acting as her usual loose self. Nothing new. Typical really. So why was he bothered? This shit was getting really nerve racking and truly irritating. What was going on with him? He had to get some type of control over these unexpected emotions immediately.

Three hours later, Pharaoh spritzed on his signature YSL cologne and gave himself a once over through the full length mirror hanging on the back of the bathroom door. Approving of his look, he was ready for the Miami night. Picking up the courtesy phone, he dialed Z's room number. After 5 rings, it went to her voice mail. Pharaoh assumed that she was most likely in the shower and instead made the decision to head down to the Tiki bar for a before dinner top off.

Making his way down the hallway, he opted to take the stairs to the first floor. Pushing open the back door to the property, the humid tropical air hit him hard. Thankful that he had decided to keep his look casual with his khaki shorts, short sleeve polo shirt, a fisherman hat and of course a fresh pair of Tims, he took a seat at the bar and ordered a double shot of 1738 straight up. The cute little bartender was very attentive as she poured a little extra in his glass.

Taking a sip, he stared out at the beauty of the moon reflecting onto the Atlantic. The leaves of the palm trees danced in rhythm with the light breeze. It was the perfect night for some South Beach action.

The buzzing of his phone notified him of Z's text advising him that she was waiting on Kai and would be down shortly. Surprised that Z was able to convince Kai in joining them, Pharaoh took another swallow. He sat a twenty dollar bill on the counter to close out. Taking the last swallow, he waved the bartender off when she returned with change. "Your tip Sweetie." He lifted his frame from the bar stool and made his way into the lobby. Z and Kai were stepping off of the elevator just as he was getting ready to walk past.

"All set and ready to roll." Z announced linking her arm inside of his. She had decided on a silky, light, airy sun dress that fit her waist and flowed around her ankles. Wedge sandals completed her outfit. Her hair was pulled out of her face into an unruly bun with tendrils framing around. Her make-up was natural and flawless. She looked amazing. Classy and flyy.

Her cousin had opted for a completely different, more dramatic and absolutely stunning look. Her make-up was a bit more colorful with various shades of green and gold around her eyes, a beautiful ombre lip, a blown straight hairstyle with tons of texture flowing down her back, a short, mini dress that put every perfect curve on broadcast and lastly, tall stilettos enclosed her feet. Pharaoh forced himself to look away but within five seconds had to take a second glance. The girl had literally turned every head in the lobby in her direction. Holy shit she was BAD!!!! Her ass, all natural where many shelled out tons of cash to imitate, bounced with every step that she took, indicating that she may be pantyless underneath.

Taking a deep breath to control his thoughts and to redirect his focus, Pharaoh, plopped down on the sofa next to Z, waiting on their transportation to arrive. Kai opted to stand by the front door looking out.

With Nyris being done with his shift for the night, a Grand Cherokee pulled up in place of his Blazer. Pharaoh and the girls hopped inside and headed for South Beach.

Walking the strip on Ocean Drive, they had decided on a nice Italian restaurant. Everson and DJ were to meet them at Wet

Willie's after they completed dinner. Nyris had also agreed to meet Z.

They ordered drinks and appetizers. Kai snapped a few photos of her and Z and recorded a Snapchat steam.

"I love it here," Kai turned to Z, seeming more relaxed with a buzz after finishing a shot of Ciroc and a huge half glass of Pineapple Margarita. "Not to live but definitely to visit."

"Yes. I agree." Z responded. "Really nice vacation town."

"Reminds me of home. Warm year round." Kai reminisced over the beautiful weather that Louisiana offered all seasons. "Winters in Milwaukee are dreadful."

Pharaoh opted to people watch, unsure if it was safe to engage in conversation with Kai acting so anti-social earlier. He also did not want to tip Z off to anything being "out of the norm" between him and Kai, so he decided that silence would be best in that moment.

The waitress returned to take their dinner orders. Pharaoh ordered the full lobster after the waitress had set a plate containing the delicious looking dish in front of one of the customers at the table dining next to them. Both Z and Kai had ordered pasta dishes.

South Beach's nightlife was underway. Many party goers were walking past, up and down the famous strip, lined with a number of restaurants, shops and nightclubs. Admiring an all white Lamborghini as it sped down the popular street, Pharaoh enjoyed taking in the lights, camera, action style in his view. It reminded him of being back home and in Manhattan.

"Pha, you good?" Z asked with concern in her voice. "You seem unusually quiet tonight. What's up with you?"

"Yeah, I'm straight. Just a little jet lag, he responded which wasn't entirely a lie. He would sleep well once the night had been called.

"You need a bit more inspiration in your life." She decided, calling the waitress to their table for a second round of drinks.

Pharaoh eyed Z with a half smirk on his face. "Oh so this what we on tonight? Well in that case," he ordered shots for the table.

Kai's eyebrow raised but she still didn't speak a word to him. Z pouted.

"I said drinks, not shots!!!"

"Careful what you step into Lil Lady. Let this be your lesson. Now turn the fuck up."

Z not being a straight alcohol drinker went with Kai's suggestion of Ciroc. Pharaoh ordered his usual.

"Oh and make those doubles."

"Boy you are wil'lin!!!" I'm not drinking all of that!!!" Z proclaimed. But was shut down by Kai, leaving Pharaoh in a position where he did not have to speak.

"Cuz, you are good. I promise. The Watermelon flavor that you ordered is super chill." She assured her cousin. For a split second she looked at Pharaoh but immediately turned her attention to those who were passing by.

Pharaoh could sense the discomfort that she had in his presence, but there would be no tortuous internal questions to suffer through this time around.

The shots arrived rather quickly. Taking the glasses in their hands, Pharaoh swallowed his in one large gulp. The ladies opted to sip and savor.

"How's everything going with the job?" Pharaoh asked.

"The recruiting is going great. We hired ten new workers who completed the cycle, with no fall off, just this week. My Assistant has been a Godsend. She will be fantastic for whoever takes over my position when I return home. We have quite a few interviews scheduled for next week. Things are really falling into place nicely." Z confirmed what he already knew would be the case.

"Think you will miss Miami when you head back?"

"The beauty, the weather……...Nyris……..yes." Her voice trailed off which caused Pharaoh a bit of concern.

"You know you are to just have fun with this nigga right Z? You not getting serious are you?" He asked receiving looks of disdain from both of the girls. Kai rolled her eyes and excused herself from the table, heading to the bathroom taking everyone's attention with her.

"Pha, remember that I told you that I got this." Z squinted in warning.

"Come on now. You gotta be smart with this shit!!!! Have fun while….."

"Pha, STOP." Zaire said with finality, cutting his statement short before he could finish.

"Aiight. You got it." Pharaoh will allow her to learn her own lessons. He didn't like where this was headed at all. But out of respect, he made the choice to leave it alone and let it all play out. If she wasn't receptive, then he would have to let her be free to hit her head hard.

A few minutes later Kai returned from the bathroom.

Thirty minutes after, they were finishing their meals, and requesting the check. Pharaoh covered the tab with his credit card. Z was giggly and ready to party. Kai was definitely more social, but still not speaking to him.

Walking down the strip, Z held onto Pharaoh's arm while engaged in a louder than normal chatter while Kai kept her pace, walking ahead.

"I'm buzzing like crazy," Z spoke loud followed by a giggle. Pharaoh laughed while walking slow to help keep her balance steady.

"Hey, you asked for this. Remember that when you find yourself wanting to play the blame game tomorrow morning."

She giggled again. "I said buzzed not DRUNK Silly!!!"

"Just don't go in to hard. We got an early start to the day tomorrow." Pharaoh reminded her.

"Oh right. So, one last drink and then I quit."

Walking into Wet Willie's, Z stopped them on the steps leading up to the top level bar to take a group photo.
She tagged both Pharaoh and Kai on FaceBook. The notification hit his phone as they waited at the bar to order their drinks.

"Hey Z, careful with tagging me. That shit will hit my timeline. I don't want a few people to know where I am right now."

"You must be hiding out from the Fan Club?" Z joked.

"I might be." Pharaoh said matter of factly. Kai's eyes made the connection again displaying that same unreadable expression. She, again, turned away fast.

Pharaoh was sick of trying to figure Kai out.

He finally was able to order himself a drink named Call A Cab, Zaire a Shock Treatment and Kai a Sex on the Beach when the bartender approached them.

Sex on The Beach had an fantastic ring to it in a city where it could easily become a possibility. The thought caused his eyes to graze past Z and onto Kai's ass. Yep. A definite possibility.

Everson and DJ walked in with bro hugs and lots of love for their childhood friend. Introductions were given along with welcoming hugs for the ladies.

Nyris's appearance came just minutes behind.

"So what's been good witchu Pha?" DJ asked, looking to catch up.

"Trying to make it. Same story, different day."

"When was the last time that you went back home to visit? I heard Mr. Goyner passed away last month." DJ referred to their beloved Principal from the school that they had all attended. He had been a favorite, providing most with either a second father figure or the father figure that they unfortunately weren't able to have as a part of their upbringing. The sad part was that the latter was the story of the majority's. He had worn his heart openly on his sleeve. The many lives that he had touched was evident in the number of guests that had attended his funeral according to the photos posted via Social Media.

"It's been a few months but I did see the news on the Book." Pharaoh had seen that other classmates had posted about Mr. Goyner's death on Facebook.

"Yeah, that was sad news. Dude was like a father to us. Real chill cat."

Pharaoh nodded in agreement. " He will definitely be missed. Last time I was there, I had attended our Family Reunion. There just for the weekend."

"The hood has changed. A lot of new families have moved in. Overrun and drug ridden. I'm not pressed about returning back to visit there. I now mostly go just to shop." DJ said, which caused Pharaoh to nod in agreement.

"Pretty much everyone has moved out, onto other things and other places. But the shopping will always be ON!!!" Pharaoh turned to check on the ladies, Z was in safe care snuggled with Nyris who was rubbing her feet while engaged in conversation. Pharaoh realized that Everson had sparked up what looked to be flirtatious conversation with Kai. A reggae joint was being played by the DJ when Everson asked Kai to dance who accepted the invitation.

The gut wrench hit, causing an uncomfortable surge of energy in the pit of Pharaoh's stomach. What the fuck?!?!

"So, are your plans to stay in Milwaukee all of your life, or are you moving on to other avenues?" DJ asked, pulling Pharaoh's attention back to the current convo.

"As of now, I'm chillin. Business is good and I have settled in. Not sure what the future holds." He answered and took a long sip of his melting frozen cocktail.

"I may have to get up to visit with you soon My Guy. Me and the wife are looking for somewhere new to visit. How is the city?"

Pharaoh took a glance over in the direction where Kai and Everson were winding low and having a good time. He turned his attention back to DJ. "The city is cool. Small, but cool. Definitely a nice place to visit. Y'all should stop up. You know I got you fosho, God. You won't have to ever worry bout shit in my domain."

Turning back to the dance floor, the song had ended and both Kai and Everson were now at the bar waiting to be served. Trying to shake the unfamiliar feeling, Pharaoh was unsuccessful. Not liking the feeling one bit, he forced himself to turn completely away, checking notifications on his cell phone. It wasn't long before they two made their way back over, drinks in tow.

"Man, what's the story on Kai? She's a BADDIE!!!" Everson sat next to Pharaoh at the table with a determined expression on his face.

Pharaoh responded cooly. "Why don't you ask her? I'm sure that she can fill you in."

"Z's cousin right? Damn. She thick as shit!!! I WANT her."

In that moment, Kai looked over at Pharaoh with an expression that he knew well. One he had seen from many chics in the past who resorted to pulling schemish antics in hopes of making him jealous or getting a rise out of him when they were feeling some kinda way. The nonchalant look on her pretty face, was the "slip up" that gave her away. He shifted in his chair and leaned back. "Go for her. Tell her that I sent you."

A confused look crossed Everson's face at the weird response, but his one track mind was being controlled by his dick, an infiltration caused by Kai that Pharaoh knew all too well. He shot back over to her without a moment's hesitation.

Pharaoh made the promise to himself, to not give a fuck about her actions for the rest of the night.

Back at the hotel, Pharaoh helped a stumbling Z from Everson's vehicle. Kai who was sitting in the front passenger seat, spoke a thank you and goodnight to Everson, closed the door while he was still in the middle of speaking with her, and made her way through the lobby doors and inside the 24 hour restaurant. She was all attitude and sour mood.

Z held onto Pharaoh's arm as he spoke his own thank you, knowing that he would see him again on the ride back to the airport. He turned heading for the sliding glass door.

Inside of the lobby, Z plopped down in one of the chairs and removed her wedge sandals. She immediately went into massaging her aching feet.

"Oh MY GOD, remind me to never wear high heels while walking in South Beach ever again." she whined in her loud, drunken voice. "I don't see how Kai does it. She's a certified pro. For me, it's an entire negative."

"But did you enjoy yourself at least?" Pharaoh sat in the chair next to her.

Z smiled. "I did!!!!" Her loud giggling caused the clerk to look over in their direction disapprovingly. Pharaoh apologized to the clerk with his eyes.

"Okay cool. That's wussup." Pharaoh laughed at his inebriated friend.

"Your guys were really cool. I liked hanging out with them. They were real smooth."

"Yeah, E and DJ have always been smooth cats. That's why I fucks with them hard as I do. Everytime I drop down on them it's a good time."

Z smiled, continuing her foot rub.

The sound of Kai's heels clicking across the tiled floor with a vengeance, caused Pharaoh to look back. She carried a foam container in her hand as she made her way to the elevator. In passing the two sitting in the lobby, she turned catching Pharaoh's eye, she sent a look of utter anger in his direction. Fuck was that about?

Z interrupted his thoughts. "Well damn, that was rude. We were sitting here waiting on her and she justs marches her lil butt right on up to her room. Wow."

Pharaoh, still disturbed by her expression mumbled. "No thanks or acknowledgement in anyway. Yeah, she is rude."

From that moment on, everything seemed to have switched to slow motion. Z rubbed her foot two more times. In the middle of the second rubbing motion, she abruptly stopped, allowing her mind to fit situational puzzle pieces from the day's occurrences together. The tickets for the cruise. The jewelry from the shop. The weird looks that she had caught pass between the two of them. Not to mention all of the drinks, the full check for dinner, the fact that Kai had controlled herself and didn't spazz when Pharaoh had made the comments about how she should be handling Nyris at the dinner table and even more drinks at Wet Willies to end the night. Now, his response to Kai's rudeness was to show that he cared about not receiving an acknowledgement from her. Pharaoh cared about her ACKNOWLEDGING HIM!!!!! Since when?!?!?

She slowly, almost animatedly, raised her head to look Pharaoh square in the eye. She stared at her bestie whom she had known like the back of her hand for a number of years now, knowing that his eyes would give her the answer in which seeked. His expression told her everything.

"You LYING………..SNEAKY………..CONNIVING……..SON OF A BITCH!!!!!!!!!" Z pointed her finger at her startled friend. "YOU FUCKED KAI!!!!!!"

Every head in the lobby turned in their direction. Pharaoh looked around with his mouth hanging open.

"Wh...what are you talkin' bout? YO, Z YOU BUGGIN!!!!" His face and strong pronounced accented voice was a dead giveaway.

"Oh MY GOD PHA YOU DID!!!!" She laughed out loud and completely out of control. "What the FUCK!?!?! HOW? WHY? WHEN? HOLY SHIT!!!! YOU GOT SOME EXPLAINING TO DO!!!!" She jumped up from her chair almost knocking it completely over. She started leaping up and down like a wild animal until her offbeat balance caused her to fall, rolling around on the floor.

He pushed himself up from his seat and took a few steps away. "Fuck outta here Z, you really buggin!!!! I told you about drinking that white shit. Never drink Ciroc, that shit kills your brain cells!!!" Pharaoh's act of denying fell on deaf ears.

Z was cracking up, rolling around on the floor. "Haaaaaaa you can't even lie straight!!!!! Oh my God YOU ARE SO HORRIBLE!!!!! You really slept with her!!!! WOW!!!!!!!!!!" She was on a roll, literally. " I need ALL of the DETAILS!!!!"

Pharaoh gave up, knowing that he couldn't lie to Z and accepted that his secret was out. The clerk caught his attention and Pharaoh nodded another apology. Grinning, he walked back toward Z and scooped her into his arms from the floor. "Come on Lil drunkie, bedtime for you. We have a long, early day in just a few hours."

Z was still laughing and now, singing "Pha and Kai, sitting in a tree...........K-I-S-S-I-N-G.......!!!!!!!!"

Pharaoh couldn't help but laugh at the goofy singing coming from the intoxicated girl.

Pharaoh carried her to her room, setting her down to stick her key in the scanner. Once the door opened and she was safely inside, he headed to his room for some much needed sleep of his own.

Chapter Thirteen: Pharaoh (Love All Over Me)

Love All Over Me- Monica (Album: Still Standing)

The alarm chimed on his phone faster than Pharaoh could have ever imagined that it would. 4:00am.

Slamming his finger against the display to end the irritating sound of birds chirping. He noted that he needed to change his alarm notification tone STAT.

The birds chirping took his mind back to the before bedtime interaction that he had with Z. Replaying her drunken singing in his head, he laughed out loud at the foolery.

Sitting in the tree huh? We'll see about. Pharaoh pulled himself from the oversized bed to start his prep for the day ahead.

After showering, he sat on the edge of the bed and punched in Z's room number on the courtesy phone.

"Get up Z!!!" He called out upon hearing her barely audible voice.

"I'm up." She responded lack lusterly, causing Pharaoh to again motivate her to rise from bed.

"Okay okay. I'm getting up now."

"You know that Nyris will be here in 45 minutes. Call Kai."

"Aye Aye Sir." She replied in a sarcastic voice and hung up the phone.

Pharaoh continued his routine, dressed and pulled his locs into a single banded ponytail. He opted to be without a cap, knowing that the temperatures in the Baha would be much more steamy than that of temps in Miami. A light weight tank, Nike basketball shorts and a fresh new pair of kicks completed his look.

Thirty minutes later, he sat in the lobby waiting for the girls to make their arrival. Kai arrived first looking tired and of course, her usual anti-social self. She walked through the front doors and sat on the bench outside.

Z came down just as Nyris was pulling up. To say that she was dragging was an under-statement. She slipped into the passenger seat, greeted Nyris and immediately rested her head to nap on the way to the Port of Miami.
Kai sat on the back seat next to Pharaoh. Her gaze was focused out the window as Nyris pulled into traffic.

Pharaoh pulled his phone from his pocket and played a few levels of Candy Crush Friends. Again, unintentionally, especially with her sitting so close and smelling her fruity perfume, his mind wondered where exactly she was with her thoughts of him. Why was she so turned off from speaking to him? That look last night. It was damn near frightening. Why was she so angry with him? He hadn't done anything wrong to receive such a bitter response. Enough was enough. Sick of wondering period and just tired of going looney trying to figure her out, he put his phone away and made his move.

Slowly and discreetly reaching his hand out, he brushed hers, receiving the look that she had been so unwilling to give. He laid his head back against the rest and held her gaze for a long moment. There was so much sadness in her eyes. Their silent conversation was all eyes only. Her expression was relaxed, but yet the sadness.....the sadness was so noticeable.

He touched her hand again, wanting her to speak with him. To tell him what was bothering her. She parted her lips but no sound was produced. Slightly leaning his head to the side, he squinted in his way of asking her if everything was okay. The question would not be answered as Nyris had pulled into the parking structure for the port, breaking the silent exchange.

Releasing his seatbelt, Pharaoh pulled himself from the car and raised his arms above his head in a much needed stretch. Turning towards Z who had also stepped out of the car, she had a smug smile on her face.

"Ummmmmm hmmmmmmmm." She mumbled in her way of letting Pharaoh know that she had seen a bit of the interaction between him and Kai.

Pharaoh gave a half smile, closed the door and walked the first few steps backwards, looking at Z with his hands in the air. If his expression would have caused a song to start playing in the background, it would have been Shaggy's 'It Wasn't Me.'

"Tuh." She rolled her eyes teasingly and closed her own door.

After clearing the customs check in process, they sat patiently waiting to board the ship. Twenty minutes later, they were all aboard the water navigating passenger vehicle. Once the ship pulled from dock and into the open water, Pharaoh settled into one of the reclining chairs with his earbuds in, listening to some light meditation tracks. His slumber came quickly.

Two hours later, he was awaken by children screaming and causing a ruckus by the snack bar. They were throwing tantrums for one reason or another.

Removing the buds from his ears, his music had stopped long ago. Looking around, the area where he sat , it was vacant minus a few others who had the same idea that he had just a couple hours before.

Standing and yawning, he walked over to the snack bar and purchased an orange juice. Taking his item, he walked around the confines of the ship. After one full exploratory lap, he still had not seen Z, Nyris or Kai.

Heading towards the back of the ship he smiled at an elderly couple who were snuggled close watching a movie on their tablet. Passing the couple he stepped up to the door leading to the outer balcony portion of the ship. From the doorway, he saw Kai.

She was leaning against the balcony, staring out into the neverending massiveness of the Atlantic Ocean's Carribean Sea. The strong winds pelted her body painting the picture of her hair blowing around her shoulders and neck, flowing sundress pasted to her frame as if it was actually form fitting. He stood and marveled at the sight of her for several minutes before stepping through the door and onto the balcony, making his way over to her.

She didn't move.

Pharaoh stood next to her, appreciating the same beauty of the sea as her eyes took in.

After a few minutes, he spoke.

"To imagine that this very water that we are atop of is thousands of miles deep." He shook his head. "It's truly unbelievable. The depths of it. 70% of the planet is covered in it. The real world is all that's underwater. We are just shepherds on floating volcanic deposits that miraculously rose forming disks on top of all this massiveness."

Kai slowly turned to him. The sunlight in her golden eyes created an almost unnatural glow.

She took him in. He stood nearly a full foot taller than she. His arms were strong and muscular, his chest was firm, his signature cologne carried in the wind.

He wasn't sure why he all of a sudden felt angry in the connection but it crossed him hard and swift.

"Why haven't I heard from you Kai?" His accent was strong even though his voice was controlled and light.

A slight frown crossed her features. "I could just as easily ask why I haven't heard from you."

"But not only had I not heard from you, you have also given me STUPID silent treatment since I arrived." He mentioned. "What's that about?"

Kai shifted and turned back towards the water. "Listen Pharaoh, let's not do this okay. You fuck women all the time and dog the hell out of 'em. I am making this shit as easy as possible for you. You could always act as if I never existed as you always have. That should be really easy, especially since it had always been that way."

Pharaoh studied her, taking her completely in. Now it all made sense. Her opinion.....her thoughts about him said all.

"Wow." Was the only response that he could conjure up.

He continued sizing her up. It was eye opening that her opinion of him, was equally as bad as his opinion had been of her. Even though he had known that she had not cared for him for a long number of years prior, it was still dawning to hear her say it.

Especially now. And if she truly felt that way, then why would she have done it?

"Then why me Kai? Tell me, why me?" She turned to him again in sadness with his pressing question. "Why would you fuck me? Why give your virginity to me?"

She shook her head, not being able to bare the detecting glare in his eyes. "I don't know. It all happened so fast. I still honestly have not been able to process it. Maybe it shouldn't have happened. It was a mistake."

Her last words cut to the bone. Wow. The shit felt like a full fledged knife. First time that he had ever heard that sleeping with him was a "mistake." Her response to him that night, along with the fact that she had 32 years worth of time to make that same "mistake" in what he was sure were many other opportunities, and the fact that she hadn't, said otherwise.

He took her face and turned it to his full attention. "A mistake. Really? Was it?" His gaze took on a dangerous expression. "Look me in my eyes and say that shit to me again."

Kai tried turning away but Pharaoh wasn't having it. Her truth was all over her face, which was the answer he had been looking for and he would not let her run from it.

Turning her eyes from his, she snatched away and tried heading for the door. Obviously Wrong words. Definitely Wrong move.

Pharaoh caught her arm before she could make her get away, pulling her into his embrace, he leaned down and immediately covered her mouth with his. She struggled a short moment until she couldn't struggle any longer. Her body, her heart would not allow her to fight any longer. She crumbled under the intoxication of his kiss. Her emotions were on overload and uncontrollable.

Pulling back to look into her tear rimmed eyes, Pharaoh softly spoke. "Now look me in my eyes and say that shit to me again."

She blinked several times but couldn't stop the tears from escaping her eyes. Her heart was flipping and going crazy. She raised a hand to wipe her droplets, but Pharaoh beat her to the punch. He tenderly used his thumb to wipe the AWOL tears that had fallen onto her cheeks. He afterwards leaned in to kiss her right where they had been.

"Was it a mistake Kai?" He asked her softly.

She sat in the moment silently. He allowed her the opportunity. He held onto her a while as she laid her head against his chest, deep in thought.

"Now I really hope this ends the little tantrum you have been throwing." He tried lightening the mood with a teasing smirk that irritated her soul but her heart would not allow her to be angry any longer.

She playfully pushed away. "That little kiss don't mean anything. I still can't stand your ass." They were approaching the banks of the island. She could see lounge chairs on a private beach in the distance as they passed.

Pharaoh laughed and moved behind her wrapping his arms around her waist. Leaning, he whispered in her ear, "Settle down, Lil Mama before I bend you over and take you on this deck. You can't stand my ASS huh? Well I'mma be smacking you on yours."

Kai turned around to SMACK him on his arm. "Boy come on now, so we can exit this ship." Her southern accent was highly emphasized.

Happy to see her receptive and finally out of her funk. He took her hand in his as they made their way back inside.

Nassau, Grand Bahama Island. Beautiful. Rich. Colorful and Lively. Pulling into dock, the first thing they saw was their current destination, huge, salmon in color and a true staple of the island, it was recommended by Nyris. The Atlantis Paradise Island Resort.

Kai and Pharaoh had found Z and Nyris on the inside. At spotting her two favs holding hands, Z was giddy with happiness.

"Yay!!!" she clapped her hands together like a two year who had received a Baby Shark toy for Christmas. Pharaoh and Kai had both rolled their eyes at Z and smiled at one another.

Now, on solid ground, they followed Nyris's advice in catching a tour van to the famous resort location. In order to find an available vehicle, they would need to take a walk past the dock and into the shopping area of the outer island. Z and Nyris walked ahead of Pharaoh and Kai.

"Have you ever been to the islands before?" Kai asked.

"Yeah, but this is my first time visiting Nassau." Pharaoh answered.

"What other islands have you visited?"

"I've pretty much hit all of the U.S Virgins, including you." Pharaoh unsuccessfully tried dodging another playful smack that Kai planted on his chest.

"You are such a Jerk!!!" Kai laughed.

Pharaoh continued. "But on the real, most of the US Virgs, Cozumel, Mexico, Aruba and Curacao."

"Wow. I have never been. This is my first time outside of the country besides a training that I attended once in Montreal, Canada." Kai let go of Pharaoh's hand to try capturing a beautiful, blue butterfly that had been following alongside them. "I love the richness of the land. So colorful in every living thing.

Pharaoh watched her intently as she kept unsuccessfully trying to clip the butterfly.

"This butterfly reminds me of a flying flower. It's so gorgeous. Seems as if the closer we get to the equator, the more the color is prevalent in the surrounding environment."

He loved how she seemed so excited and in tune with the sights.

"So, Lil Mama, tell me, what makes you tick?"

She looked back at Pharaoh from her paused kneeling position that she took to smell a magnificent Yellow Elder flower. "Hmm……great question. Let's start with this." She spread her arms around her. "Beautiful landscapes created by beautiful wildlife. There is nothing more relaxing than the beauty in nature. Looking out at the water soothes my soul. I am an Aquarius you know. So I am naturally attracted to bodies of water." She paused, giving thought before continuing. "Learning things that I hadn't known before. Education never ends in life and continues until our dying day. I'm always open to new experiences…...new ideas. Seeing new things. Living life to the fullest. Having fun. Enjoying being me. It's really all in God's plan…..to live life to the fullest. I don't believe the intention was to sit around, do nothing…...grow old and make an exit. Life, I believe is truly what you make of it. We only have one here on this planet. There is no way of knowing what the after life has in store. But what we do know is about life in the here and now. So we have to live it up to top potential." she paused again.

Pharaoh watched her, listening to her every word. Engrossed in her views. Her opinion.

"Family makes me tick. I love my family!!! We are all so close knit. When one suffers, we all do. I will ride and roll HARD for my peeps, as you know." She laughed then continued. " I also love children. The innocence of them. They are like human sponges, living, learning and imitating the behaviors of those closest around them. The laughter…the realness. I swear a child will tell you the truth…will blurt it out with a straight face and not a single regret." She laughed again. "I love my home in the bayou. I know where I come from and it is branded in my blood. My mom is French and black, my Dad was pure negro. But he could throw down in the kitchen, so good he put my mom to shame, and that's amazingly hard to do!!!!" Her face lit up reminiscing. " It's where I learned to cook. In the kitchen with him."

"What happened to your Dad if you don't mind me asking?" Pharaoh collected her hand again in his, knowing that he was asking her to tread in sorrowful waters.

Kai was silent for a long time before responding. "He passed away when I was fifteen. An accident on one of the barges in which he worked." She appreciated the fact that Pharaoh held onto her hand a bit tighter. "Even though I've had time to recover, I still miss him everyday. He was my best friend." Her voice trailed off.

Pharaoh sat in her last statement for a while, thinking about the loss of his own best friend. He was interrupted by a squeeze of her hand.

"I truly understand Pha. I've been where you are now when the death of my Dad was fresh. He was my everything as well." She looked into his eyes with a caring expression. "Time. That's the answer. Nothing heals wounds like the medicinal properties in time. And trust me that even then, the loss will still affect you. But, you have to take the pain that is residing in your heart and harvest it until it produces love and only love. Just think about the good times. The good times will be that which will remind you of the love."

Pharaoh let her words sink in. Harvest the pain until it produces love. What a process. But he knew that the lessons in her own experience was the absolute truth. He stopped walking and turned to face her. Taking her hand into his, he kissed her softly on the forehead. He then released her hand and wrapped her in his arms. "Thank you for sharing your wisdom."

Kai looked up at him and planted a soft peck on his lips. "You are most welcome."

Z and Nyris was up pretty far ahead when she stopped and turned back to her favs. " Catch up you two love birds." She called out, loving their embraced moment.

Pharaoh and Kai released one another and started their trek to catch up to the couple ahead. Once they had joined them, they continued around the corner, through the shops and out to the open road where several passenger vans awaited.

Hopping into one of the vans that was already loaded with quite a few tourists, Pharaoh allowed Z and Nyris to take vacant seats. Sitting next to them and taking the last seat, he helped Kai up into the van and onto his lap.

The driver closed the door behind them and took his throne in front.

"Welcome to Paradise!!! Welcome to the Bahamas!!!" He announced in his thick Caribbean accent. "I'm Fritchie and I will be taking you all to breathtaking Atlantis!!!" He greeted his smiling guests. "Hold on tight to your loved ones because HERE WE GO!!!"

Fritchie pulled from the curb and into traffic. He pointed out many details about the island and its rich culture along the way.

Kai observed the impoverished areas riding through the town. Pharaoh was used to the sight as he had long ago learned by being up close on all of the other surrounding islands that he had visited, that the story pretty much stayed the same. The areas that weren't shown via broadcast television. Tourism was a major market for the natives and for many, their only means of feeding their families. Whether they provided services of transportation, local goods, food or other crafts made available for purchase, if the tourists weren't visiting the islands, many would starve.

Pulling up into the grounds for the resort, Fritchie drove past a part of the resort that consisted of a skywalk that connects two of the buildings together.

"That skywalk is an actual $25,000 a night room. The most luxurious on the grounds. The entire bridge is one whole suite. Celebrities such as Michael Jackson, Jennifer Lopez, Shaquille O'Neal among many others have all enjoyed the comforts while staying in Nassau." Fritchie announced.

Kai's had her phone out, snapping away at almost every part of the resort that the vehicle drove passed. Pharaoh had to hold onto her waist to keep her steady and from slipping off of his lap. Z was also snapping photos but her eyes couldn't help but to connect with Pharaoh's. She wore a smile so bright that her eyes seemed to be twinkling. She squinted, reading her friend.

"What?" he mouthed to her, slightly shaking his head.

Z didn't respond. She just continued with her beaming.

The van stopped in front of the front doors to the elegant resort. Turning his long legs at an angle so that Kai could step out comfortably, Pharaoh stepped out behind her. Z and Nyris followed right after.

Fritchie called out, advising everyone that he would return to pick them up at exactly 3pm. They had 5 full hours to explore.

Z took Pharaoh's hand and pulled him to the side.

"I love it!!!" She could barely contain her excitement.

"Ummmm what exactly is it that you love so much?" Pharaoh played his game, although he knew that Z was one who knew him all too well.

"Pha, you are really feeling Kai. I can truly tell. Wow. I'm shocked at all of this. You know you have to fill me in on what the hell happened to make this a possibility."

"I'm enjoying the day. Isn't that what you have always wanted? For us to GET ALONG?" He teased receiving a knowing frown from Z.

"This is GET ALONG to the tenth power Sir!!! Pha, you're holding her hand and kissing her in public for Christ's sake!!!! You NEVER have done that with any girl you have EVER introduced me to!!!"

"She's your cousin Z!!! Of course I am going to respect her." His acceptance of his own actions and behavior was not there in the moment.

Z gave up. "My cousin right? Because of that you will respect her…..hmmmmmm…...just remember that you said that Homie." She winked and walked over to Nyris.

Kai was still walking around taking photos and selfies when Pharaoh walked up behind her throwing the peace sign up with his two fingers for the photo bomb.

Kai laughed and turned to him. " I thought you didn't want any photo action in the case that your FANS may see." She smashed her lips in the corner on one side of her mouth as she waited for his response.

"Oh yeah right." Pharaoh played along. "Don't tag me in that shit."

Kai's expression was unreadable when Pharaoh grabbed her by the hand and pulled her along into the building.

The beauty of the interior quieted her thoughts immediately. The lobby was ivory and gold with several pillar columns surrounding a Gold domed top opening where beautiful seashells carvings made up the entire inside. The lobby looked as if it was created to mimic what one could imagine that the home of the Mythical Greek God of Water, Poseidon, would look like. The construction. The decor. The billions of dollars that were obviously spent to create such a marvelous masterpiece could not go unnoticed.

Z and Nyris walked over while Pharaoh and Kai was exploring the brilliantly constructed lobby.

"Did you guys bring your swimming attire?" Nyris asked.

"Nah, I didn't have a clue that I would need it." Pharaoh responded honestly. Kai also shook her head to having hers.

Z frowned apologetically. " Nyris and I both brought ours."

"That's cool. You guys heading for the pool?" Pharaoh asked.

"Yeah, we are going to start there. Beautiful day for a swim." Z wasn't lying. It was a steamy tropical day. If Pharaoh's common sense had awaken at the same time as he had that morning, he would have grabbed a pair of trunks.

"You two please come hang with us. We can have some drinks and chill poolside for a while." Nyris suggested.

"Nah Boss. You two do your thing. Don't let us stop you from getting your swim on." Pharaoh encouraged. "My phone is right on my hip. Call me if you need ANYTHING." He looked squarely at Z with his last word spoken.

Z ignored him. "Let's meet here in the lobby at exactly 2:45pm." They all agreed and split for their separate ways.

"So what do we do first Lil Mama?" Pharaoh asked looking at the pamphlet in which Kai handed him.

"There's an aquarium on site that I would love to see." She answered excitedly.

"Okay according to this map and the signs on the wall, it's this way," Pharaoh led the way to the underground lagoons.

"This brochure says that there is a total of 14 Natural habitat lagoons. Wow." Kai face lit up with her anticipation.

"Yeah that sounds dope. Definitely want to check that out."

Upon entering the lower level, the huge Aquarium surrounded by thick glass appeared in front of them.

"Oh my Lord," Kai's mouth hung open at the enormous structure that seemed to go on and on twisting down the wide open hallway. Huge sea creatures swam free and unbothered behind the protective glass. The decor created in the Aquarium was on point, truly mimicking a naturally, undisturbed underwater scene.

Kai walked over to the glass for a closer look, as Pharaoh's phone buzzed, notifying him of a call coming through. It was Tre.

"Yo, wussup?"

"Pha, when you coming back Boss?" Tre's voice sounded panicked.

"I will be back tomorrow evening. Why was going on?"

"Ms. Holmes left out this morning heading to the grocery store and left the water running in a clogged sink. Mannnnn Water is EVERY muthafuckin' WHERE!!!!"

Pharaoh removed the phone from his ear and counted to ten to keep from exploding. "Yo, are you FUCKIN KIDDING ME RIGHT NOW?!!!"

"I wish that I was but unfortunately I am not," Tre sighed.

"Is everything okay?" Kai rushed over to check on her obviously struggling, angry companion.

"Yeah Kai, I'll be good." Pharaoh sat on the bench by the wall returning his attention back to business. Kai returned to her exploration after he nodded to her that he was okay.

"You got it covered Boss? At least until I return?" Pharaoh asked, knowing that his return home would now be a hectic one.

"Yeah, a few of the guys are over there now, extracting the water and performing clean-up. It should be good until you return. I will schedule an appointment to have someone come out to access the damage."

"Alright cool. That's wussup." Pharaoh felt his blood returning to a normalized pressure.

"Yeah, don't worry. Just wanted to give you a heads up on what's happening. That's all. Definitely don't let this spoil your vacay." Tre assured him that he had it all covered.

"Hey Pha, before you go, was that just Kai that you were speaking to?"

Pharaoh paused before responding, now noticing his mistake. FUCK!!!! He could not and would not lie to his Bro.

"Yeah. It was. Long story that need to be told over drinks." Pharaoh rubbed his left temple. "Let's link up when I return tomorrow."

Tre's response took a few torturous seconds before it came. "Okay cool. Let's do exactly that."

After the call ended, Pharaoh felt horrible. One for the issue with the flood, but the illest of the feeling came from the disappointment that he had detected in Tre's voice. He opted to sit still on the bench for a little while.

Even though Tre didn't know the full extent of what was going on with Kai being in his presence, what Pharaoh knew that he DID know was that they were speaking pleasantly to one another which in itself was cause for alarm.

He would have to tell him the truth whether he wanted to or not. The thought of it stabbed him in the stomach with a jagged edged knife. Tre had been crushing on Kai for a long time. This would not be a good meeting, but it would definitely be one that he would schedule as soon as he returned home.

Kai walked back over to where Pharaoh sat, taking a seat next to him.

She rubbed her hand over his shoulders, helping him to relax. "Are you sure you are alright?"

"Yeah, got a flood to deal with upon my return home." Pharaoh told the story, intentionally omitting the part about Tre.

"Oh wow. That's a headache and a half." Her southern charm was music to his ears. She continued to rub his shoulders until she switched, and started playing with his locs.

Her hands were working magic in lifting his mood. A few minutes later, Pharaoh stood and took her hand in his, pulling her to her feet.

"Let's continue our walk."

Kai smiled happily joining his side.

"I saw this HUGE Stingray a bit further down. Looked as big as an elephant."

"A Giant Stingray. Had to have been," Pharaoh searched the pool for the creature.

"Isn't that the same kind that Steve Irwin was swimming with when he was killed?" Kai asked.

"Yeah. We need to be careful with any animals larger than ourselves. Guess he knows that shit now."

"And some of the smaller ones as well," Kai said matter of factly. Pharaoh agreed.

They walked the winding strip and still did not see the elusive Stingray. Growing tired of looking, they decided to head back up to their next destination.

"Your turn, you choose a spot." Kai passed the ball into his court.

"Okay cool." Pharaoh rubbed his hands together. "Onto that Playa shit!!!!" Kai looked confused. Pharaoh laughed. "The casino. Here we come"

"I don't gamble. Don't know how." Kai smiled at the now transferred excited expression on Pharaoh's face.

"You will learn today Lil Mama. Maybe you will bring me some of that infamous beginner's luck."

"I sure hope so. But it wouldn't be me, it would be you because you will be the one telling me what to do."

"Even still, you will be playing along beside me."

They walked into the busy casino but first stopping to have their photos taken in the huge golden thrones that sat as decor out front.

Starting off light, Pharaoh walked over to stake out the Black Jack tables. Making his way around, he found one that didn't look to be hitting consistently. Knowing that his and Kai's addition would cause a major card shake up and preferably for the best. He took a seat, pulling Kai onto his lap.

Pulling from his wallet, he removed 20 crisp $100 dollar bills. The dealer counted the funds and provided him with his chips. He placed his chips down to start his bet. The dealer dealt Pharaoh a King and Queen of spades out the gate.

"A twenty pop in perfect representation of the gentleman and his Queen here at the end." The dealer winked. Pharaoh looked at Kai who smiled. The dealer then flipped himself an Ace as his facing card, the second he placed face down. "Insurance anyone?"

Pharaoh opted to let the cards fall, no insurance taken.
Great call. The dealer flipped himself over a six of hearts. Pharaoh collect his winnings while Kai sat watching, lost.

"So, the goal in this game is to get as close to 21 without going over," Pharaoh whispered in her ear.

"I know most of the basics," Kai started. " I was just confused with the insurance thing that the dealer just did."

Placing his chips up for the 3rd hand after landing a twenty one on the second, he explained to her about the insurance offering.

"Anytime that the dealer flips over an Ace as his first card, of course it is possible that his second card could be valued at ten, giving him a score of 21. So before flipping up the second card, he has to ask all players if they would like to take out an "insurance policy" in the case that he does have Black Jack. It ensures that the player who takes it, breaks even on the hand. But in order to take the insurance, the player must automatically wager half the value of their original bet. If the dealer has a BlackJack, the player who has anything lower and has purchased the insurance breaks even, but if he doesn't have a Black Jack, the player loses the amount that was wagered for insurance." Pharaoh put more chips

222

up for his now fifth bet. He leaned into her ear to whisper again. "Truth be told, taking insurance is usually the worst bet that is taken on the table."

Kai shook her head. "I can see why. It's too risky. I prefer the slots by the way."

Pharaoh laughed ."Is that what you want to do Lil Mama? Play the slots?" He took his hand and rubbed it over her bottom. She turned to him with narrowed eyes.

"Yeah, let me head over to the slots Free Feel Will, before you find yourself in some serious trouble." She stood and took a couple steps away.

Pharaoh chuckled before grabbing her hand and snatching her aggressively but playfully back towards him. He pulled her in and whispered in her ear. His lips brushed her lobe as he spoke. "Now don't go writing checks that even ALL that ass can't cash." He smacked her on the rear.

Kai's cheeks were blushed. Pharaoh smirked at the pleasantly frightened look on her face. Reaching in his pocket he handed her Six fifty dollar bills.

"Have fun. Play smart. And, tread carefully before you find YOURSELF in some real trouble. Don't forget we are already inside of a hotel." Pharaoh licked his lips.

Kai slowly spun on her heels, not before tossing him the middle finger. She turned back with a grin on her face as she took a few steps toward the slots.

Pharaoh chuckled and mouthed. "I will gladly handle that request later on Smart Ass."

They stayed, playing in the casino for the next three hours. Pharaoh had collected an additional $6700 on top of what he initially started with. Kai had lost $100 of the $300 that Pharaoh had given her. She tried handed the remaining funds back to Pharaoh who declined. He advised her to buy something nice for herself in the gift shop. She decided to instead use it buying souvenirs for those back home.

At exactly 2:45pm, the four had reconnected in the lobby as agreed upon. Z and Nyris seemed rather romanticized and completely absorbed into one another.

"So, How was your swim?" Pharaoh asked receiving a wide smile in response.

"It was really nice. The pool was lovely. It had this waterfall slide extending from the top of a step pyramid structure reminiscent of the ruins in Teotihuacan. You would have loved seeing it," Z responded. "It was gorgeous."

"That sounds dope." Pharaoh could imagine what a beautiful sight it must have been. He noted his need to return for exploration.

"What did you two end up doing?" Z asked

"We visited the Aquarium and of course the casino." Pharaoh recited the details of his and Kai's visit.

"Oh wow. I missed a lot. We must return and soon." Z stated, reading his mind. Pharaoh completely agreed.

The ride back to the dock was a quiet one. They had the entire van to themselves this time around as the other passengers had taken an earlier return transport. Z and Nyris were sitting in front snuggled while Pharaoh and Kai sat in the back seat. Kai had her legs across Pharaoh's lap playing a game on her phone.

With a bit of time to spare before having to head back to board the ship, they all agreed to walk down to Senor' Frogs for meals and drinks. The lively, packed bar had a theme similar to Jimmy Buffett's Margaritaville. Adult games were being played including: a sexy balloon pop, beer drinking and a variety of other contests. Z and Nyris competed in the Balloon pop contest coming in second place and receiving an award of 2 Foot long Margarita tubs. Z passed her drink over to Kai, opting not to risk sipping again with having already started the day with a mild hangover.

Pharaoh and Kai shared a huge bowl of Guacamole made fresh, table side with chips.

The time went fast. They were back aboard the ship pulling out from dock in record time. On the sail back, the four decided to play Spades with the set of cards that Kai had purchased from the gift shop at Atlantis.

Pharaoh was disturbed and disgusted with the fact that Nyris and Kai wanted to play without using the Jokers.

"Who the fuck plays Spades without the Jokers?" He protested. "That's rookie shit. Put the damn Jokers in for crying out loud!!!"

Kai laughed. "My deck, my rules. Ace High. No Jokers."

He did not win the debate. Nor did he and his partner Z win the game. Kai and Nyris gloated in their win.

"Of course we lost, we were cursed out the gate. That janky ass Ace High bullshit." Pharaoh hated losing, especially with the amount of shit he had talked through the entire game.

"Awww Luv," Kai kissed his cheek and used her thumb to remove the glossy residue that her lips had left behind. "Get your game up and maybe you'll have a chance next time."

Pharaoh rolled his eyes heavenward. "Get my game up. Stop it!!!! You are sitting in the presence of a Spadeologist. Been doing this shit since the Big Bang. Get YOUR game up Lil Mama and stop taking the easy way out by playing Ace High. Shits for the inexperienced."

Their laughter continued the entire sail home.

Back in Miami and at the hotel, Nyris dropped Pharaoh and Kai off while he and Z drove on, headed to a party that a friend of his was throwing in honor of his Wedding Anniversary.

Pharaoh and Kai decided to take a walk on the now dark and secluded beach. The moon again reflected beautifully on the calm tide. Stars littered the clear skies above.

"I could seriously never get tired of living a beach life." Kai loved the sensation of the sand under her bare feet. "I truly hate to return home tomorrow. I promise that I need just a few more days."

Pharaoh smiled. It did seem as if the weekend went by in a flash. It just wasn't enough time. Another two to three days would have been perfect. But unfortunately for him, his time was winding and coming to a close.

"I must say that I do appreciate the company that I was blessed to have today," Kai looked up into his eyes. "Thanks for making this day truly memorable."

Pharaoh stopped walking, sizing her up. He was struggling with the abrupt change of once, just so recently, feeling so much irritation at the very sight of her, and now actually agreeing with her statement and truly admitting that he, also, had indeed enjoyed her company as well. It was an almost bipolarized adaptation.

Kai smiled, tucking a strand of hair behind her ear. Her expression quickly changed to one of deep considerations. "It's so weird how things work. Pharaoh I must be honest in saying that I am still a bit unsure about ...everything. This. Whatever this is." Her voice trailed. Pharaoh saw the concern on her face. He listened thinking that maybe she could provide some incite to the questions that they both seem to be having trouble with. "You asked a valid question of me earlier in why. Why?" She paused, jumping up to pull her weight onto a huge rock that sat on the beach in front of them. "I truly don't know why…..or what…or even how this all happened with us. It was so fast."

Pharaoh watched her as she struggled with her understanding of the place they were in. And he too had no clue where that place

227

actually was. Had he enjoyed spending time with her? Absolutely. Kai was a completely shocking surprise. He had never known that she had so much more to her under the surface. She was smart, sweet, caring and genuine, everything that his guys had seen in her from the start. Everything he had not.

His mind went back to that night in his apartment. He had been so upset with her and the drama that she had brought to his doorstep. Why had he hated her so? Why had he never given her a chance?

As if reading his mind she asked, "Why did you hate me so much Pharaoh? Could you explain that to me? Yes I had snapped regarding you being so tough on Z when we first met, but you were never able to get passed it. Why?"

He could see the hurt in her eyes. He wondered how long she had been asking herself that question. Wanting to ask the question of him. Thinking back to the day that Z had introduced them, he remembered that she had been rude to him from the very start. Arms folded, eyes rolling ...her attitude was so snotty for no apparent or explainable reason.

"Honestly Lil Mama, I had played off your energy. Your vibe. I hadn't done shit to you, but yet your attitude was completely unreceptive of me." Pharaoh shook his head. "Never was completely sure what that was about." He shrugged his shoulders.

Kai looked at him, also allowing her thoughts to travel back to that day outside of the Marquette campus. She had to be honest in admitting that her display of rudeness was completely intentional. When Z had first told her about her bestie Pharaoh, her goal was to prepare her cousin, who was known to be a hot head, for the encounter. Z had known that her best friend had an arrogant and egotistical nature. But even with that, she had wanted her cousin

228

to understand how harmless he actually was. Kai had automatically prepared herself for the worst in hearing Z's usage of the words "Ladies Man" and "Cocky." Z would not realize her mistake until it was too late.

In all honesty, nothing really could have prepared Kai for her first run in with The Infamous Pharaoh. He had literally sucked her breath away with just how attractive he actually was, Z's description had not done him any justice whatsoever. He was a true masterpiece. How could just looking at someone cause her panties to collect so much moisture? He was amazingly fine!!! The guys that she was used to back home were not cut from the same cloth and no where near measured up.

Feeling nervous and panicky, she had to act fast. Although truly attracted to him, she had not wanted to fall victim, ending up as another notch on that long list of ladies that Z had described who were constantly falling at his feet. The only defense that she could come up with in her young and immature mind, was to play hard to get and force herself to act as if he had not affected her in the way that he had. Unfortunately, her acting in that way, had set the sour tune that had continued playing as their norm.

On Pharaoh's end, he was truly taken aback by the way in which she had treated him. It was the first time that a chic had outright rejected him, immediately, with no explanation from the start. When Z had walked him over to meet Kai, he had been stunned by her attractiveness. Kai had been beautiful beyond words. A moment that lasted just seconds because her attitude and smart mouth had immediately turned him down and ultimately turned him off. They had been at each other's throats ever since. Until now.

Pharaoh walked up and stood directly between her legs. "Listen, there are of course questions, but none of these questions are really of importance. We're adults now and that was all child's play." He assured her. "I'm cool on that shit from the past. We just have to move forward from here. It is what it is."

She nodded in agreement. "You're absolutely right Pha. And I completely agree." She nodded and decided to just enjoy the moment.

A cool breeze came through from off of the water. Holding onto to Kai, Pharaoh looked into the night sky, he spotted Orion immediately.

"Question. Let's see how well you pay attention Young Lady." He pulled away just enough to comfortably tilt her head upwards. "Point Betelgeuse out to me."

Kai studied the stars in the sky above. She pointed. "The large star there, above the first belt star on the right." She paused in thought before looking back down into Pharaoh's beaming face. "Right?"

"Good job Ma." He rewarded her with a peck on the lips.

Kai turned her head to the side now studying her handsome Instructor. "So, now I have a question for you."

Pharaoh took his fingers, intertwining them in her flowing mane, marveling at how much she had impressed him this weekend. "I'm listening. What you got for me?"

"So, I'm thinking, since this the second date and all, that maybe you can tell me about this Orion character and how he came to have a constellation in the sky." She pushed her face into his with an over exaggerated angelic expression. Hoping it would help to get her way.

It was hard denying her with the super sweet look she wore upon her face, but Pharaoh could not help but to use the opportunity as pay back.

"This," He leaned down and kissed her forehead. "My," Kissed the tip of her nose. "Dear," Kissed her right cheek. "Is not," Kissed her left cheek. "A date." Kissed her lips. He pushed back with a smirk for emphasis. "This…..is a session."

"Oh really Pha?" The pouting expression on her face was priceless. "Well let me collect my things and head on inside. I'm going to need to speak to Your Manager because my session does not include the same type of services as I had received before."

"Oh yeah?" He licked his lips causing her heart to skip a beat. "So what exactly is it that you are missing? I am trying to obtain your BEST overall review plus rating Miss?"

He reached his arms around her waist and pulled her body down from the rock so that her legs wrapped around him for balance. Smoothing his hands from her waist and around her back, he did what he had been wanting to do since he had seen her pantiless in the dress that she had worn the night before. Pressing his now hardness into her sweet spot, he cupped her ass in his hands.

She gasped subtly at his aggressively bold move. Knowing that he had her where he wanted, he grinded into her so that she could feel the full power of him. Looking deep into her eyes, he licked his lips again and smirked.

"Go ahead. I'm listening." He voice was low and deep. "And you were saying?"

Kai had lost her entire train of thought. Not a single word escaped from her mouth. It took her a few seconds to run the appropriate interference, cancelling the transfer of thought from flowing to her now soaking wet center and back to her brain.

Pharaoh was still smirking in amusement when she opened her eyes.

"Right here. Like this, Pha?" She looked around, making sure no one was around to see them.

"Your wish is my command." He obliged, lifting her completely from the rock and setting her down in the sand. "Let's get you more comfortable and move this to the inside."

Kai reached down to retrieve her sandals from the sand before allowing Pharaoh to take her hand to lead her back towards the hotel entrance. Once inside the elevator, Pharaoh pressed the button for the fourth floor. Moving back against the wall of the car, Kai was already pressed against the opposite wall. Their eyes met. So much was communicated there, within that single connection, even though not a single word was uttered.

The doors opened to the elevator, Pharaoh took her hand and led her to his room door. Slipping the keycard in the scanner, he turned the handle and allowed her to step inside first.

"After you."

Kai glanced around the huge room, impressed with the amenities. "Well somebody been living rather lavish on this end of the hotel." She joked, taking in all that the suite offered.

Pharaoh walked up behind her, kissing her on the neck. "You like?" She nodded truly loving the makeup of the room.

Wasting no time, he reached down, lifting her sundress over her head, leaving her in just her bra and panties. Facing her towards him, he unsnapped her bra while he leaned in covering her lips with his. His tongue slipped inside of her mouth intertwining with hers. She placed her arms around his neck to keep from falling from the drugging spell that his kiss was creating.

He lifted her, purposefully carrying her into the bathroom, placing her on the ledge of the sink. He walked over to turn the knobs in the shower, activating a relaxing, steamy spray. Removing his shoes, socks and tank shirt, he dropped all items to the floor as Kai watched.

His body was so perfectly cut. The six pack present in his midriff region had not a single can missing. Just below his navel, there was a thin line of hair leading into and disappearing inside his shorts. It was one of the sexiest things that Kai had ever seen with her own two eyes. She wanted to kiss his chest, to kiss that sexy trail of fur...to love on him, to worship him with her mouth.

She watched him closely as he slowly made his way back to her. This man was a True Adonis indeed!!! Reaching for him, she allowed her hands to explore his arms, his chest, his abdomen...He watched her every move, with soft, seductive eyes as her hands traveled the hard core of his body.

Finally making her way to that furry trail that started at Pharaoh's navel, she stopped there and turned her golden orbs upwards locking onto his eyes.

She slowly used her hands, dragging them across his sagittal, ensuring that she kept her eyes on him the entire time, wanting to see, wanting to learn every place on his body... paying close attention to what made him flinch, what made him moan, what turned him on. His eyes closed as her hands continued their journey, down into his shorts, into his boxers and brushing the head of his diamond hard dick. She massaged the shaft with one, while using the other hand to reach further in, cupping and lightly rubbing his scrotum. She used her thumb in a clockwise motion, being extra careful with the most sensitive place on his artfully sculpted body. He was firm and thick in her palm. She noted how she could not close her hand around the entire width.

Taking her hand in his, he removed them from his shorts and placed them at her sides, planting a soft kiss on her lips. Leaning down, he removed his shorts and lastly his boxer briefs. He lifted her frame from the countertop and set her on the floor, guiding her over to the now steam filled shower. Pulling on the handle and sliding back the glass door, he turned back to her, lowering himself to remove her silky thongs. Stepping outside of the undergarment, she stepped onto the tiled floor of the shower confines. Pharaoh followed suit, sealing the door shut behind him.

Walking up to take his place in front of her, he tossed her a thousand watt smile.

"Hey there beautiful."

She shyly returned the smile. "Hey there handsome."

"How are you feeling tonight?" He pulled her into his thick, strong arms.

"Naked. Does that count as a feeling?"

Pharaoh laughed. He kissed her forehead, wanting to make her as comfortable as possible. "Naked's good."

He sucked her bottom lip between his. The simple action caused a tingling sensation deep within her core. The moan escaped her lips, coming from a place deep within. He continued his mastery, swirling his tongue deep into the confines of her mouth. Trailing kisses down her neck, he tenderly found the sweet spot beneath her ears and lingered his attention there. Her whimpery moans were drowned out beneath the sound of the running water. Returning to kiss her chin…..her cheeks……..he rotated her body so that her back was facing him. Grabbing a bar of Raw African Black soap, he conjured up bubbles between his palms before slowly and gently working the lather onto her skin. Taking a hand and pushing her now damp curly hair to the side, he made room for his mouth as he continued his sensual wash, showering kisses around her neck and shoulders. His hands worked magic, rubbing soap across her chest, her breast, around her nipples...Turning her head for an over the shoulder kiss, her lips sought out his, needing to taste his nectar. He obliged, allowing her full access to receiving the amazing kisses that she had grown so accustomed to.

His journey continued trailing soap along her stomach, her waist, her back, her ass, and lastly…..

He turned her once again face forward. Leaning her head back into the streaming water, she allowed the water to run over her face and into her lioness mane. Pharaoh watched the unintentionally and unknowingly seductive movement. If only she knew just how sexy she looked with the clear liquid running over her face. But she was so new to this arena of passion, he doubted that she had the slightest clue what a complete turn on the show that she was performing, right in front of his eyes was. Setting the bar down and picking up a bottle of the same brand of Frankincense scented Raw African Black shampoo, he started at her scalp, massaging the product into her long, thick mane.

He was so careful with the way that he was handled her. So masterful. In her mind, she was his rare jewel and he cared for her as such. Precious. Fragile. Gentle.

After ensuring that all of her hair was coated with the purity of the all natural shampoo, she again leaned back into the stream and stayed a few minutes until she could no longer feel the softness of the bubbles cascading down her frame.

Retrieving the soap, he took the entire bar and pressed it against the very part that made her a woman. Her lips parted ever so slightly. His fingers slipped between her folds, rubbing across her clitoris and into her soaking, slippery wetness. He allowed his fingers to explore her there for a few moments, loving the sounds of her heavy breathing and soft, barely audible moans.

Grabbing the soap from his hands, she returned the favor, rubbing the lather over his chest, his shoulders, his back, his neck, his love line, his dick, his butt, his thighs…

Switching places, he stepped into the water to rinse the suds from his body. He finally shut the flow of the water off, before sliding the door open and stepping out, pulling her with him.

Grabbing two towels from the rack, he wrapped one around her dripping wet hair and the second around her body. The Frankincense scent from the shampoo smelled heavenly radiated from her mane now restored to its original natural state. Covering himself in a towel after drying his own locs, he opened the bathroom door to allow the steam to drift out into the open bedroom area.

Pharaoh walked out and took his place on the edge of the bed while Kai ran the towel over her hair, soaking up as much of the moisture as she could.

She turned to him and smiled. So simply, yet so beautifully.

When she had finished, he motioned to her with his index finger.

"C'mere Lil Mama." His accent was noticeable and heavily seductive.

It took only seconds for her to make her way to him. She planted her frame directly in front of his awaiting profile.

Reaching up as if unwrapping a prized Christmas gift, he untucked the towel and watched as it fell to the floor. His eyes scanned her body, causing her to shift uncomfortably. Her auto response kicked in. Her shyness caused her to raise her hands in an attempt to cover up, he caught them midway, and pulled them back down to her sides.

"Not tonight Kai. Just stand right here and be absolutely beautiful." He kissed her navel before pulling her forward, into his arms and down onto his lap, straddle position.

His rock hardness was directly set at her entry point. Running his hands up her cheeks and into her wet hair, he grabbed a handful as he moved his lips again over hers. Deep, wet, probing kisses invaded her mouth as he took his free hand, placing it on her waist and pulling into him so that the tip of his hardness broke through and into her awaiting wetness.

Her moan was deflected into his mouth. Kissing her deeper and entwining his tongue with hers, he pushed further into her tightness, enjoying the sensation of the place, where only he, had been. Her moans grew heavier as he pushed again, finally breaking past, halfway into her well.

He paused, giving her time to calm and adjust to his thickness. He knew that this time would be no different than the first. A period of adjustment was required.

Once she seemed to have settled, Pharaoh leaned the upper half of his body back, lying flat on the bed. Kai looked frightened, not sure what to do. But Pharaoh was patient. He would give her the first lesson on how to ride his dick tonight.

"Look at me Lil Mama." He turned her face to his. "Remember that I still got you."

She nodded her head up and down.

"Kai, do you really REALLY trust me?"

"I do." Her words were soft and light.

"Then follow my lead, okay?"

"Okay." Her reply was soft in her nervousness.

He kept his eyes connected to hers as he placed both hands on her waist. Slowly, he guided her hips back. Then once again forth. He repeated that same movement. Again. And again.

"Just like that. Back and forth." he explained. "Go slow until you feel comfortable enough to pick up pace."

Kai followed his instructions, going slow. In just minutes, she had seemed to have gotten the hang of it, looking into Pharaoh's eyes and listening to the messages being received from her own body, which was screaming out for more of a faster rhythm.

She picked up pace, moving her hips as if her favorite song was playing, and she was on the dance floor with all eyes on her. In this case, her audience consisted of just one. The most important one in her entire world at that time. His name: Pharaoh.

Finding her flow, the grinding felt natural. The deep friction that was being created inside her canal caused both her and her chocolate recipient to moan in pleasure.

Finding that she had gotten the hang of the basics and fast, Pharaoh was ready to take her to Phase Two.

"C'mere. Kiss me."

Kai responded to his request immediately. Taking her tongue into his mouth to smolder what he knew would come, he raised his bottom up, pushing every single inch deep and hard inside of her, she nearly flipped off, trying to get away.

"Ohhhhhhhh FUCCKKKKKKKKK!!!!!!!" She yelled out pulling her mouth from his.

Pharaoh lowered his bottom back to the bed. He pulled out from her canal knowing in that moment that she was not ready to take the full power of him while in that particular position.

He pulled her back to him and planted soft kisses all over her flushed face to calm her down.

"I'm sorry." He kissed her lips. "It's okay. I'm so sorry"

Once she had settled down, he raised his upper body to look leveled into her eyes.

"There are two positions where you will be able to feel EVERY single inch with no brace whatsoever. You being on top is obviously one. The second is doggie style." He tried explaining. "Don't worry, I promise that I am going to get you to eventually handle both no problem. Just not tonight." He kissed her another time and flipped her so that she was now lying on the bed and he was on top.

"Are you okay Boo?"

She shook her head, trying to control the beating of her heart and the painful throbbing deep within her well.

"Are you sure?"

She nodded again, although feeling as if she had failed some sort of test. How could she be a ripe 32 years of age and still damn near be a fucking virgin. What she had once held onto as a prize, now seemed like a hindrance. She felt helpless. Shameful.

She had wanted to please him.

He had been with so many girls. How could she ever compete with that? She knew he was studying her with his always and forever probing glare. But she couldn't help it. She was a hopeless and emotional wreck. She felt so inadequate. So inexperienced. Before she could stop it, a tear slipped from her eye.

"Lil Mama," He pulled her to him feeling horrible. Maybe he had gone too far. The last thing he wanted was to seriously and physically hurt her. "Come here Babes."

She had never felt so embarrassed and so under measured by self. God!!! What was going on with her. Why did she feel the need to impress him. The need to make him want her. This whole thing was fucking stupid!!! From the stupid dress that she wore the night before as an attempt to get his attention, to this entire undefined shit that she was feeling!!!! She would never be able to measure up or match with someone as prime and as experienced as he was. What was she thinking? He had always demanded and required more than just good looks. What did she bring to the table? She was a 32 year old, country ass almost virgin who couldn't take a full dick pushed inside of her. Maybe he had told the truth when she standing outside in his hallway. Maybe he was in a different league. Of a different caliber. She wanted to pick up all of her things and make an exit. Quick!!!!

Pharaoh held onto her, rocking her and feeling terrible. It wasn't until this moment that he realized just how much he truly cared for this girl. How had she been able to get to him in this way? To matter to him so much? How was it possible that he cared so much for her in such a short time? Or maybe he had always cared for her. He was just so tired of feeling so conflicted around her. He didn't understand these emotions. This shit was for the birds!!! Every fiber of his being was advising him to run away and not look back. That he was in entirely too deep. But his need to have her near him, to care for her, to make her all better was wearing him thin, yet obviously winning the self created war going on inside his brain. Seeing her tears had snapped him immediately into action.

He had felt as if he had violated her in some way or another and that thought made him feel loathsome and foul. What the fuck was going on with him!!!!????? It was fucking Kaimery!!!! When had he started buggin over her like he was?!?! He was usually so smooth. What was it about this chic who had him losing all of his composure? Pulling and stomping all over his player card damn near every single encounter. The fact was, that she had always been able to get under his skin in one way or another. Why did she affect him so heavily?

But yet still, he was losing the war and about ready to call in, pulling his remaining, but wounded troops. He was a goner.

Laying her back, he apologized again.

"I promise to make it better." He looked into her tearful face. "Let me make it better Lil Mama"

His trail of kisses started at her thighs. She resisted at first still continuing to beat herself up. But his masterful mouth wouldn't stop. He kissed and sucked away at her thighs, planting the huge red marks all over. Marking her. Branding her. Sucking away until blood pooled at the surface just underneath her toffee hued skin.

It took seconds for her moaning to return.

Taking two fingers and spreading her lips apart, flicking his tongue across her clitoris, tasting her and kissing the unintentional and thoughtlessly inflicted pain away. He kissed and sucked her pussy, as if his very life depended on it.

After she had cum once, he continued, circling her clit and dragging his tongue down forcing it deep inside of her, as if trying to get to the very place in which he caused her pain, needing to kiss and make it all better. Make it all go away. Using his thumb, he continued the circling motion on her clit.

This act that he was performing was making her goes nuts. Holy shit he was whipping some form of magic on her that she was not emotionally prepared for. No feeling had ever been as great as the one that he was giving her now. His mouth was conjuring up spells so potent, that she was sure that he was a Witch Doctor. When his finger slipped inside of her rubbing and pressing against her G Spot, her composure had completely checked out.

"Ahhhhhhhhhhh Pharaohhhhhhhhhhhhh!!!!!" She screamed out, her emotional state caused her voice to crack, in pleasure as she exploded. More tears...more throbbing...but in a completely different place of high.

Pulling himself level with her he kissed her tears away.

"Did that make it feel better?"

His concern was the cutest and sweetest thing she had ever witnessed.

Not verbally replying, she reached for him, motioning him up until he was in the right position.

She finally spoke. Tears streaked her cheeks. "I need you."

He stared into her eyes for a long time before his entry. He took his time. Super Slow. Steady. He pushed inside her. Grinding gently.

"Ohhhh." Kai's moans matched his tempo.

He kept planting his soft sweet kisses all over her face. His slow grind continued as she rubbed his back, massaging his muscles.

"Oh shit Kai." Pharaoh was amazed at how willing she was even after his slip up. She gave him everything that he needed in that moment. Her forgiveness was loud and clear.

His pace remained slow as he pushed a bit deeper, wanting to feel all of her. She opened wider so that he could. In the same moment, she needed all of him that her pussy would be willing to take.

He kissed her fingertips, her elbows. He kissed her eyelids. Her ears. Raising her leg and placing her foot on his chest. He sucked and kissed her toes making her squirm in absolute, unquestionable pleasure. She was so ridiculously wet at this point, he was damn near slipping out from her overly lubricated womanhood. Hmmmm. Imagine that.

Feeling his own climax building with the abundance of fluid accumulating within her pussy, Pharaoh's moans grew louder. His vocals weren't far behind.

"You like this dick?" He asked looking into her eyes that provided him with all the answers that he needed, yet still he wanted to hear her say it.

"Yes. I love this dick."

"You love it?" He looked in eyes to detect her truth. It was written all across her face.

Her voice was low and soft. "So much. I love it so much."

He sent a finger to rub on her clit. Feeling her climax coming on.

"What's my name Kai?"

"Oh My Goddddd…...Pharaohhhh."

"Say it louder, I can't hear you." He increased the pace of rubbing against her clit all while increasing the pace of his pumps.

"Pharrrrrrraaaaaaaaoooooooohhhhhh!!!!" She closed her eyes feeling herself on the verge of exploding.

"Is this my pussy Lil Mama?" Pharaoh pushed in just a little deeper, building on his own climatic finish.

She dug her nails into his back. "Oh shit I am about to cum."

"Look at me," he demanded, forcing her to open her eyes to reveal her truth. "Is this my pussy?"

"Oh God yes …it's yourrssss," she screamed out as she exploded. Pumping harder and faster, he came along with her, but not before getting the info that he needed to know from deep within the depths of her eyes.

His Great Old Man had always told him that in looking someone in the eyes, their entire story could be revealed. "The eyes are the entry way into the soul. Lies would always be rejected there for they have no place."

Kai's eyes did not lie. He just needed to figure out why that particular question had become one of most importance.

———————————————————————

Pouring 1738 over ice into the glasses, and grabbing a cigar Pharaoh stepped out onto the balcony. He handed one glass to Kai and took one for himself.

She was all light breathing and relaxation, stretched out on the wicker lounge chair covered in his tank top only.

Taking a seat next to her, he took a much needed sip from his drink.

Setting the glass on the table between them, he clipped the top from his treat and used a torch to ignite the end.

His habitual gaze traveled towards the stars above.

"Orion, son of Poseidon, The God of Water, is a Giant being of Greek mythology." Pharaoh started. "The stories are conflicting surrounding his tale." He pulled from the cigar, sending the traditional smoke into the still air. "It is said that he was a gifted huntsman whose good looks had earned him his way with the ladies via many affairs. He is said to have fathered 50 sons from his numerous run ins. The man was a Don!!!" Pharaoh chuckled. Kai rolled her eyes and smiled. "His admiration of the Goddess Artemis is what ultimately brought on his demise. A great huntress herself, she killed him with her own arrow after his attempted attack on her, sending him and his faithful dog, Sirius, to live in the cosmos for all of eternity."

"His dog has a constellation as well?" Kai listened intently. Her eyes lighting at the possibility.

Pharaoh took another long pull and set his cigar in the ashtray atop the table.

Turning to Kai, he took her hand in his, motioning for her to join him on his lounge. Once comfortable sitting between his legs, he lifted her chin upward, focusing her eyes in the direction in which he intended her to look.

"Not a full constellation, but a single star at his side." Pharaoh kissed her sweet spot under her ear. Kai laid her head back against his chest, her eyes never leaving the twinkling stars of the Orion constellation above.

"Find Betelgeuse for me again." He directed. Kai pointed at the bright star dancing above. "Good. Now find the first belt star aligned just a ways down from it." Pointing again, she traced her finger down in alignment with the first belt Star. Pharaoh was blown away by how much she had taken in on his home balcony that night. "That's wussup. Now trail your finger, again in alignment straight down, pulling away from the constellation to the right of his body." Grabbing her hand, he helped to guide her finger in the right direction, stopping down below on the largest and brightest star visible in the entire sky. "That is his right hand man that sits just to the right of his body. The name of that star... is Sirius. The Dog Star."

Kai relaxed her body against him, staring into the brightness of the glowing wonder.

"Orion. Original. Origin." He continued whispering in her ear. "Our ancestors of Ancient Egypt were connected to this entire constellation. It was prevalent in all of their writings, the hieroglyphs...the pyramids...so many references. During the time of The Great Sphinx, The Great Age of Leo, when the statue was said to have been constructed in honor, the pyramids were built there after in perfect alignment with the three belt stars of Orion." Each pyramid represents a perfect placement of each belt Star."

Kai turned her eyes up to his, engrossed in his abundant wealth of knowledge regarding the cosmos and their linkage to the Ancient world. "Wow. That's amazing. So was Leo the only Great Age or were their others?"

Pharaoh picked up His cigar again and took a puff. "Every single astrological period has an Age. All twelve. From Aries, being first, and Pisces, being last. The cycle continuously repeats. Each Age's cycle is thought to last approximately 2,150 years, according to the details of the precisely constructed Mayan calendar. The Mayans were Beasts with recording events and keeping track of time!!! The were so dope with it, that they were able to record as far into the future as with our own current time, which is thousands of years after their own disappearance."

The look on her face was of pure interest and he loved her insatiable appetite for knowledge. Kissing the tip of her nose, he continued.

"Remember back when everyone was tweaking and going crazy back on December 12, 2012, preparing for the end of the world?"

Kai nodded, remembering that everyone had run out to stock up on non perishable food items in the prediction that the world would end that day. Her mom was also one who had taken with the craze.

"For some strange reason, the Mayan calendar was recorded only through until that day. Everyone automatically assumed that since every other recorded prediction that the Mayans had on their calendar had come to pass, that there had to be some reason why the calendar ended on that particular day. End of calendar, end of recorded time, end of days." Pharaoh chuckled. "Made sense huh? But one thing scientists and other self proclaimed know it alls will never do is admit their wrongs. Well, obviously they had misinterpreted the entire meaning of that last day on the calendar."

Taking one last pull from the cigar, he pressed the burning tip into the tray until the fire smoldered.

"The Mayans were also avid keepers of knowledge regarding Astrology. All around the perimeter of the calendar, the Astrology signs are framed in various sizes. Some a bit larger in size than others. These signs represented the Ages, which also were to be included in the full and accurate record of time. When I say that the Mayans shit was on point, that shit was down to a science!!! Not sure why, but the recording of Astrological Ages move backwards in cycle for some strange reason." He shook his head before moving on. "Before that quote "end of day," we were known to be functioning in what was said to be the current Age of Pisces" He paused before continuing. "Made sense to me as the current state of mind and events are said to be reflective in the traits associated with the astrological sign. Pisces, being moody, rigidly controlling, having strong, pushed upon religious beliefs, follow this or you are WRONG!!! Enslavement. Forced views. All of these things have occurred within our time. Within the last couple thousand years. All are traits of the fucked up nature of Pisces." Pharaoh passion came through in the appearance of his strong accent. "Well, I believe along with many others that what the Mayans were really recording was the last day in the rigid Age of Pisces. It's hard to say for sure because no one has anyway of knowing exactly when the Age of Pisces begin. We only had known that we were definitely 2000 plus years into the Age. That is the only accuracy we have ever had."

"So if we are in fact moving out of Pisces, then what Age are we moving into and what are the traits associated with it?" Kai sat up, turning to face her handsome, passionate Instructor.

Pharaoh smirked and took a sip of his drink before responding. "Some traits are prevalent even now from the new Age. Change. Open mindedness. Extreme intelligence. Seeking of the truth. Exploration. Innovation. The Freedom to be who you are. The freedom to believe what you want. And soon to come, humane treatment of mankind, love for one another, togetherness, the over throwing of control and rigid governing forces. The joining of all, together for the greater good. Key reference: The Humanitarian Age."

Kai's smile started small, checking his face for truth, she saw no lies. Her smile grew wide and bright in knowing.

Wrapping her arms around his neck she kissed his lips. "Well now."

Pharaoh laughed at her obvious excitement with knowing the answer. His last description was a dead giveaway.

"Gotta love an Aquarius right?"

He continued laughing, shaking his head at the charm of his southern Aquarian counterpart.

"Yes, and you, being a Daughter of Aquarius and all other Sons and Daughters, will have an important role of spreading yourselves around and teaching us others how to be the best in order to capitalize on all of your beautifully gifted traits."

Kai finished the last of her drink and raised herself from the lounge.

Pharaoh teased. "Where you going? Just leave the money on the nightstand and bounce?"

Kai stopped in the frame of the door. "I'm refreshing my drink. I will need another strong one in preparation for the next adventure."

Pharaoh frowned. "The next adventure. What's that?"

Kai reached and grabbed Pharaoh's glass for a refill as well. "You will hit this," she smacked herself on the ass. "doggy style.

Pharaoh's eyes widened in surprise. Although excited about the opportunity, his concern of possibly hurting her caused him to decline the offer.

"Nah Lil Mama, you are NOT ready for that."

Kai pouted, not wanting to be looked at as being fragile. She wanted to at least give it a try. Hell, she had to be pushed into more than just missionary. And she knew in her heart that Pharaoh would be more than gentle with her. She was ready to explore. Even if that meant biting into a pillow and ripping the sheets apart with her bare hands, she was determined to have him to take her from behind, THAT night!!!

"No. I said what I said." She turned and headed in before he could object to her decision.

Pharaoh sat back in his chair and considered her request. He was excited just thinking of her ass being raised in the air in the most submitting position. But he did not want to over exert her. The last scare was enough to make anyone think twice about traveling that road again. He was well aware of his own power and his well endowed size. Kai was a newbie and he couldn't bare the thought of causing her pain again.

"I don't know Kai," he spoke through the doorway. "I'm not good wit that."

She reappeared shortly with glasses in tow. Setting them on the table, she took her place between his legs turning her body facing him. Lifting her hand to his cheek, she had pleading eyes. "Listen, I'm ready. Please, just go slow and give it a try. I Want you. In that way."

There was no way that he could deny her with the current look that she wore on her face. That cute, adorable, pleading look alone was enough to get her what she wanted.

"Sipping from his newly refreshed drink, he nodded. "Under one condition."

She smiled. "And what is this condition of yours?"

Pharaoh smirked. "That you call me Daddy while I'm in that shit."

Kai laughed. "Pha, I cannot take you serious. I swear."

He laughed along with her. But suddenly, his expression grew dangerously mischievous. Taking her by the waist, he pulled her ass back into his hardness.

"Oh but you will take me serious Ma," he accent was deep. His voice dangerously low.

Kai's stomach churned with the butterflies that were now fluttering around in her gut. The look that crossed his face left her speechless.

Removing his hand from her waist and placing his arm above his head, he leaned back into a rested position. He motioned with his head toward the table.

"I suggest you go on and finish that drink."

Something about his cocky and threatening stance turned her on to no end. She wanted to be everything that he needed. To give him everything he wanted. To eventually be able to confidently match him wit to wit and stroke for stroke. But she knew that before she would be able to get there, she needed experience. She was now determined more than ever to push her limits. To go places that her body wasn't prepared to go. A little more each time.

Pharaoh couldn't be more impressed with her willingness and determination. Boy she wasn't lying when she had mentioned that she was open to learning new things earlier in the day. Her quest for knowledge and having new experiences were admirable beyond understanding. This girl continued to surprise him every single second. Being with her was interesting. Fun. New and Exciting.

Wow.

All this time, Lil Kaimery was a force to be reckoned with. "Let me find out." His thoughts were spoken aloud.

Kai squinted. "What's that?"

"Let me find out that you got a bit of spunk and spontaneity bout yasself."

"Plenty."

Her simple response was dripping with challenge and sass.

He patted her on the bottom. "Well, let me find out what this thing do?"

"Plenty."

Pharaoh grinned at the audacity of the feisty Lil Lady. She had no clue, he thought to himself. It would be just seconds before he literally knock that smug look from her face.

Lifting her from her sitting perch, and rising from the chair, he picked her up and tossed her over his shoulder, carrying her inside. She was squealing helplessly when he tossed her onto the bed. Flipping her over face forward, he removed his boxer briefs.

He leaned forward and whispered into her ear. His voice low, demanding and seductive, "Now be a good Lil girl and raise that ass up for me."

Kai climbed onto both knees, following his instruction. Her heart was beating as if it would explode through her chest.

Pharaoh lifted the rim of his tank from over her mound, revealing the prize.

Dayum.

She was in trouble.

Pushing her upper body flat against the bed. He spoke. Now don't you move."

Using his hands, he pushed her cheeks apart revealing her center. Kissing her soft, firm flesh, he worked his magic in warming her, getting her to the place where he wanted. Where he also needed her to be in comfort.

Raising into position, he placed his curved weapon at her center. Spreading her flesh apart, he slowly pushed inside, reading her signals: her breathing, her moans, her gasps, her movements to ensure that she was okay.

Once all had checked out, he reached, grabbing a handful of her hair and pulling her upper body to his chest. His kisses devoured her neck. Lifting the rim of his tank, he removed the garment from over her shoulders and lastly her head. Tossing it to the floor, he continued devouring her back, as she moaned in pleasure.

Aggressively, pushing her upper body back into position, flat against the bed, he started his movement. Slowly, grinding into her. Her hands clutched the bed spread, holding on for all of her life.

Working her slow until she had adjusted to the feeling of him taking her in the most animalistic way, he gained momentum in pace. Her moans grew more vocal.

"Huhhhhhh…. Huhhhhhhh….ohhhhhhh…..hooooooooo."

She was taking it like a champ.

Her pussy had gotten so wet, he could see his dick glistening, covered in her honey each time he pulled out. The scene, her moans, the amazing feeling that her snug walls were causing surrounding him, was enough to send him cursing.

"Shiiiit. You feel so good."

His moans seemed to make her wetter, if that was even possible.

She clutched the comforter, biting down hard to keep from screaming. His dick was so massively thick. It just couldn't be real. And the curve of it was rubbing against places within her walls that was creating so much pain, and so much pleasure at the same time. She was spinning out of control. This man was super powerful.

Reading her signals, he could tell that she was on the verge. Mastery kicked in. He was determined to take her there.

"Ohhhh God Pharaoh.....this dick is so big!!!!"

"Yeah? Then say it Boo........say the magic words." He smacked her on the ass. Firm but commanding. "Whose pussy is this?"

"Yoursssssssss!!!!!!" She yelled digging her nails into the mattress of the bed.

"Wrong response."

Pharaoh smacked her just a bit harder on the ass in punishment and reached down, grabbing a handful of her hair, tugging enough to cause her body to move a bit further onto the fullness of his dick.

"Ohhhhhhhh Goooooddddd," she took the pain, digging harder into the mattress.

"Whose pussy is this?" He asked with a more commanding voice than he had used initially.

"Pharrrraaaaoooohhhhh it's yourrrrrrssss," she called out. Unfortunately for her, it was the wrong answer yet again.

Tugging her hair harder and smacking her on the bottom again, he asked. "Is this Daddy's pussy?"

"Yasssss."

Pharaoh knew that he had her where he wanted her.

He pulled her hair, enough so that her upper body was once again raised from her position against the bed. Placing his lips against her ear he spoke low but firm. His accent was extremely pronounced. "Kai, you will learn not to play with me. You understand. This is my domain. I am The God Pharaoh Knight I will tear your lil pussy UP!!!!" Pushing her upper body back flat into position, he smacked her on the ass again, slowing his pace but grinding a bit deeper. Her climax was unstoppable.

"When I ask you whose pussy is this? You respond, "Daddy's" Now who pussy is this?"

Kai cried out in her climax. "Daddddddddddyyyyyyyyyyyyyyy'sssssss"

7:14am.

Pharaoh watched as she slept. So sound. So peacefully. He stopped counting the number of rules that he had broken, as it seemed as if in just being around this woman, rules weren't in no way applicable.

He wondered what was happening.
He wondered what this woman had done to him.
What type of voodoo had this Creole vixen put on him?
He needed to make it stop.
He didn't want for it to stop.
He needed for it to stop.

It was the first time that he had outright branded a woman.
He had placed hickeys, certified territory markers on her thighs.
He had marked her as his.
Branding her in his name.
Making her pussy his.
What had he done?
Why had he done it?
He had wanted to do it.
He should not have done it.
He knew that he would have to face the aftermath.
He would have to answer for his crimes.
It was the first time that he felt the need to.
It was the first time that he had ever been completely terrified of his own conflicted heart.

Chapter Fourteen- Zaire (Best Friend)

Best Friend- Tweet/Bilal (Album: Southern Hummingbird)

Zaire couldn't contain her excitement as she watched the Jag pulled to a stop at the curb in front of Milwaukee's Mitchell International Airport. Almost skipping over to the vehicle, Zaire dragged her carryon behind her, tugging on the handle. Her dread head bestie climbed from the driver seat with a huge smile pasted upon his face. Meeting him at the trunk, he reached over to envelop her into a huge hug.

"Hey Birthday Girl." He greeted her with extra love.

Zaire's smile covered her entire face. It was her first time touching down back at home since her leaving for Miami. Although her stay would be short, lasting the weekend only, it still felt great to be back on familiar turf.

Pharaoh placed her bag in the trunk and slammed it shut. Walking around to the passenger door, her opened it, allowing her entry into the car.

Zaire fastened her seatbelt and rested her purse comfortably at her side. Pharaoh entered at driver's side just seconds later.

Pulling from the curb and into traffic, he turned to Zaire and grinned. "Welcome Home you."

"It feels so good to be back." She matched his grin. "Seems like it has been forever!!!"

"Way longer than two weeks since I last saw you."

"I know right."

Zaire was home in celebration of her birthday. It was hard to believe that her special born day of July 12th had come so quickly. She was officially 35 years of age. It seemed as if it were only a few years ago that she had turned 21. Where did the time go?

Naomi had been more than understanding and had approved her request immediately to return home to bring in her big day. She would return back to Miami on that Sunday morning to begin wrapping up her assigned duties. She was now down to thirty more days at the plant. Then, she would return home for good. It would be a bittersweet countdown.

The weather was absolutely gorgeous, perfectly cooler than the temps that she had endured during the last couple of weeks in the tropical city. The low 80 degree weather was a welcomed perk of being back in the midwest.

"How does it feel to be back in Cream City?" Pharaoh asked sparking one of the Cubans he had purchased in Little Havana to life.

"It feels so good. I actually get to frolic around in my own apartment for a little bit. That's fabulous."

Pharaoh laughed. "I guess being away for so long can make you appreciate the comforts of home. I can see that."

"I'm telling you," Zaire sighed. "It's a true birthday treat."

"That's wussup." Pharaoh turned onto the ramp leading to I-794 from Layton Ave. "It's all about you this weekend. Whatever you want."

"In that case, I'll first have a frickin Cousin's Sub." Zaire stated matter of factly.

Pharaoh chuckled. "Maybe later on. I promise I got you. But let me get you home first so that you can drop your bag off and check in on your shit."

Zaire didn't protest.

Minutes later, they pulled into the parking structure leading to her apartment. Taking her bag from the trunk, Pharaoh followed as she made her way to the elevator shaft. The lifting car seemed to have been expecting her.

Pharaoh sent a text from his phone once inside, while Zaire pushed the button for the 7th floor. Walking down the hall, they stopped in front of her door. Pharaoh had the spare key out, sticking it inside the lock. Clicking it open, he stepped in first, with her bag. She reached for the switch to cut on the lights.

"SURPRISE!!!!!!!!"

Zaire's heart leaped from her chest. Surveying her apartment, she saw all familiar faces. Trays of food covered her kitchen counter, a gift table had been set up in the corner of the living room. Gold and her favorite color blue balloons decorated the entire front area.

Turning to Pharaoh, a look of innocence accompanied a large grin.

Zaire beamed. "You guys!!!!!"

Her guests rushed over for hugs. All family members and friends stepped forward.

"Who is responsible for this?" She asked after hugging everyone and catching her breath.

Everyone turned to Pharaoh with smiles.

"Of course you were." She wrapped her arms around his neck and kissed his cheek. Her bestie was the absolute bomb.

"Welcome back Babygirl," Her Dad walked over to her with a small, neatly wrapped box in his hands. "Your birthday gift from me and your mom." He was happy to see his only daughter.

Zaire accepted the gift from her Main Man and hugged both him and her mom who stood grinning behind. Removing the wrapping and opening the box, she discovered a beautiful set of gold earrings in the shape of the motherland.

"Oh my God, they are gorgeous!!!" She hugged both her parents again. Thanks so much."

"I picked them out." Her mom announced."I thought they were absolutely perfect for you."

"Indeed they are. I can't thank you two enough."

"So deserving Sweetie. You make us proud every single day." Her Dad's face said all.

Music flowed from the Bluetooth speaker sitting on her cocktail table. Reg had connected his phone and opted to play some 90s R&B to get the party started.

A few friends from school pulled her over to catch up while a line started for food service.

A bit later after settling down with her own plate, equipped with that Cousin's sub that she had been requesting earlier, she sat next to Pharaoh who had his own bowl of tuna salad and veggies.

"Dude, you are too much." She nudged him in the arm. She was amazed at the obvious lengths that he had gone to pull off the surprise.

"Anything for you Babes." He planted a kiss on her cheek. "Are you enjoying yourself so far?"

"This is everything that I needed. Seeing everyone here." Her eyes misted over. "Thanks so much for this."

"Aww now don't go tearing up." Pharaoh sipped from the cup of 1738 that he had in his hand. "You know that I had to make your 35th year of existence special." He pulled her into his arms for a long hug, then playfully pushed her away "Now get off of me before you transfer your sensitive ass cooties to me."

Zaire laughed turning her attention to the door that her Mom had opened to let Tre inside. Her was carrying Nala in her cage who was crying wanting desperately to get out. Jumping up, she sprinted over to her cat daughter whom she had not seen in weeks.

Nala was screaming and crying at the sound of her Mama's voice. Opening the door on the front of the cage, Nala climbed out and into her arms.

"Hi there Baby," Zaire was on her knees holding her spotted kitty for dear life. Nala rubbed her head against her Mama's cheek.

Kai made her appearance walking through the wide open door.

"Happy Birthday Cuz!!!!" She called out, sinking onto the floor to wrap her arms around her cousin. "So sorry that I am late. I was taking care of a few last minute arrangements before the morning."

"No need for an apology. You know I completely understand. Really, I had no clue that this was even scheduled as a part of my day." Zaire laughed honestly. "This was all Pha."

Kai scanned the room at the mention of his name and spotted him sitting on the couch. Their eyes met. He sipped his drink, looking away.

Zaire caught the exchange between them regardless of how short it was. Kai wore a plastered smile over what Zaire could tell was a sad and bothered expression.

"Are you okay Cuz?" Zaire had several conversations with her cousin since she had left Miami. She was already aware that she and Pharaoh hadn't had much communication since being back home. Kai had made several attempts, only to be shut down by Pharaoh. He was either too busy for conversation or not answering his phone at all, sending Kai to voicemail. Zaire wasn't sure what was going on with her bestie. He wouldn't speak with her about anything concerning Kai as part of the topic. Zaire was extremely worried about Pha. But she was even more worried about the victim, her baby cousin Kai.

"Not sure why he would even invite me. Or at least have Tre to invite me." Kai spoke her thoughts out loud. She shook her head coming back into the moment. "For you of course I am here." She quickly tried disguising her sadness with another huge plastered smile.

Zaire hated whatever game Pharaoh was playing. The damage that he had done to Kai was irreversible.

Taking Kai in her arms for another needed hug. She allowed Nala to wander off and over to the bowls that Tre had filled with both food and water.

"I'm cool Cuz, really." Kai raised from the floor and stood to her feet. "Don't worry please. I want you to enjoy your day." She walked over to hug her Aunt and Uncle before Z could respond.

Looking over at Pha, Zaire watched as his eyes followed Kai and then forcefully look away, engaging in conversation with Reg as a distraction. Zaire shook her head. She had to allow Pha to learn his own lessons. He would learn hard and fast. That she knew.

The guests stayed well into the night. Her mom and Dad left after a couple of hours, leaving the younger ones to continue without them.

Reg departed not to long after, needing to get home to deal with his angry son's mom.

Zaire and her brother, Dayshun were running the table in their eight round of spades.

Kai was sipping on her drink while conversing with their cousin in the corner.

Pharaoh and Tre were out on the balcony smoking cigars.

Taking a break from playing cards, Zaire turned over her spot to her youngest brother, Armari.

Sitting next to Kai who was now perched on the couch. Zaire checked in.

"You good?"

Kai gave a feeble laugh. "Yep. I'm as good as I will be."

Zaire frowned at the weird response. "Did you get a chance to speak with Pha?"

Kai's expression turned sour. "Briefly but long enough to get the picture."

Zaire watched as Kai tucked a strand of hair behind her earlobe. She looked genuinely devastated.

Zaire raised from the couch, taking Kai's hand and leading her to the master bedroom. Closing the door, she took a seat next to her on the bed. Nala looked up from her resting place at the head of the bed but quickly turned back over to continue with her nap.

"What happened? What did he say?"

Kai sat silent for a moment collecting her thoughts before starting. "He basically told me that we were just fucking. That we should just leave it as what it was. A fun time. And let it be."

Zaire's mouth hit the floor. "Are you kidding me?"
"Nope." Kai pressed her lips together. Her eyes were cloudy.

Zaire couldn't believe it. What in the entire hell was Pharaoh doing? There was no mistaking the emotion that she had bared witness to during their stay in Miami. For the life of her, she didn't understand.

Kai sat silent for another moment before forcing yet another smile and grabbing her cousin's hand. "Enough about me and this bullshit. How are things with you and Nyris?"

Zaire's heart broke for her cousin. She deserved so much better. When would Pha learn? When would he grow up and finally stand on his two feet as a man. He had complained about women not striking his fancy or being able to hold his interest in the past. Now he finds one who has, but cut her out in the exact same manner as he had done all of the others. Not Kai!!!!

Zaire answered her question, needing to change the direction of her thoughts.

"Everything's cool with us. Nyris is still the sweetest. He took me zip lining the other day. Imagine that." She laughed. "He actually told me to tell you guys hello."

Kai tried sucking up some of Z's happiness but struggled. Zaire could see the pain in her eyes.

"Hey Babes," She reached over putting her hand to her cousin's cheek. "I love you. And if you need to take off, I advise you to do so. You have to finish closing out anyways."

A tear slipped from Kai's foggy golden eyes. Quickly wiping the droplet away. She stood. Zaire stood with her. She hugged her Big cousin for a long time before letting go.

"I love you too Cuz. Take care and enjoy the rest of your party. I will call you when I make it back home."

Zaire watched as she sprinted from the room before she had the chance to respond. Moments later she heard the front door close.

Fighting her anger, Zaire sat rubbing Nala for some time before heading back to her guests. Spotting Pharaoh who sat in the corner facing the door, having the nerve to have a ridiculously hurtful look on his own face, she stopped herself from walking over and cursing him out on sight. She took a deep breath, calming her nerves. She would let him learn a valuable lesson. She had to.

Pouring herself a glass of punch, she went back to entertaining her guests.

Saying goodbye to her brothers as they walked down the hall to the elevator, Zaire closed the door. Tre was in the kitchen washing dishes. She was so thankful that he had volunteered to stay behind to help with clean up.

She mouth a "Thank You" showing her appreciation. Tre smiled and nodded.

Turning towards the guest bathroom, Zaire entered to check on Pha who was snoring hard in his drunken slumber. His locs fell wild around. They seemed to be everywhere above and all around his head. Shaking her head, she turned off the light and closed the door.

He had gone IN, consuming damn near a whole fifth of 1738 by himself. The negro had lost his entire mind. His slurred speech and stumbled steps led Zaire to confiscate his car keys and jail him in her guest room for the night. He had the nerve to drunkenly laugh himself to sleep as if his antics were some sort of comical routine. It was so stupid and completely unlike him. But of course, she knew why he had done it. Precisely. Dealing with dumb ass decisions was a tough pill to swallow no doubt.

Heading back into the kitchen, Tre was placing the last of the tupperware dishes that stored the leftovers into the frig.

"Tre, you are a GODSEND!!!" Zaire walked around the counter and kissed his cheek. "Thank YOU!!!!"

"I got you girl." Tre closed the door and grabbed a sheet of paper towel to dry his hands. "How's Pha?"

Zaire rolled her eyes in disappointment. "He's sleeping now but he will feel it in the morning."

"Yeah, I'll bet." Tre grinned. "Kai really got him fucked up in the head I see. Wow. I'm speechless. I'm amazed to bare witness. I'm actually a bit worried about him.

Zaire agreed and grabbed a bottle of water from the frig, heading over to sit on the couch. Tre joined her to continue their conversation.

"It's crazy. I have never seen him like this over any girl in the past. He keeps denying his feelings of course, but I'm not sure why because it is written all over his face." Tre was just as lost as Zaire. "I hope it's not because of me. I am genuinely happy for him and

269

want nothing more than to see them together. I just couldn't have ever imagined the two of them actually getting together. But that makes it all the more fascinating. Shits like an unlikely fairytale from the depths of hell." He laughed. Zaire joined in with him.

After Pharaoh's return home from Miami, the guys had gotten together for their chat over drinks as promised. Pharaoh had been sure to include Tre in regarding his involvement with Kai. What Pharaoh had been shocked to discover was that Tre was not in the least bit upset and was actually extremely happy to hear that the two had linked despite their beef in the past. He thought that the two together was a good look.

"Yes, a major shocker." She agreed, picking up the remote control for her television, she flipped to find a movie.

"Can I be honest?" Tre asked.

"Of course. You better be." Zaire responded.

"I thought you and Pha would be together." He laughed. "I believed that you two were destined to be married. Hell, everyone did!!!"

Zaire rolled her eyes again and smiled. "Pharaoh and my friendship is just that. A FRIENDSHIP. He is my brother. There is nothing that I won't do for him." She explained. "I love him dearly, but I can never in life imagine us being together in any romantic type of way. That is disgusting!!!" She laughed. " The thought makes me want to throw up. It's no different than in the way that I feel about my blood brothers. There will never be a Pha and I. Never!!!!"

Tre chuckled. In that moment, he somehow knew that her words were positively real.

He changed the subject. "The party really turned out nice. Did you enjoy it?"

"I did. Y'all got me good." She laughed. "I wasn't expecting you guys at all. And Pha of course didn't speak a word about it."

Nala jumped up on the couch and into Tre's lap. She purred as he stroked her fur.

Zaire frowned. "Oh really Nala, you traitor? You having seen me in weeks and you jump into the Babysitter's lap? Okay, I see where this is going."

Tre smirked with his now over animated petting. "Yeah this is my little buddy. We always sit up at night and watch movies. She know what time it is. Ain't that right Nala?"

Nala responded with a meow.

"Wow. Ain't that about nothing"

Tre laughed. Zaire was playfully pouting with her arms crossed, fake angry at the kitty who was content, perched on Tre's lap.

"You will be back for good soon and the routine that you two had will pick up right where it left off."

"Tuh." Z poked out her lips, play swatting at the spotted kitty.

"Oh no you don't," Tre took action defending Nala. "Don't you swat at my foster daughter Missy."

"Would you prefer that I swat at you?" Zaire playfully punched Tre in the arm.

Nala meowed. "Okay, let's get her Nala," Tre lunged over grabbing a giggling Zaire, tickling her. "Where you at cat, we jumping her. Don't go hiding now." He laughed at Nala who was now hiding under the cocktail table, startled.

Zaire tried breaking loose but Tre continued to hold her down, calling Nala back to "take her lick" and continuing to tickle her when she tried getting away.

"Oh my Godddddd stop!!!!" Zaire giggled once his fingers dug into her extra sensitive sides of her stomach again.

"Say that you are sorry." Tre warned of another tickle attack if she didn't comply.

"I'm sorry." She gave up her fight.

Lifting his hands he started pulling away, Zaire took her chance. Too late, he had caught her hands pulling her back down and into another attack.

"Okayyyyyyyy!!!! Okayyyyy!!!! I quit," She giggled with tears streaming from her eyes. Her flailing and trying to get away caused them both to fall off the couch and onto the floor. Tre rolled on top of her.

Looking in her eyes. Her smile. Her sweet nature. A wanting feeling took over, coming completely and positively from left field. His response came from nowhere.

His lips covered hers. So soft and so fast. Zaire's breath caught in her throat but the sensation of his pillow soft cushions would not allow her to pull away. She wrapped her arms around his neck, needing him to come in closer to her. He deepened the kiss, devouring her mouth, tasting her, desiring her.

Nala's meow, brought them back, breaking the contact of their kiss.

They both looked over at Nala who seemed just as confused as they were when they looked back at one another. What had just happened?

Tre raised his body from over Zaire's giving her room to sit up. She wiped a finger across her lips in her confusion.

"Ummmm.....okay....." Was all that she could manage.

Tre stared at her with wide eyes. The shock was evident on his face as well. Taking a hand, he rubbed it over his bald head, biting his lip. Holy hell!!!

"Ummmm, maybe you should go," Zaire finally spoke words that made sense. She sat frozen staring at him a moment longer with a look of total disbelief.

Tre shook his head, shaking his brain back into function. "Uhhhh yeah.....okay.....yeah......cool........" He rose into standing position, collecting his keys from the kitchen counter. He looked back at Zaire one last time with an inquisitive expression on his face. What the hell was that?

Zaire stayed posted on the floor as Tre closed the door behind him.

273

She stayed planted there for minutes, trying to understand where the kiss had come from and why she had accepted it. The butterflies were hatching rapidly inside of her stomach.

Wow.

Chapter Fifteen- Pharaoh (Gone)
Gone- N-Sync (Album: Celebrity)

The pounding that occurs from the effects of a hangover induced headache is one that the recipient would always remember.

Blinds drawn, fetal position, Pharaoh's prayer to all of the mighty NRT was more of a negotiation. If only the pain could somehow miraculously evaporate, he would never go within two feet of a bottle of 1738 ever again. The Gods must have detected his ill endorsed lie, as he clutched his head waiting for the Ibuprofen pill that he had orally consumed to kick in.

The night before had ended with him slamming back pure shots of the dark liquor as if his body were of the same makeup as Marvel's Jessica Jones. But, he learned rather quickly that he unfortunately was not one who was gifted that form of super ability.

The smoky smell of bacon upset his stomach further. After throwing up three times in the past two hours, he just had to be honest with himself and conclude that Zaire was indeed trying to purposely kill him. Yes. That had to be it.

Still not being in any condition to drive home, even at the late hour of ten o'clock the next morning, he would have to sit and suffer the consequences of his poor decision making the night before.

Turning over and lying face up with his back planted flat against the Queen sized mattress, he pulled his locs, which he had tied in a ball on top of his head, a bit towards the front in order to allow for a more comfortable resting position.

What the fuck was he thinking?

The knock on the door came, followed by the twist of the doorknob. Zaire walked in carrying a plate on a tray accompanied with a glass of Apple juice.

Pharaoh moaned.

"You need to eat something to soak up the rest."

He acknowledged her with one eye closed as she sat the tray on the nightstand next to the bed.

"I'm good Z. Just really need for this pill to take effect so i can make my way home." Pharaoh covered his eyes with his hand, using the other to fan her off.

"Eat something Pha. You will feel so much better." She insisted plopping down next to him on the bed.

Pharaoh moaned again.

Holy shit!!!! An entire Go Go band was performing center stage in his brain. The pounding was out of fucking control.

Zaire reached over and kissed his forehead, feeling sorry but not sorry for her friend. She wanted to gloat. To tell him that this is what he deserved but knew that what he truly didn't deserve was her pettiness during his time of turmoil. He was suffering in many ways. No gloat necessary.

Removing the plate from the tray, she held it out to him as he closed his one propped open eye.

"Come on Pha. Just a few bites would make a world of difference."

"You know I'm not fuckin' with that swine shit!!!"

"And you know that I have not placed any on your plate so stop being dramatic for no reason." She rolled her eyes.

Knowing that he would not be able to get rid of her until he ate, he reluctantly sat up and accepted the plate.

"See, just egg beaters and toast. Now eat up."

He took a forkful of the discombobulated scrambled omelet that included tomatoes, onions, mushrooms, peppers and cheese and forced it into his mouth. Okay, the shit was pretty fiah.

Zaire silently watched him for a bit. She had so much that she wanted to say and Pharaoh purposely avoided her disappointed eyes.

"Pha, you are going to have to help me to understand because I am having so much trouble." Her voice was coated in that same disappointment when she finally spoke. "Why?"

"What are you talkin' bout?" His voice was low, but accent well defined. He continued to avoid her gaze, shoving another forkful into his mouth.

Zaire touched his arm, causing him to look up into her waiting eyes.
"We are not going to do this Pha. I will not allow you to bullshit me. You know what I am asking."

Pharaoh looked away again. In front of him sat the one who he knew he could not run from. He decided to utilize his right to remain silent.

Z continued, her voice soft and honest. "You love her Babes."

Pharaoh listened as she spoke the words that he couldn't bring himself to accept as his truth. What he did know is that whatever it was that he was feeling, it was definitely not love. Now that was a stretch.

Pharaoh shook his head. "Nah Z, not quite that."

"Okay, not quite love. Some other shit caused you to take a bottle to the head. Okay. Let's roll with that."

"Another stretch," He was looking for anyway to beat around the bush.

"Fine. I'm done." Z leaped up from her sitting position on the bed in anger with the way that Pharaoh was trying to avoid what was real.

"What do you want me to say Z?!?!" He asked before she walked through the threshold.

"I want you to stop with the bullshit!!!! That's what I want!!!!" She yelled, throwing her hands in the air. "You may not have been ready but you have fallen hard for Kai, Pharaoh!!! That's the bottom line. Miss me with all of that Male Ego bullshit you try to toss around. I'm not these tramps that you deal with in the streets!!! You are talking to me right now!!!! You are constantly tracking me and what I do but you aren't receptive when I approach you. I know you Pha!!!! You know that I know you!!!! So why would you let her go?!?!?"

"I didn't let her go. Fuck are you talking bout?" Pharaoh placed the plate back onto the nightstand and grabbed the glass of juice, taking a sip. "I just told her that we need to chill a bit. Not like I sent her packing and shit!!! What the fuck?"

Zaire laughed. What an evil sound escaped her lips. "You silly silly guy you. Well in that case, call her and have her to come over right now."

Pharaoh frowned trying to decipher the weirdness in his friend's last statement.
"If you want her over then you call her."

Zaire laughed evilly again. "Wow."

Pharaoh was genuinely confused. "Talk Z!!! Say what you need to say. I don't do well with all this subliminal shit. What the fuck is it?"

"I guess you don't know. So here's your wake up call Sir. YOU CAN'T CALL HER AND NEITHER CAN I BECAUSE SHE IS

GONE PHA!!!!!" Zaire walked back over toward the bed, standing in front of him to ensure that her point was directly received.

"Gone?" Pharaoh shook his head at the angry girl standing in front of him. "Now what is that supposed to mean?"

Zaire took a few deep breaths to calm herself. To fools who know not what they do. She closed her eyes shut, counting to ten before reopening them. Pharaoh was patiently waiting on her response.

She slowly started in a soft, calm voice. "She's gone Pharaoh. Her flight left this morning over an hour ago. She's gone Back home to Louisiana to care for her mom who has been struggling as of late."

"I'm sorry to hear about her mom, now that I truly am. Wow." Pharaoh sat silently a bit before shrugging. "But with prayer, she won't have to stay long and will be back shortly. Let's hope."

Zaire shook her head, knowing that her headstrong friend did not quite understand. She sat in the same place next to him on the bed, taking his hand in hers.

"No, you don't understand." The look on Zaire's face caused his heart to start racing. "There won't be a situation where she returns."

Pharaoh's heart skipped a beat before pounding as if he had swallowed a handful of steroids instead of the Ibuprofen that Z had given him earlier. "Huh?"

Zaire dropped her head sadly before delivering the news that she knew would devastate her obviously oblivious best friend.

Looking up and back into his now frightened eyes, she spoke. "She's gone for good. She has moved back home. She is not coming back."

Pharaoh's mouth fell open.
What????
NO.
Why would she do that?
How could it have happened so fast?
Why so FAST?
Why didn't he know?
Why didn't she tell him?!?!?
Not coming back.
What the fuck!!!!
She's GONE?
Z had to be joking with him.
Her look said otherwise.
She would never lie to him about something like this.
Gone.
Kai was Gone.

He looked up at Z with heavy eyes and an even heavier heart. She had unintentionally taken on the role as a hired hitman, shooting a bullet straight through his heart. She had succeeded in her plot to murder him.
She had officially committed a homicide.

AUTHOR'S NOTE:

At the tender age of 13, Keisha Powers wrote her first book which unfortunately went to ruins in a flood, after sitting in the basement at her parents' home for a long number of years. Now, after continuous motivation from her family and loved ones, she followed her passion by once again tapping into her universally gifted talent to deliver her first novel to the masses, All The Stars. She currently resides in her home town of Milwaukee, WI.

Other Titles by Keisha Powers:

All The Stars Part 1
All The Stars: Supernova- A Novella
All The Stars Part 2: In Retrograde
All The Stars Part 3: The Alignment

Made in the USA
Lexington, KY
02 December 2019